the
BOATHOUSE

the
BOATHOUSE

R. J. HARRIES

Matador
9 Priory Business Park
Kibworth Beauchamp
Leicestershire LE8 0RX, UK
Tel: (+44) 116 279 2299
Fax: (+44) 116 279 2277
Email: books@troubador.co.uk
Web: www.troubador.co.uk/matador

ISBN 978 1783064 076

British Library Cataloguing in Publication Data.
A catalogue record for this book is available from the British Library.

Typeset in Minion Pro by Troubador Publishing Ltd
Printed and bound in the UK by TJ International, Padstow, Cornwall

Matador is an imprint of Troubador Publishing

MIX
Paper from
responsible sources
FSC
www.fsc.org   FSC® C013056

www.rjharries.com

For my family

CHAPTER ONE

Sean Archer sensed he was being followed.

He ran alone, late at night, as it helped him clear his thoughts and forget about the past. He liked the hypnotic rhythm of his feet hitting the streets like a drum, the air rushing in and out of his lungs, body parts working as one – on autopilot.

The midnight chimes of Westminster echoed behind him and he focused up ahead, through the misty autumn chill, towards the tapering row of lamps that stood tall on the granite river wall.

The Victoria Embankment was too quiet. There had been no passing traffic since Westminster Bridge and the rising pitter-patter of another late-night runner was gradually getting louder.

He entered the shadows beneath Charing Cross Railway Bridge. Two uniformed policemen parted and turned sideways to let him through. The gap was more than wide enough, but the thick-set copper on the right flinched and moved his right arm back. Archer glanced towards him as the truncheon swung round towards his head. He leaned away and tried to swerve out of reach, but his shoulder crashed into the other man's chest as the baton smacked him just above his left eye.

He woke up under the bridge, slumped against the wall, with his chin on his chest and a dense throbbing headache. The pressure intensified as he lifted his head up and tried to get his bearings through kaleidoscope eyes.

The dirty cops must have dragged him there when he was out cold. He heard voices in the distance and started to turn his head, but the vice-like grip tightened, so he stopped. The cold and the damp were numbing his lower body and his eyelids closed automatically as he drifted off into a swirling vortex of darkness.

A train rumbled across the bridge overhead and he slowly opened his eyes. When his mind stopped spinning he realised he was holding something in both his hands. There was a knife in his right hand and what felt like a postcard in his left. It was dark and he couldn't see exactly what it was, so he slowly unzipped his jacket and placed both objects inside the net pocket, took some deep breaths, leaned to the right and dry heaved in short spasms.

He pushed himself up with his arms and legs, like a punch-drunk boxer struggling to beat the count. Bending forward slightly he coughed and spat out the stomach acid that had burned his mouth and ripped his throat raw. He zipped his jacket back up and took a deep breath as he started what would be a long walk back to Walton Street, SW3, clenching and unclenching his fists, gritting his teeth and keeping his gaze low to the ground.

After a few hundred yards of slow deep breaths he broke into a light jog without even thinking. The movement was mechanical and familiar, helping him ignore the pain. Regaining his speed and rhythm alongside the river; hammering the street like a drummer keeping perfect time. Breathing the cool damp air in, and the warm moist air out, with a visible cloud of vapour; zoned out from the random clusters of cars heading home.

Finally, alone inside his renovated South Kensington townhouse, he double dead-locked the solid front door, set the perimeter alarms and stretched his aching leg muscles towards the pain barrier, removing the lactic acid to prevent them from cramping up. As he leaned forward, slowly working his burning calf muscles, his thoughts gravitated towards Alex, but instinctively he closed them out. Compartmentalising was a skill that enabled him to function whenever his brain was overloaded with vivid memories from all five senses.

The white plantation blinds covered the bottom half of all the sash windows and were always set at an angle so that nobody could see inside. He opened his jacket and studied the knife. It was a Fairbairn Sykes fighting knife, used by elite British forces. He had one just like it upstairs in his study, and he used it as a letter opener. This one had something on the blade.

It looked like dried blood.

The postcard was actually a glossy photograph. A dead woman in a running kit splayed on her back with the knife sticking out of her neck, her wrists and ankles tied with clean white sailing rope to the four corners of a double bed. Her face had been blurred by some trick of Photoshop. The seven-inch steel blade must have hit the carotid artery as blood had sprayed in a wide arc over the white bed sheet, while a darker patch had formed above her shoulder. On the back of the picture someone had printed in thick black capitals:

DROP IT OR DIE LIKE HER.

Two weeks ago an anonymous caller had threatened to have him silenced if he didn't drop his personal investigation into Alex's unsolved murder. He hadn't taken much notice, but this threat was different. This time he should call the police.

He carefully placed the knife and photo inside separate Zip-loc plastic bags and put them at the back of a kitchen drawer, deciding to forget about them until later. Two aspirins and a small bottle of Evian took care of the dull residual headache.

After his daily routine in the compact basement gym of fifty push-ups, sit-ups and pull-ups, he stretched, went upstairs to the first floor, kicked off his size twelve Asics, undressed and tossed his sweaty combat-style running kit on top of the laundry basket.

Naked, he walked into the slate-tiled en-suite bathroom and turned the shower on as hot as he could stand it. He scrubbed himself with a hard sponge to rid himself of the disturbing encounter with the cops. Then he turned the shower down and stayed under the freezing cold water until he could bear it no longer. Within two minutes he was back on autopilot as he dressed in fresh boxer shorts, pale blue polo shirt and flip-flops; until a drop of fresh blood landed on the back of his left hand.

He studied himself carefully in the bathroom mirror. His cobalt blue eyes revealed nothing but calm. The inch-long gash above his left eye was still bleeding. He found a packet of butterfly stitches in the cabinet, squeezed the wound closed, wiped the blood off with a tissue and stuck a small piece of sticky tape across it to hold it together. Ruffling his fingers through his short brown hair, he thought about shaving, but decided to leave it until the morning.

Back downstairs in the large open-plan living area, he opened an ice-cold bottle of Peroni and selected some music to break the silence: on deck one he'd left *Kind of Blue* by Miles Davies since he'd moved in over a year ago. He loved the moody sax solos by Coltrane. It was the best album he had for late-night background music whether relaxing or working. He started the turntable and brushed the dust off. But first he needed a shot of blistering blues guitar; something restless to match his unsettled mood.

On deck two he placed *The Sky is Crying* by Stevie Ray Vaughan, positioning the stylus above the smooth dark grooves that indicated the gap before the fourth track *Little Wing*. He relished the mesmerising blues-rock guitar riffs with intricate phrasing, greasy distortion, chomping wah-wah and frantic blues slaloms.

The renovated Victorian house had thick walls to absorb the sound and several retro features including a double vinyl hi-fi rig as an alternative to the more convenient digital system. Both sounded good, but the uncompressed dynamics and strong links to the past won on this occasion. The touch and smell of the twelve-inch disc made it a far more intimate experience than digital.

His own blues guitar was gathering dust on the stand next to the rig. He gently brushed his finger across the strings of the customised black Stratocaster, but still wasn't ready to pick it up. It had been fourteen months and he'd lost the calluses on his finger-tips.

He flipped the lever on deck two. The stylus dropped and washed the room with the warm fluffy sound vinyl makes before the music starts as he took the first sip of beer.

The guitar sound filled the room as he wandered over to the large touch screen on the wall and turned it on. It showed a map of Great Britain and he stared at all the coloured dots. Each one depicted a potential location for the Boathouse, along coastlines, rivers and lakeshores. Different colours signified various levels of cross-referenced research materials. Four sites were coded red.

He recalled his personalised field training by a retired SIS officer who needed to top his pension up. He'd written a Sun Tzu style memoir that hadn't sold well, but he still held the record at Fort Monckton: *Know your enemy and know what they want.*

The Boathouse was off-grid, a facility that nobody wanted to talk about. How many people had been tortured and killed there? It was an obsession, and finding it would help him find Alex's killer. He should have stopped her investigating it before it was too late, but she wouldn't have listened to him or anyone else. His body tensed as his mind projected the ghostly image of her pale dead body. He'd accepted the fact that he couldn't change the past, but he was fiercely determined to change her killer's future.

CHAPTER TWO

Sean Archer's office was a convenient two-minute walk from his house and on the same meandering street in the heart of South Ken. He always felt comfortable walking down Walton Street, with its two- and three-storey stucco townhouses, boutiques and art galleries. It had that relaxed village feel to it, but was also upbeat, with wealthy Russians heading towards Knightsbridge and fashionable locals who always made out they were in the know.

He ordered two large Americanos in Le Bistrot opposite the office and stared out of the window at the white painted building where he worked. His office was above two bespoke sole traders; Morgan's Fine Art Gallery and Farnsworth Antiques.

Londinium Lux Limited comprised of Sean Archer and his business partner Zoe de la Croix, originally from Luxembourg and sacked by GCHQ as an intelligence analyst, caught utilising their powerful resources for personal use.

He used the front entrance and ran up the stairs two at a time without spilling any coffee through the flimsy plastic tops. The office space was open plan with two private meeting rooms. The parquet floor was honey-coloured oak and the walls white painted brick, covered with flat screens, framed posters of movies and old computer games he had developed called *Psycho Killer*, *Vigilante* and *Man Hunt*. Club chairs and leather sofas gave it a relaxed Manhattan-loft-meets-special-operations-centre feel.

It was unashamedly anti-corporate.

Zoe was an elegant brunette, dressed in a black skirt and white blouse. She was sitting upright at her work station, operating multiple screens, and frowning at images of the three investment bankers they'd been investigating for the past week, for a Dutchman who ran a dodgy hedge fund in Charles Street, Mayfair, but paid out on a good percentage. One of the screens showed them having breakfast in their favourite café in the Barbican. Archer had planted the tiny camera, microphone and transmitter there – inside a light fitting. Most hedge fund clients were after satellite imagery and analysis. This one wanted more.

"Morning, Zoe." He placed her coffee next to her desk phone.

"Thanks." She looked up at the scar above his eye. "How did you do that? Let me put some make-up on it."

"It's nothing. Found anything useful yet?"

"It's coming. Take a croissant."

She opened her red leather handbag, took out a large make-up brush and held it in front of her with an impatient look. "Come closer." Archer obeyed and bent forward as she gently dusted around and over the butterfly stitch. "There."

She gazed up at him and smiled as she played with her pearl necklace from Majorca. A material reminder of the only time they had been intimate together. She sighed and turned around to her computer, put the brush away and resumed working. Her red fingernails rattled across the keys at speed, alternating between two keyboards as the screens around her flashed up new images and information. Pictures, videos, satellite imagery from tracking their phones and confidential files stolen from various networks.

Archer was fascinated by her ability to hack into anything without getting caught. She'd learnt her lesson and was fearless with technology and completely comfortable with the unconventional techniques they used to solve cases. Despite being tall she always wore high heels, a lot of make-up, bright red lip gloss and designer clothes. The only framed picture on her desk was one of herself playing the cello at one of her burlesque shows. Archer always had to hide a smile when he stole a glance at it; he'd enjoyed her last public performance far more than he'd let on.

His iPhone rang out with a bell-like ring tone. The image of a chunky old man with wild grey hair and red-framed glasses, reading in his study, showed that it was his old family friend and Nobel Prize-winning psychologist, Professor Miles Davenport, OBE.

"I'll take this in the meeting room."

Zoe paid no attention to him as she continued working the case in her animated style, which meant talking to herself and shouting at screens.

"Sean."

"Miles, I was just going to call you. Fancy lunch?"

"It's not a social call, Sean. I've just recommended you for an assignment."

"Your old pals at the Home Office lost someone again, have they?"

"No, it's a kidnapping case unfortunately, a friend's wife – he can't get the police or any of the well-known crisis management consultants involved. He asked me for help and I told him I knew just the man."

"When was she taken?"

"Yesterday."

"Who is it?"

"Peter Sinclair. He's in the chair again at my lodge."

Sinclair was also fifteenth on the list that he'd been given last week. He was a highly secretive figure, surrounded by layers of security and lawyers making him almost impossible to reach without introduction.

"I'll think about it."

"The poor fellow's desperate and needs expert help."

Sean walked over to the window, rotated the white slats in the blinds and peered down at the narrow street. Directly below him was a large black Mercedes waiting outside on double yellow lines, a twin exhaust plume showing that its engine was running.

"He's also impatient."

CHAPTER THREE

The black Mercedes S600L had dark tinted windows and a strong smell of high-quality leather. It reminded Archer of the old-fashioned shoe shop he used on Sloane Avenue. He put his seat belt on and stretched out comfortably in the back seat. The stiff-looking driver with the obligatory shaved head turned around, introduced himself as Jones, set off, and made a brief hands-free call.

"I'm on my way, sir, with Mr Archer on board."

Jones had to be an ex-soldier. His tone was deferential so he was probably talking to the boss. If Sinclair was somehow linked to the people behind the Boathouse then this was a strange coincidence; either exceptional good luck, like winning the lottery, or he was being set up. And if it was some kind of elaborate trap, then Archer was on his own without backup. Nobody would know where he was, unless Zoe tracked his phone location, as she often did when he was alone in the field. He felt the shape of his iPhone in his right trouser pocket for comfort. As long as it was switched on it would leave a digital trail of his whereabouts.

They headed east down Walton Street, cruising calmly through heavy traffic on Old Brompton Road and Knightsbridge before entering a one-way street into Mayfair. Not another word was spoken until they stopped outside the back entrance of a mansion block on Park Lane between the Dorchester and Grosvenor House Hotels.

"Where are we going?" Archer asked.

"Mr Sinclair's penthouse," Jones said.

They got out together and stood on the pavement outside Sinclair Mansions. A heavy-set man in a dark grey suit stepped out of the lobby, got into the car and drove it away. Another heavy bald-headed man held the door open as Jones escorted Archer into the building and pressed a button for the lift. The lobby was decorated neutrally, but soft lighting showcased glass cabinets of hand-painted china, two large oil paintings of old sailing ships and four white marble Grecian-style busts on square columns. It was like visiting a private museum reserved for wealthy patrons; an off-limits elitist's paradise.

"Have you worked for him long?" Archer asked, inside the lift.

"Long enough," Jones said. Not giving anything away to a stranger, like a typical ex-soldier finally onto a good thing and afraid to lose it.

They got out on the ninth floor and Jones led the way straight ahead. A tall silver door opened automatically and a shining square plate next to it said: The Penthouse. It felt like entering a state apartment inside a palace and had to be worth at least fifty million.

Inside the entrance, minimalistic-looking spaces were visible beyond in various shades of grey. The apartment was a tall airy space with a white and grey marble floor. A long lobby lead to a square entrance hall where an expressionless woman dressed in black sat behind a rococo-style desk. To the left, a rectangular living room and terrace overlooked the park. The furniture was modern with table lamps providing soft lighting and comfortable-looking sofas. The artwork was also modern and the only feminine touches were occasional groups of family photographs in silver frames and prominent cut-glass vases of white lilies.

Four men were seated at a dining table at the far end of the room. Two wore dark grey suits and two were in dark jeans and black leather jackets. Hard-nosed bodyguards who exuded a ruthless military bearing just like the SAS. A lot of muscle for a property tycoon.

All four turned sharply to stare at Archer, then at a fifth man who was standing next to a desk by the window. This had to be Sinclair, an older man in a light grey suit, pink shirt and pale blue tie. He had short white hair and a white, elegantly trimmed beard that worked well with his sun-tan. He looked fit but distressed, still and straight, hands spread out on top of the desk as if he was about to keel over if he moved them. He was staring vacantly at the black triangular-shaped conference phone in front of him.

"This is Mr Archer," Jones said.

No answer, just silence.

The man at the desk stared as if hypnotised by the phone. Then he turned round dramatically, clamped his eyes on Archer and walked straight towards him. He was blatant, checking Archer up and down, measuring him, judging him. When done, he extended his right hand and smiled.

"Peter Sinclair," he said. "I'm pleased to meet you, Mr Archer."

His accent was clipped public school, probably Oxbridge, but it also had a dramatic cadence, as if he had studied at RADA. Archer shook his hand. It was cold with a firm grip.

"Tell me why I should hire you," Sinclair said.

"You shouldn't, you should call the police."

"But why should I hire you and not some other consultant or investigator?"

"I think there must be some sort of misunderstanding. I came here on a personal recommendation. I don't do interviews or beauty parades, Mr Sinclair. I thought you wanted my help based on a direct referral from our mutual friend, Miles Davenport."

"So what makes Davenport think you're so good?"

"Maybe you should ask him."

"How do you know him?"

"I've known him all my life. He knew my parents and grandparents."

"Hmm. Can you expand on your association with him or your credentials for being the best person for this job?"

Sinclair was testing him. Expecting him to sell himself. This was a unique opportunity to see if Sinclair was connected to the Boathouse. Best to play it cool. Make him do the work.

"Not really, no. I don't mean to be rude, but like I said, I don't do interviews. You see, I'm selective too, so I think I'll pass."

"Oh please, Mr Archer, have the courtesy to stay for a few more minutes so we can pick your brains a little."

"Okay. But you really need a team of investigators."

Sinclair looked deflated as he was clearly used to getting his own way.

"What are you then?"

"I'm a self-taught criminologist and software developer, more of a digital profiler and analyst than your typical private investigator."

"Hmm. What happened there?" Sinclair pointed at the butterfly stitch.

"Triathlon. Fell off my bike."

"What did Davenport tell you?"

"Your wife has been taken and you need help to get her back."

"She was out shopping and failed to turn up at the hairdresser's for an appointment. Then a man called and asked for two million pounds in cash. If we call the police or any of the big kidnap and ransom consultants, they'll kill her, but if we do as they say, they'll release her in a few days, unharmed."

"How much time have you got left to pay?"

"It's already been paid."

Sinclair folded his arms and stared harshly into Archer's eyes. After a minute of silence, Sinclair's men started to shuffle uncomfortably in their seats until Sinclair smiled again and unfolded his arms.

"Davenport tells me that you're brilliant. Your profiling software is used all over the world and he also mentioned that you've consulted on major kidnap and ransom cases before. So tell me more about yourself, humour me, like you would any other wealthy client."

"Like I said, I'm a boutique-style consultant, operating on word of mouth."

"Who have you worked for that I would have heard of?"

"The Met, their kidnap unit, SOCA, the Home Office, Interpol, FBI."

"I don't understand. Why do they hire you if your software's so bloody good?"

"Well, first we can customise the software, but there are lots of tools out there: forensic profiles, psychological profiles, digital profiles and huge data bases. It takes a long time to integrate profiles and cross-reference big data. They bring me in to speed things up."

"Hmm, all right, you probably already know that I'm chairman of the Sinclair Group of companies. Property mostly."

"I've heard of you." Who hadn't? His obsession for privacy was well-publicised.

"So what do you advise, Mr Archer?"

"Call the police. Right now. I can call them for you if you like. I know some people at Scotland Yard. Their specialist kidnap unit is excellent."

Sinclair looked away for the first time. He stood still and looked out over the park for a long time. Then he looked back at Archer and smiled, as if he wanted something.

"I'd like you to help me Mr Archer, not the police." His tone condescending.

"I'm sorry about what's happened, Mr Sinclair, but you need serious help and serious resources. I'm just one consultant. You need a team."

Sinclair turned and walked back to where he had started, back to the table and the telephones. He stood in the same place with his hands flat on the table again and stared at the triangular-shaped conference phone, as if willing it to ring.

"Have you got any idea who's behind this?" Archer asked.

"Why would you care?" Sinclair sounded petulant now, like a child not getting his way. He moved his hands from the top of the desk, walked over to Archer, and motioned at a stunning portrait on the wall.

"That's my wife."

Archer looked at the portrait of a woman with blonde hair and green eyes. A classical beauty with prominent cheek bones and full cherry-red lips stretched into a radiant smile.

"Her name is Becky," Sinclair said, puffing his chest out. The room was so quiet you could hear him sigh quietly.

All eyes in the room were on Sinclair.

"They promised to let her go unharmed if we met all their demands," Sinclair said, his tone became harder. "But they haven't called back yet and I don't know what to do next."

Sinclair walked away towards the window. Nobody else moved or made a sound.

"Do you think she's dead, Mr Archer?" Sinclair asked, with his back turned.

CHAPTER FOUR

Archer watched Sinclair's head drop and his shoulders sag. He looked back at the large portrait hanging proudly on the living-room wall that somehow managed to capture Becky's vivaciousness. She was much younger looking than her husband; a cliché trophy wife.

"She's probably still alive."

"She's my soul mate," Sinclair said. "I waited a long time to find the right woman to marry and I want her back."

But why did Archer not believe him?

"She's your first wife then?"

"Yes."

"When did you have the portrait done?"

"About two years ago at our house on Sandbanks."

The four hard men at the table were turned towards Sinclair, still silently watching his every move like sentinels.

"You need to promise me something," Sinclair said.

"What's that?"

"Whether you decide to help me or not, I need your word that you won't go behind my back and get your police friends involved."

Archer nodded. "Okay," he said, casually.

"I want your word." A harsher undertone.

"Okay, you have my word, no police."

"Is that a problem?"

"No problem."

"No friends from the Met or Special Branch, no police contact whatsoever," Sinclair said. "We'll handle this situation ourselves. Is that clear?"

"Yes."

"If you break your word and anything happens to Becky because of it, I'll have you killed. Do you understand?" he said, and looked over at his pack of guard dogs.

"You have my word."

Sinclair's persistence was untrusting. He was a total control freak.

"And you know what I'll do if you call the police?"

Archer looked over at the guards. The four men stared back without expression. They were hardened killers whose loyalty had been bought and paid for.

"I already gave you my word," Archer's tone sharpened defensively.

Sinclair screwed his face up as he spoke. "It's not an idle threat. I could have you taken out any time I like. Always remember that."

Archer didn't blink.

"Why are you so afraid of the police?"

"I don't trust them, or the so-called justice system. Not here or anywhere else, so if anything happens to Becky, I'll organise my own justice. Anyway, you're probably a better investigator than their burned-out dickheads."

"I don't have anything like their level of resources, but it's your call."

Archer glanced over at the phone and then back at Sinclair.

"And they asked you for two million in cash?" he asked.

"That's right."

"You were able to get two million in cash that quick?"

"Of course," Sinclair scoffed, and gestured casually as if it was nothing.

"How big is that? I mean, what did you put it in?"

"A Louis Vuitton suitcase full of fifties. It weighed forty-five kilos on the scales."

"I assume you're insured for kidnapping?"

"Yes, of course, but if I call the insurers they'll contact the police or a kidnap and ransom consultant and I can't risk that, so I'm on my own."

"Okay then," Archer said, a little over-enthusiastically, consciously trying to show more interest in the case, but detesting every moment of being in the same room as Sinclair. "I'd like to know more about what happened yesterday."

Know your enemy and know what they want.

"Have you decided to help then?" Sinclair smiled, as if he'd won the first round.

"No not yet," Archer shot him a stern glare to keep him on his toes. "But they're going to call you back today and you need to be ready for them when they do."

"What makes you so sure?"

"They'll want more money. Lots more, in fact. You're worth too much to settle for a lousy two million pounds, so sit down and tell me what happened yesterday."

Sinclair sat in a chair with his back to his men and started to tell Archer about the previous day. Archer sat on the sofa looking at them all. Jones sat bolt upright with the others at the table. On the same team, but not in the real hard men's clique.

"Becky went out around ten in the morning," Sinclair said. "She went to Harvey Nichols as she had a hair appointment nearby at noon."

"But she failed to show up at the salon?"

"Yes."

"Was she alone?"

"As far as I know. I don't have her followed – well, not often enough anyway." Sinclair scoffed at his own joke and then stopped abruptly as if he didn't want to give too much away.

"Who drove her there?"

"Jones, the same driver that picked you up today, same car."

"Where was she dropped off?"

"The side entrance on Seville Street."

"Does she go there often?"

Sinclair tilted his head back and closed his eyes, appearing to be frustrated by the questions. "When we're in London she likes to go there. Harrods, Selfridges, Bond Street, any one of those about once or twice a week, hairdresser's every week, and lunch once or twice most weeks. She also spends a lot of time in the gym and being pampered at the spa."

"Who does she lunch with?"

"Her sister mostly, if she's in London, but she's out of town a lot on business. She owns a travel company. She has a set of Sloane Ranger flunkies they do lunch with."

"Is there anything that you have or can get hold of that somebody else wants badly enough to do this?"

"Like what?"

"Art. Information. Property."

"Well, I own plenty of buildings other people seem to want."

"Do you have many enemies, Mr Sinclair?"

"Why? Do you think someone's out to get me?"

"Maybe," Archer said. "Tell me more about the phone call."

"They called at three in the afternoon. It was brief. They said I have to pay to get her back. They threatened to kill her if I called the police, as I already told you."

"What did the caller sound like?"

"They used an electronic voice changer. It was mechanical, slow and deep."

"How did you respond?"

"I asked them how much they wanted. They said two million pounds." Sinclair closed his eyes. "I agreed without even thinking and the man said he would call me back within the hour with further instructions."

"And did he?"

Sinclair closed his eyes again and nodded. "At four o'clock. I was told to wait until seven and put the money in the trunk of the Mercedes and have it driven around London while waiting for further instructions by mobile phone. They instructed us to drive a clockwise circuit around Hyde Park. We gave them a mobile number and that was it. If we called the police they said that they would kill her without hesitation."

"Anything else?"

Sinclair shook his head solemnly.

"Nothing else, no proof of life?"

"I asked to speak to her, but they said that she was sleeping as they had drugged her when she put up a fight. She's quite feisty, you see." Sinclair smiled with a deeply etched frown on his hard lived-in face.

"How do you know for sure that they have her?"

"A motorbike courier delivered her handbag with her purse and phone inside. Cash-in-hand job off another motorbike courier. All the cards still intact. Then they called on the private number reserved for friends and family rather than business."

"We can't track the cards or phone then. Where was the drop-off made?"

"Hyde Park."

"Who drove the car?" Archer asked.

"Jones volunteered," Sinclair said, and nodded over at him for support.

"I followed their instructions," Jones said. "I drove around until they called the mobile and they told me where to go. They had me driving around Hyde Park for over an hour, probably checking to see if anyone was following."

"Where exactly did you make the drop?" Archer asked.

"South Carriage Drive, in the park – you know, by the barracks."

"How was it made?"

"I stopped and was instructed by phone to open the boot from inside the car," Jones said. "A van pulled up and parked right behind me and a hoody got out of the back, took the suitcase out and put it in the back of the van."

"What kind of van?"

Jones nodded knowingly as if he had known what the next question would be.

"Dark blue Volkswagen Transporter, new-looking – well, the latest shape anyway."

"Did you get the licence number?"

"Yes, fake plates, we already checked. It's registered to an older van in Scotland."

"Can you describe the hoody?"

"Medium height, broad shoulders but slim, probably early twenties, faded jeans, Nike trainers, faded light blue hoody, with the hood up completely hiding his face, the sort of outfit that blends into the background. Nothing out of the ordinary."

"And then what?"

"He closed the back doors from inside the van and they drove off."

"They?"

"It moved straight away so he wasn't the driver."

"Which way did they go?"

"They went north towards Lancaster Gate."

"Can you describe anything else about him or the van?"

"He jumped out of the back of the van, took the case out of the boot, put it into the back of the van and then jumped back in. In all it only took about ten seconds."

"Okay, thanks," Archer said. The hoody was at the bottom of the food chain, but it would be worth checking the cameras for facial recognition.

"So Mr Archer, will you help me?" Sinclair said.

Every eye in the room was clamped on Archer now. He looked directly into Sinclair's steely grey eyes and tried to read them. His instincts told him that Sinclair was a ruthless manipulator and a naturally competent liar. But why was he fifteenth on Alex's list?

CHAPTER FIVE

"Your wife needs all the help she can get. I will help you, but by my rules. You pay me as a consultant, but I don't take orders from you or anyone else. Is that clear?"

Sinclair sneered and folded his arms. "You'd better be bloody good." A hint of East End occasionally crept into his polished accent. He was all about façade.

Archer loathed Sinclair, but couldn't allow his wife to be killed. He also had to find out if he was connected to the Boathouse, or at least if he could lead him there. In Archer's reckoning this case was not as it first seemed. He still felt like he was being set up.

"And if anything happens to her, will you help me find the men responsible?"

This was confirmation that this case was more complex than just a kidnapping for ransom money. Sinclair was not just concerned about his wife's welfare. There was more to it. His new client wasn't telling him everything.

"Yes."

"Thank you, Mr Archer. I'll pay you whatever it takes to find her and get her back."

Money seemed to be a vulgar concept to this ruthless bastard.

"And I want to find the men who took her. Who do you think they are? Professionals, some sort of criminal organisation?"

Archer's hackles rose, but he stayed calm. He immediately knew that revenge rather than rescue was the primary motivator on display before him.

Know your enemy and know what they want.

"This was not opportunistic, it was targeted and they knew her routine. Either they knew exactly where she was going or they followed her there. In that case they'll know plenty about you too."

"Why's that?" Sinclair asked.

"They knew you could get two million in cash together in a couple of hours without time to go to a bank. And they know that you can and will pay more."

"So they've either been watching me or perhaps you think they know me?"

"Probably both. Have you swept this place for bugs today?"

"It's clean. What else have you got?"

"It's definitely a gang. There has to be at least three of them, two in the Transporter van, probably stolen, and at least one watching Becky, somewhere in London or the Home Counties. Somewhere close to the motorway system."

"How do you know that?"

"They need to have access to the drop-off, unless there are two crews, but kidnappers usually work as a close-knit team. They're either still based in the city, or somewhere out in the country, with access to fast routes back for the ransom drops."

"How do you know they'll call back? They could be long gone already."

Know your enemy and know what they want.

"They'll take you for as much money as they can and it's going to be a lot more than two million. Unless they do in fact want something more specific from you. They haven't shown their real intentions yet. They're building up to something."

"So why haven't they called back then?"

"They'll call, but in their own time. They're showing you who's in control. This could go on for a long time, weeks even. Does anyone know exactly how much cash you can get hold of?"

"Not accurately, no. I deal with many people. But nobody knows everything."

"But it's a lot more than two million, right?"

"Of course, much more in fact," he said, unable to hide his smugness. Sinclair was a more arrogant bastard than he'd initially imagined.

"Then Becky is safe for a while anyway, at least until they've taken enough money or whatever they're really after. Getting her back safe is the hard part and that's what we need to figure out. I'll stick around until the next call if that's all right. I need more information before I can start looking for them."

"Okay. What do we need to do next?"

"Wait for the phone to ring and then ask to speak to her. Stay calm but be firm and don't back down. Try to buy as much time as you can to get the money together. And give me the number of that phone so we can trace the call."

Sinclair wrote the number on the back of a business card and organised for sandwiches to be brought in by his assistant. They arrived in twenty minutes on a large silver platter from Claridge's, but Sinclair didn't eat any. He just sat back at the desk and stared at the phone while the bodyguards eagerly tucked into the free food.

Archer walked out to make a private call on his mobile. He called Zoe from the terrace and asked her to hack into the local exchange and trace the next phone call to the penthouse. He also asked her for a full background check on Becky and Peter Sinclair and to keep digging until she found everything she could. All other jobs would have to wait, including those that boosted their profit margins with the provision of insider information. This case had just become their number one priority.

CHAPTER SIX

Archer quietly interviewed members of staff out on the terrace, while keeping a watchful eye on his new client through the window. He hadn't eliminated Sinclair yet, but the kidnapping seemed more likely to be motivated by ransom money or revenge. At three p.m. he heard the phone and saw Sinclair jump awkwardly to his feet and hit the speaker button after the third ring. Archer ran inside to listen.

"Sinclair," he said calmly, despite the sudden movement.

"Listen carefully. If you want to see your wife again you need to get five million dollars in cash in a suitcase like before plus a half-litre flask of flawless cut diamonds, just like the hot ones from Botswana." The electronic voice changer lowered the pitch and made the call mechanical and far more threatening than a natural voice.

"I want to speak to my wife," Sinclair shouted.

"Shut up and listen," the distorted voice snapped back.

"No, you shut up and listen. Put her on the phone now otherwise you'll get nothing else and I'll come after you with everything I've got."

The line went dead.

Sinclair stared at the phone in shock and then glared at Archer. His face tightened and flushed red in anger. He picked up a crystal paperweight and threw it down at the desk. It bounced off and landed on the floor. Jones jumped up and put it back in its place. Sinclair sat back uneasily with his eyes closed and his head resting on his chest.

Five minutes later the silence was broken and the phone rang again. Sinclair braced himself, sat up straight and pressed the speaker button after two rings.

"Peter. Are you there?" A woman's voice, undistorted, nervous, out of breath.

"Becky. Is that you?" Sinclair started trembling.

"Help me. Do whatever they say. Please help me. I want to come home." Everyone in the room heard her scream and then a muffled sound and a bang like the phone had been dropped. Sinclair jumped to his feet, thumped the desk and kicked his chair backwards.

The distorted voice returned. "Get the money and the diamonds and we'll call you in two hours with instructions on where to make the drop."

"When will I get her back?"

The line went dead.

Sinclair was shaking. He made a private call on the cylindrical handset next to the conference phone. He turned his back and spoke quietly, but Archer overheard him mention five million dollars and a half-litre flask of diamonds from Botswana in half an hour.

"Make sure we're ready to go again in two hours," Sinclair ordered.

Archer walked to the lobby and called Zoe. The kidnapper's call had been too short. She couldn't trace it back far enough. She would try again with the next call.

"I'll call you when I find something useful," she said and ended the call.

Archer returned to the living room. Three of the men walked out to the terrace and started smoking. The other two including Jones sat in armchairs and waited in silence.

Sinclair was still seated, staring at the portrait on the wall.

"Can we talk somewhere private?" Archer asked.

Sinclair got up stiffly as if in pain and said, "Follow me." Archer followed him to the rear hallway and up the stairs to the tenth floor. A quiet floor with what looked like guest bedrooms and a large private study. Was this the retreat where he schemed and plotted?

The study was full of trophies, including a picture of Becky riding a horse through the surf on a beach, with a bronze sculpture of a female rider and horse below. It was a classical study in contrast to the rest of the modern apartment. The walls were light oak panels and the shelves were filled with old books, artefacts and sculptures. The art on the walls was also classical, more Canaletto's Venice than Picasso's Cubism downstairs. Sinclair sat down wearily at the desk and Archer sat in the green leather armchair opposite.

"There has to be an insider," Archer said.

"How do you know that?"

"The kidnappers have inside information. First, they know you can get hold of substantial amounts of cash in sterling and dollars."

"So can plenty of other people in London," he said, with disdain.

"Plus they know you can quickly get your hands on cut diamonds."

"Okay, less common than cash, but still not unique. Carry on."

"Specifically, they know you have some illicit diamonds from Botswana."

"All right, not so common, but I still can't form a shortlist on that basis alone."

"How much does your wife know about your business dealings?"

"Too much," Sinclair blurted out quickly, before his face reddened. "I mean too much for her own good." The recovery failed to mask his apparent discomfort at this revelation. But if his wife did know too much and he wanted to bump her off, there were far easier ways than faking her kidnapping and putting on a complex show like this. The same would be true if she was running away from him.

Sinclair turned and looked out of the window.

Archer thought through his potential suspect list: Sinclair, Becky, Relatives, Staff, Friends, Enemies and Opportunists.

The phone vibrated twice in his hand with an incoming text from Zoe. He made an excuse to call the office about the trace and Sinclair walked back downstairs in a trance. Archer stayed seated in the study and speed-dialled his office.

"Hey, what's up?"

"Sinclair hides a lot of his deals. He's careful, but I'll find a hole in his armour somewhere, don't worry. There has to be one. There always is."

"What are the signs?" Archer said.

"The usual stuff when something bad is being covered up by immoral lawyers and bankers on massive fees. It takes a poor moralistic hacker like me to find them."

"Like what?"

"Layers of offshore shell companies with transactions through numbered bank accounts in Switzerland, Aruba and the Cayman Islands. He's well connected in several countries via lobbyists and agents. And I just found a trail of property deals leading back to Washington D.C. and the CEO of a major defence contractor. Be careful, Sean."

Sinclair was definitely connected to cold-blooded killers. But was he connected to the cold-blooded killers behind the Boathouse?

CHAPTER SEVEN

Sinclair sat bolt upright at the desk. His stare switched between the phone and his solid gold Rolex with occasional glances towards the large portrait on the wall. At five p.m. the phone rang as promised. Sinclair pressed the speaker button after the third ring and listened carefully to the instructions to drive around the circuit. At the end of the call he quietly said, "Okay, so when do we do the exchange?" The line went dead.

As he stood up he took a deep breath and addressed his team. "Load the money and the diamonds into the car and drive around the circuit again, like before. Start in an hour. Who wants to make the drop?"

"I'll do it," Jones said.

"I'll go with him," Archer said.

The other four men at the table started talking quietly and then one walked towards Sinclair.

"Shall we follow them, sir?" asked the biggest one.

"No, not yet," Sinclair said.

"What's the circuit?" Archer asked.

"Basically it's a clockwise route around Hyde Park," Sinclair said.

He walked off towards the master bedroom. It was on the same floor as the living room, across the entrance hall. Archer was still waiting to see inside it. The four men at the table openly discussed the call while Jones walked over to Archer.

"Be ready in half an hour," Jones said, and walked off.

The stockiest of the four men broke away and nodded at Archer. "So are you going to help us find out who's behind this?" he said.

"Yes," Archer said.

"You find them and we'll sort them out," he said. "Once Mrs Sinclair's back safe we'll get the money back and then shut them down for good. They won't be bothering anyone after we've finished with them."

Archer looked into the stocky man's dark eyes and believed he meant it.

Then the man stuck his arm out to shake hands and a huge bicep flexed into action beneath the silky grey suit.

"John Haywood," he said. "Pleased to meet you." His crushing grip lasted a moment too long. Archer wondered if the excessive muscles and handshake were over-compensating for some hidden weakness. The ice was broken, but only by a hairline crack. The rest of the men slowly stepped forward to introduce themselves. Adams was the biggest, Best the shortest and Clarke the nastiest. They shook hands with Archer, but he sensed they were still keeping their distance. There was not a hint of warmth or a welcoming smile. He was still the untrusted outsider.

"So do you all work for a security firm or what?" Archer asked. No reply. "What kind of security do you guys do?"

Archer focused on Haywood. But he just stared back without expression.

"You're all retired SAS though, right? Archer asked.

"Not too difficult to guess, but Clarkey here was a Commando."

Archer asked them some light questions and they answered curtly until Peter Sinclair came back into sight. He was pulling a large suitcase that looked stretched full and heavy. Five million dollars just like that, Archer thought. Some cash machine this guy has access to. He estimated that it weighed about fifty kilos. The case had two wheels, not four, and was bulging to its expanded limits, like elasticated trousers on a mud wrestler. Sinclair wheeled it out to the entrance hall, where it fell over and crashed onto the marble floor with a dull thud.

Jones flinched and the four guards instinctively reached for their weapons. Archer noted the exact locations of their reflex actions and followed Sinclair into the entrance hall.

"Can I see Becky's room now and her personal effects?"

"Why?" Sinclair said, over-defensively.

"It's called investigating. I'm trying to help you, remember?"

"Okay, follow me." Sinclair frowned and tapped his leg nervously as he led the way.

He followed Sinclair to the modern master bedroom across the entrance hall. More of the same grey and neutral tones. Again, nothing feminine except a heavy-looking crystal vase of white tulips and some tastefully framed holiday photographs of the Sinclairs.

"Any children?"

"No." Sinclair snapped.

The bedside tables told two stories. One had an alarm clock and a photograph of Becky looking radiant. The other had several photographs and recent hardbacks. The photo of Peter Sinclair posing with a shovel at a construction site was dwarfed by one of three women preparing to ski down a mountain.

"Who are they?" Archer asked.

"That's her sister Louise and her niece Amanda."

"Are they close?"

"Is this really necessary?"

"Yes."

"Very," Sinclair said, and grimaced as if he had a bad taste in his mouth.

Archer took a photo of it and sent it to Zoe. He skipped the all-marble en-suite bathroom with its giant marble bath and in-built television. Instead he headed straight for the walk-in closet full of designer clothes and shoes. Hundreds of shoes and handbags lined up on show. Archer started to look through the drawers in the closet, causing Sinclair to raise an eyebrow. One of the drawers was full of jewellery, another of watches. Several contained expensive-looking underwear, mostly matching sets of silk lingerie. Archer wondered if Becky was naturally well proportioned or surgically enhanced, but decided not to comment.

The bottom drawer, about the size of a briefcase, was full of neatly stacked money, bundles of new twenty-pound notes.

"How much is there?"

"Two hundred thousand."

"Why all the cash?"

"She has expensive tastes and a limitless charge card, but sometimes only cash is king. She has instant access to it if she needs it."

A fortune to most people, but he thinks it's just some spare cash stashed in a drawer.

"Okay, thanks. I've seen enough for now," Archer said. "I'll need to speak to the rest of your staff, but I can do that later."

Archer followed Sinclair back to the living room. The suitcase was still on the floor, in the entrance hall. A small stainless-steel flask had appeared next to it. Jones and the other men were still sitting quietly in the living room. Jones nodded that it was time to leave. Adams and Best took the case and the diamonds to the car. Clarke and Haywood stayed seated with Sinclair in the living room. Archer assumed they were his most trusted bodyguards.

At ten minutes to six, Jones drove the black Mercedes out onto Park Lane in bumper-to-bumper rush hour traffic with Archer in the passenger seat. Five million dollars in cash in the boot and a small flask of sparkling diamonds between his legs worth well over two million dollars. The second drop was underway.

CHAPTER EIGHT

Jones drove the Mercedes around the congested street circuit exactly as instructed by the kidnappers. Knightsbridge was still busy with shoppers as Archer stared out of the window. Throngs of tired-looking commuters still travelling home from work. Cyclists in suits with their computers in rucksacks. Joggers who left their suits in the office. People in office outfits wearing trainers to walk easier and faster, some even overtaking slower people out exercising. The pace of commuting had increased dramatically over the years. These fit commuters were seriously focused on minimising their journey time as they elbowed tourists and dawdlers out of the way, as if they had a birth right to be first wherever they happened to be. He noted the contrast as they passed the overweight smokers and drinkers standing outside pubs calmly waiting for the rush hour to pass. It was all easy to watch from the comfort of a luxury air-conditioned sedan.

Becky would be used to the remoteness of wealth, accustomed to the finer things in life, like being whisked around in style and never getting too close to the workers. She was probably struggling with her ordeal on several levels. Being held prisoner, not in control or comfort, but far too close to strangers and fearing what they might do to her.

The route around Hyde Park took between ten and twenty minutes per lap depending on the traffic and the lights. Archer counted the fourth lap out loud and checked his watch. They had been driving for exactly one hour and it was getting dark, but still no call.

"Do you always drive the Sinclairs around?" Archer asked.

"I'm mainly Mrs Sinclair's driver, but sometimes I drive Mr Sinclair."

"Does she always keep to the same routine every week?"

"She favours certain shops and restaurants, normally after her workout."

Jones was a steady driver and held his nerve well during an hour of mild interrogation. He kept hitting Archer's questions back over the net without taking his eyes off the road or showing any signs of stress, like a well-trained ex-soldier.

"Does she socialise much?"

"Long lunches with her sister, dinners and functions with Mr Sinclair."

"Are she and her sister good friends?"

"They argue like all sisters."

"Any notable jealousy?"

"Her sister's a bit envious of Mrs Sinclair's wealth I suppose but they're still close."

"What else does Mrs Sinclair like to do?"

"Keeps fit, watches movies and reads a lot."

"No clubs or charities?"

"Not to my knowledge."

"Any male friends?"

Jones took his eyes off the road for a second and gave Archer a bemused sideways glance in total disbelief.

"You must be joking, Mr Sinclair wouldn't have any of that."

Archer had finally made a dent in the stiff-lipped driver. Jones showed he had some personality hidden somewhere beneath the surface. This was the exploratory foot in the door Archer was after; he had to bond with someone on the inside. He was about to change tack and make the move, when the mobile phone in the cradle lit up. He answered it on the second ring on speaker.

"Yes."

"Turn left and park in front of the Hilton."

Archer hit the mute button.

"Turn left up there." He pointed but Jones was already indicating.

They had just passed the turning for Curzon Street and took the next left and another immediate left which brought them right in front of the hotel entrance. They reverse-parked next to two other German-made cars in front of the high-rise hotel, the boot facing Park Lane and the park. Jones turned the mute button off and the sound system's volume up.

"Okay, what next?" Archer said.

"Put the flask on the ground in front of the car while letting down the driver's side front tyre. Then take the bag to the concierge. Tell him it's for Mr Jefferson."

"And then?"

"Pump the tyre back up and go home. Don't hang around the lobby or follow anyone otherwise she gets a bullet in the head."

The line went dead.

"Open the boot and I'll take the bag to the concierge. Here, you take the flask and let the tyre down," Archer said.

Jones pressed the button to open the boot and it started to lift slowly. He took the flask and opened the door. Archer opened his door and got out. People were milling around in all directions but nobody was taking any notice of them. Taxi drivers were talking in a group, the doorman was talking to a cab driver. A group of couriers were smoking near their bikes.

Archer lifted the heavy bag out, carefully placed its two wheels on the pavement and closed the boot. He looked up at the twenty-seven-storey hotel and wondered if they were being watched. A vivid image of his friend free-falling flashed before him. He had died base jumping off the hotel roof when they were twenty. The chute had snagged and his arm was torn off on the way down. Archer had witnessed it from the rooftop and had never base jumped since.

He watched Jones place the flask in front of the car and unscrew the dust cap. Jones then squatted down beside the wheel and used his nail to depress the valve and let the air out.

Archer wheeled the heavy case past Jones and yanked it up the kerb. The doorman asked if he wanted any help but he politely declined, shimmied through the revolving door into the lobby and casually strolled across to the concierge desk. He waited in line behind a tourist getting directions to a restaurant and then stepped up to the desk. He was greeted by Sergio from Spain, or so his badge stated.

"Luggage for Mr Jefferson."

The young concierge's eyes bulged greedily and his face lit up.

"We've been expecting that one, thank you, sir, let me come and get it."

The concierge grabbed the handle and pulled it towards the lifts. He seemed to wait for a lift, but as Archer exited the front entrance he looked back and saw the concierge walk away towards the rear entrance pulling the case behind him.

Archer walked out of the front entrance and saw Jones take a small bag from the boot. He then sat in the car with the door open and opened the bag. The front tyre was deflated and the flask of diamonds was still on the ground. He was getting the pump ready as a silver BMW motorbike stopped in front of the car. The leather-clad rider was wearing a full face helmet but appeared to be male. He bent down, picked up the flask, and put it in a small rucksack.

The biker headed off down Pitt's Head Mews. Archer ran to the corner of the hotel to see if he could read the small number-plate for Zoe to track by hacking into the CCTV system. As he turned the corner he saw the biker had stopped. A lorry was blocking the road while a crane was unloading materials at a construction site. This was an opportunity to read the plate if he could get close enough. Archer sprinted down the road. The biker was only forty yards away, but wasn't waiting for the road to clear. He spun the bike around, leaving half a donut of rubber behind, and headed back towards Archer, who automatically stopped in the middle of the road and held his hands out, shouting, "Stop!" Which immediately felt like a stupid thing to do.

The fit-looking biker stopped six feet in front of him and casually reached inside his leather jacket, pulled out a yellow Taser gun and aimed it at Archer. He motioned it towards the pavement and Archer moved off the road and jerked uncontrollably as his body went into spasm. Every muscle in his body tightened and became rigid with the fifty-thousand-volt shock from the Taser. It stopped, and his legs fell away beneath him. His muscles vibrated as if he'd had a mains electric shock. His body went numb and seemed to fall asleep for a minute or two. He couldn't move, and then he felt hot, and as soon as he could move again his muscles started to tingle. He tried to stand but was too weak. Hundreds of pins prodded his skin before it was set on fire, prickling, itching. Would it ever end? He sat on the kerb with his head bowed between his knees for a couple of minutes to recover. Pedestrians passed by, but nobody stopped.

He got up, still feeling weak, and managed to stumble back to the car, slumping into the passenger seat next to a relaxed-looking Jones.

"What happened to you? You look like shit."

"Never mind, let's get out of here."

"Did you get the plate?"

"No, did you?"

"No."

"Let's tell Sinclair what happened and then come back and see the concierge."

CHAPTER NINE

They drove from the hotel via Berkeley Square, where Jones pointed out his boss's office. He waved at the doorman standing outside the Connaught, who looked like another ex-soldier, and then turned sharp left into Adams Row, stopping in front of Sinclair's double mews garage. They sat in the car with the engine running in the quiet cobbled lane near Grosvenor Square. Jones told him that the garage housed four of Sinclair's cars and had a four-bedroom serviced apartment above it which was used by his staff to stay overnight if required. Archer acted disinterested in the garage and flat, but noted all the information freely provided. There seemed to be no end to Sinclair's cash or ego.

"I need to know more about Becky Sinclair," he said.

"Like what?"

"Personal details, discussions when you were in the car with her or places that you took her. I need to know about her private life, her friends and family."

"Her sister Louise, Mrs Palmer, is her closest friend."

"Where does she live?"

"Knightsbridge. It's not far but there's no point going there as she's away on a business trip."

"How do you know?"

"I took her to the airport with Mrs Sinclair. We always take her to the airport."

"When was that?"

"Sunday, the day before they took Mrs Sinclair."

"When is she due back?"

"We're picking her up next week. The flight details are in the glove box."

"What were they talking about before she left?"

"Nothing special."

"Think harder, anything about where she was going the next day?"

"Well they were – no, I can't tell you, it was private. It's got nothing to do with what's happened anyway."

Archer decided not to push Jones in case he clammed up. But he would come back to it even if it required some leverage.

"Can you show me where she lives and get me her mobile phone number after we go back to the hotel?"

"Okay. I'll do that, but first I'm going to get a snack in that café on the corner, then we'll go. I'll come and get you after you've told Mr Sinclair what just happened."

"And try telling me everything you know. Just imagine what kind of job you'll have if we don't find her."

Jones frowned nervously as Archer opened the passenger door and welcomed the blast of cool fresh air. He got out and started walking back towards the penthouse. He took out his phone and made a call.

"Hey."

"Hey, hold on," Zoe said. Then he heard a burst of rapid gun-fire.

"Where are you?"

"Hang on, I'm at the shooting range. My flat was turned over while I was at work so I'm venting and practising in case they return."

"You okay?"

"I'm fine, I wasn't there, but you know how it is, it feels strange."

"Did they take anything?"

"Only an old laptop with nothing interesting on it. Maybe some porn. Listen, there was a fat detective with a head like a bull looking for you just before I left the office. He said he would come back tomorrow. Had some questions for you but wouldn't leave his name."

"Give him my number and I'll sort it out tomorrow. See if you can track the bike via the camera systems, but first get me some leverage on Steve Jones, Sinclair's driver, within the hour."

"Okay, I'm nearly done here. I have to get back as the locksmith is coming."

"So what else have you got for me?"

Archer noted the French-looking café on the corner, jay-walked across South Audley Street and headed towards the back of the Grosvenor House Hotel down Reeves Mews. A handy shortcut to Park Street and the rear entrance to Sinclair's penthouse.

"The Firm's old system traced the calls back to a provider within London's zero twenty exchange, but it's being bounced around again from there so I need more time. I need to borrow a better system. Tell him to stay on the phone a little bit longer, okay?"

"I'll tell him. Look, we really need to find her and fast. I need you focused on Peter and Becky Sinclair. There's something not right about this."

CHAPTER TEN

The doorman at Sinclair's mansion block recognised Archer and bowed his shaved head as he opened the door for him. He rode the dedicated penthouse lift to the ninth floor, still agitated and aching from the Taser, thinking about what had just happened at the hotel. The drop-off was all over in a flash. Professionally planned and well executed.

Who are these people?

Sinclair's door opened automatically again. Archer gritted his teeth in anticipation of a frosty reception as he walked towards the living room. He hardly knew him, but he already hated Sinclair. The man was pathetic. But he had to play the game to see where it would lead. Sinclair was the first to spot him and pounced towards him like a hungry wild cat.

"What happened?"

The four guards stared coldly from the table.

"The drop-off was at the Hilton, just down the road, right under our noses. We followed their instructions to the letter, and now they've got the money and the diamonds."

"Did you see anything, do you have any leads?"

"We're going back to talk to the concierge, he may know something."

"Didn't you follow them?"

"We had to let the tyre down. A biker took the diamonds and the concierge took the money to the back entrance."

"So you're telling me that they got away again and we've got nothing."

Sinclair's face flushed and his body was shaking. The guards conveniently removed themselves from the living room.

"We may get a lead from the bike or the concierge. We were instructed to pump the tyre up and leave. No hanging around and no following, otherwise they would shoot her."

"I need you to find her, Archer."

"I know."

"Is it about the money? Do you want me to pay you in advance, is that it?"

"It's not about the money."

Sinclair breathed heavily as he walked back to his desk and opened the drawer underneath. He withdrew a large white chequebook and slapped it down hard on the desk. He sat down and slowly unscrewed the top off a silver fountain pen. The room was silent except for the sound of the gold nib scribbling across the smooth surface and the large paper rectangle being torn out.

He held it out, shaking it dramatically in front of him to dry.

"Here, take this, and then find her."

"I'm not taking it, but I will find her."

"It's a retainer for a hundred thousand pounds. Now take it." Sinclair paused and then raised his voice again, "Take it, damn it. I just told you to take it, so do as I say." His bottom lip trembled in anger.

"No," Archer said.

"You can always frame it for posterity if you don't want to cash it." He said it mockingly and chortled openly in disgust.

"Who uses cheques these days? Wire it like everyone else. I'll write down my account number, give me the pen."

Archer wrote the name, sort code and account number for Londinium Lux Limited on the back of the cheque. Sinclair called for a laptop and one of his assistants appeared within seconds. He sat down with the laptop and a small code machine from his bank and transferred the money himself.

"There, it's done."

"Thanks. Look, we've traced the calls back to London, but we need you to stay on the call a bit longer. Try and ask them some more questions about Becky. Ask to speak to her again, get into a conversation with them, anything just make them stay on the line."

"I'll try."

"If you can keep them on the line, we can trace the call. Find them, and we find Becky. So give it your best shot, okay?"

"Understood."

"Ransom calls follow a pattern. There will be another call and that's the one you need to nail for us. My team is working on it. They know what they're doing. Trust us. We'll find them, but I need more information."

Archer was distracted as he read an incoming text from Zoe.

Jones returned to the penthouse after visiting the café and signalled to Archer with a thumbs up sign that he was ready to go but stayed out in the entrance hall away from his boss. Archer told Sinclair where he was going and followed Jones out to the waiting lift.

"Are you going to tell me what the sisters were talking about in the car?"

"No."

"Does Sinclair know you occasionally moonlight for cash in his car?"

The colour instantly drained from Jones's face.

"I'll tell you, after we've spoken to the concierge. Just don't ever mention the moonlighting thing again. I'll show you where her sister lives, but you have to promise me that you won't tell anyone else what she said."

CHAPTER ELEVEN

Archer entered the hotel through the revolving doorway. The dark-haired concierge was leaving the desk, walking swiftly towards the rear entrance. Archer sped past reception and called after him near the lift lobby. "Hey, hold on."

He turned around and frowned when he recognised him.

"Oh, it's you – look, I'm on my break."

"Can I ask you some questions?"

"Sure, but my memory is not so good, huh." He smiled confidently and licked his lips. Archer flashed his wallet and told him to follow. They went out the rear entrance where it was quiet and stood in an empty hotel parking bay. Archer gave him two hundred pounds and heard all he knew in less than two minutes.

Archer walked around the outside of the hotel and got back into the waiting car at the main entrance. Jones pulled away and gently nudged the car back onto Park Lane. They were heading towards South Kensington to Louise Palmer's house.

"So what did he have to say?" Jones asked.

"Not a lot."

"Nothing?"

"He was given the job by phone and paid six hundred in cash upon delivering the bag to a waiting taxi. Supposed to be going to Heathrow to catch up with Mr Jefferson."

"Was it a black cab?"

"He thinks it was a regular black cab driver with a cockney accent who gave him an envelope. He didn't take down the number."

As they drove along part of the earlier street circuit, Jones pointed to his left and said: "Her sister's office is down there. She lives a short walk away."

Louise Palmer's travel company was located amongst the designer clothes shops of Sloane Street. A good location for wealthy passing trade.

The black Mercedes cruised quietly down Gloucester Road before slowing down at Launceston Place. They inched carefully through a narrow wisteria-covered stone archway onto the cobbles of Kenance Mews. The sister's house was a pretty mews cottage painted off-white with pale blue shutters and woodwork. Very Provençal.

They stopped twenty yards away. The lights were on and the curtains closed. Jones told him that she always left the lights on timer and the house was alarmed.

"Tell me about the conversation on the way to the airport. I think it's important. Just what was it Becky said to Louise?"

"Mrs Sinclair was upset about something. Her sister said they would talk about it when she came back. In the meantime she should pamper herself and shop."

"What was she upset about?"

"She said that she wanted to get her own doctor. She didn't want to use Mr Sinclair's private clinic doctors any more."

"What else?"

"Mrs Palmer was in a really bad mood because she'd left her mobile phone in her office so she had to buy a new one in the airport."

A moving shadow was visible on the cream-coloured curtains upstairs. It was obvious that someone was inside the house, moving around. Jones and Archer looked at each other and Archer opened his door.

"Let's go and find out who's in the house while she's away."

They left the car a few houses down from Louise's and walked up to the front door. Jones rang the bell and they waited.

No answer. They waited patiently for a minute before ringing the bell again. Still nothing. Then another minute before ringing it again and knocking on the door hard. A woman's voice shouted: "Hold on."

Someone stomped rapidly down the stairs, rattled the chain and unlocked the door. A tired-looking woman with short orange hair, tight faded jeans and an even tighter white T-shirt recognised Jones immediately. She was the regular cleaner working late.

"What do you want?"

"Is Mrs Palmer in?" Jones said.

"No. She's away on business."

"Do you know when she'll be back?"

"Next week, I have to go."

She slammed the door in their faces.

"Polish," Jones said as they walked back to the car. Jones started the engine but didn't drive off. He just sat there as if he wanted to get something off his chest.

"What's the matter?"

"Nothing."

"What else did they talk about?" He saw Jones wince. He was clearly uncomfortable. Archer stayed silent until he spoke.

"The Sinclairs use a private clinic in Switzerland, and Becky is not happy about it."

"Why's that?"

"It has cryogenic facilities for a start."

"Really?"

"I'm not comfortable talking like this."

"You have my word that it won't go any further. It could help us find her, so tell me all you know."

"Mr Sinclair hates children."

"Okay, some people do."

"He has stem cells at the clinic for cloning replacement body parts."

Archer raised his eyebrows and Jones winced awkwardly. Was this guy for real? It all sounded a bit too far-fetched, but Sinclair was a control freak. And immortality was the ultimate control. The world was full of nutters and unfortunately Sinclair had more than enough money to live out his wildest fantasies.

"Is that what they were talking about in the car?"

"Not exactly. You see … You see, Mrs Sinclair is afraid of falling pregnant."

"Why?"

"Because of what Mr Sinclair might do to her."

"What's she afraid of?"

"She told her sister she was late and she thought she was pregnant."

"Thought?"

"She did the test and she wasn't pregnant, but she was scared and wanted to talk to the doctor about her contraception."

"Did she tell Sinclair?"

"No, she told the doctor and he told Mr Sinclair."

40

"So she wants to find a new doctor?"

"She's going to register with her sister's doctor next week."

"What did Sinclair say to her after he found out?"

"He called her a stupid fucking airhead and punched her in the stomach."

CHAPTER TWELVE

Sinclair was not in the living room when Archer returned to the penthouse. Best was at the desk manning the phone while Adams played with a silver pen. He was sitting at the table and dexterously twirled the pen around the fingers of his right hand, keeping it moving and passing it between his fingers like a magician at a children's party. The room was quiet apart from the female newsreader talking on the large screen, but the volume was down low. The lighting was soft, coming only from table lamps. Archer was irritated in seconds by Adams' mindless pen trick and waited for Sinclair outside on the terrace.

The air was chill and the park looked like a black hole preventing any light from escaping. Archer stared into the darkness and felt it drawing him in, until a stool scraped the floor nearby and startled him. Haywood was at the far end of the terrace, sitting smoking a cigarette. Archer acknowledged him with a deferential nod of the head and stayed at the railing looking down at the eight lanes of traffic below. He wondered if the kidnappers were watching the penthouse. Through a spotting scope inside a hotel room with a direct line of sight, like on the Bayswater Road. A police car siren was getting louder. When it passed it was deafening. Archer wondered how long it had been since the siren makers had gone out of control with the concept of letting people know the cavalry was coming. There was nothing wrong with the old blues-and-twos; with the traditional two-tone horn so quintessentially British and still used in some places, but not here.

His mobile phone vibrated in his right trouser pocket.

"Hey," Zoe said.

"Hey, what's up?"

He walked away from Haywood's earshot to the opposite end of the terrace and noticed that it turned the corner towards the master bedroom. He could see an outdoor sofa and a discreet hot tub partially hidden behind a topiary screen, but couldn't imagine Sinclair and Becky soaking together with champagne and candles.

"I'm sending you some more information. You need to check it out."

"What have you got?"

"No luck with the bike. But there are too many people close to him who've been killed or gone missing. It looks like he hired Oakland Security five years ago, but it's a cleverly masked contract with layers of offshore companies. There's also a link to a firm in Virginia."

"I'll read the files back at my place."

"Be careful. There's a long list of arson attacks on buildings just before he buys them and people who won't sell conveniently committing suicide. Oh yeah, and his old fiancée before he got married to Becky died in a car crash and her brother is convinced that it wasn't an accident. But nothing ever sticks."

"Where's the brother?"

"He's a hot-shot lawyer in the City."

"Get me his number."

"No problem – you okay?"

"Don't worry about me."

"Someone has to."

"All right then."

"Work is piling up, so pull your finger out and come back safe."

"Thanks, Zoe."

Archer sat on a stool keeping his distance from Haywood. He needed some space to think. There was definitely an insider involved, but who was it?

Peter Sinclair entered the living room in fresh clothes. His hair was still damp and his face was flushed pink. He had replaced his suit with grey flannel trousers and a grey ribbed roll top beneath a navy blazer. Archer thought he was grey to the heart.

Best moved from the desk to the sofa and continued watching the news channel. Archer observed them from the terrace. He could see Best lusting after the newsreader like a mindless pervert. Secretly undressing her. His darting eyes and tongue way too obvious.

Sinclair sat back at the desk, bolt upright like a proud sentry guarding something important. He placed his hands in front of him on the desk and clasped them loosely. Left over right. Archer had already noticed he was a lefty when he signed the cheque.

Archer walked in front of Best without acknowledging him and went straight up to the desk to talk to Sinclair. They stared at each other in silence for a few seconds.

"You should get some rest."

"I'm waiting for the next call. I want her back here where she belongs."

"They won't call you again tonight. You may as well try and get some rest."

"They may call, and if they do, I'll be here. Remember I'm paying you to find the kidnappers, not to babysit me."

"Okay, your call. I'll be back in the morning."

"Fucking lightweight," Sinclair muttered sharply and looked away.

Archer left the penthouse quietly, walked home via Hyde Park Corner underpass and along the Old Brompton Road to Walton Street. He immediately changed into his running kit to crank up the endorphins and pound the endless maze of late-night streets. His mind was far too active, and he wasn't tired enough to sleep. He needed to clear his thoughts and get into his rhythm. His subconscious often solved problems when he let it work without any clutter.

A car engine started up as he began his run. He glimpsed a navy Ford Focus across the street pulling away slowly. He ran through Chelsea towards Battersea Bridge. The car was still tailing him by about a hundred yards when he reached the cooler air by the river, so he changed course, doubled back and took a narrow passageway off Cheyne Walk and made a dog-legged detour before getting back onto Chelsea Embankment and crossing Albert Bridge. The navy Ford tail had gone.

He ran back towards Chelsea over Battersea Bridge, feeling as if the past was catching him like a dark cloud he couldn't shake off. He ran faster and felt a chill on the back of his neck that made him shiver. He sprinted along Cheyne Walk, but no matter how fast he ran, he knew he could never escape the past, even if he couldn't remember fourteen years of it.

As he turned the corner into Walton Street, he saw the navy car was parked across the street from his house. He tapped the passenger window and the driver shouted, "Get in."

Archer opened the passenger door and poked his head inside, as the driver thrust his warrant card at him. "DS Lambert, have a seat, Mr Archer."

Lambert wore a black leather jacket, flat cap and East End accent via West Ham, Barking or Dagenham. The inside of the car was dark and stank of sweat and stale cigarette smoke. The big man spilled out from the seat in all directions and greeted Archer with a glare and worn-out grimace on a pumped-up pumpkin of a pock-marked face.

"How can I help you, Detective Sergeant?"

"I'd like to ask you some questions about last Wednesday evening. Where were you between six and ten?"

"Is this a formal interview, DS Lambert?"

"Don't be a dumb fuck."

"I can see you're from Southwark CID, and I definitely did not make it south of the river last week. So I think we're done here."

"Watch it, Archer. We both know you were in Ruislip. And you're in deep shit. You're under surveillance. Now get out."

Archer stopped himself from responding, got out and slammed the door as the car sped off. Proper police surveillance didn't come with a health warning. This was a cheap tactic: by a dirty cop paid to intimidate him by whoever was responsible for last night's nasty encounter.

CHAPTER THIRTEEN

The next morning at quarter to eight, without breakfast or coffee, Archer headed off to South Kensington tube station, compiling and evaluating theories. He topped up his Oyster card with sixty pounds and took the Piccadilly line three stops east to Green Park. The forty-year-old tube train was hot and packed full of miserable looking commuters still half asleep. Some builders and outdoor manual workers were dotted around the carriage, but the majority appeared to be from offices and shops. Wearing the drab uniforms of their chosen professions, they all blended into a dullish grey mixture of vocational blandness.

The world's first underground was still running without proper air-conditioning on most of its routes, including the busy Piccadilly Line. Even in the autumn and winter it was uncomfortably hot at times. Especially when people squeezed themselves into the rush hour crowds, only to end up crushed inside the carriage, as they invaded each other's personal spaces, like helpless animals heading off to slaughter. Men and women pressed up against each other. Perverts copping a feel of the past as they rubbed bodies with younger, fitter women way out of their league. The discomfort was tolerated, but the mood was simmering between unpleasant and hostile.

The air in the claustrophobic carriage felt stale and heavy. After only three stops he was glad to get out. On the platform the air was still stuffy and recycled but the odd blast of cooler air from the tunnel gave him hope of getting enough oxygen to avoid suffocation. As he travelled up the escalator the air became thinner, cooler and fresher. Back out on the street the exhaust-tinged environment felt fresh like sea air in his oxygen starved lungs as he sucked it down deep and instantly felt better.

He crossed Piccadilly and strolled purposefully through random throngs of commuters towards Berkeley Square. He had discarded his usual office attire of Diesel jeans, Oxford shirt, cotton jacket and Chelsea boots for a more robust outfit. Darker jeans, rugged walking boots, long-sleeved polo shirt and his favourite black leather jacket. He stopped and sat on a wooden bench on his way through Berkeley Square. The case needed a break as his theories were about as stale as the tube train he'd just suffocated inside. Sinclair wasn't ruled out of the mix just yet, but it was far too elaborate a scheme for a bored husband to be bumping off his gold-digging wife. Becky was still a suspect, with a trusted accomplice in her sister, who might not be away on business after all. Both untraceable without their phones, but it was a complicated and dangerous way to leave a powerful husband, and less lucrative than finding a good divorce lawyer, so highly unlikely. The insider angle was still the key to catching the kidnappers. There had to be an insider and they were teamed up with an enemy or an opportunist, mainly motivated by ransom money. But he was still only skimming the surface. He needed much more information before he could run his powerful digital tracking and profiling models. Coffee, bacon and eggs required urgently.

He noted that Sinclair's cars were all still garaged in Adams Row before he stopped at Café Richoux on South Audley Street for breakfast. The décor was continental; it was like he had been transported to a café in Paris or Vienna. He sat in the corner with his back to the wall and a good view of the room and the door. The clientele was mixed. Business-people, tourists and workers. He overheard a large man in a track suit explaining to a family on holiday that he was staying in a five star hotel nearby that wanted ninety-five pounds for breakfast. "London's criminal. Full of sharks." The man owned a football club up north, but he was still shocked by the extortionate prices in central London. Archer stopped people-watching, ordered his breakfast, read the headlines and started doing the crossword. *Heartfelt appeal, from the depths.* Two and nine. He knew it. *De Profundis.* Good start.

He finished off his crispy bacon and scrambled egg with HP Sauce, drank Tabasco- and Worcester-sauce-infused tomato juice and changed papers and crosswords from *The Times* to *The Telegraph*. Two rounds of wholemeal toast, butter and thick-cut Oxford marmalade and another pot of freshly ground Illy coffee. It was half past eight and he wanted to be back at Sinclair's apartment before nine. Ready to tackle anything.

One round of toast and two thirds of the crossword to go. He was on form and was feeling compelled to finish it, until his mobile phone rang.

"Slumming it in Mayfair again, I see? How's Café Richoux?"

"Always good to know you're keeping track of my whereabouts."

"Someone has to. I've just sent you the brother's telephone number – the brother of the fiancée who came to a sticky end. His name is Julian Cavendish and his sister was Jane. He hates Sinclair with a passion. Now it looks like Becky's going down the same hole, he ought to sing."

"Excellent, thanks, Zoe, I'm going back into his evil eyrie now. I'll call you later."

Archer paid his bill and left a generous tip. As he walked to the penthouse he called Julian Cavendish, but got his voicemail, so he left a message.

He was back at the penthouse before nine. Sinclair was sitting on the sofa watching the news. His face was pale and crumpled. He looked completely exhausted. The mood in the living room was gloomier than the night before and even the glamorous presenters on the news channels were unable to ease the awkward tension.

The ten a.m. weather forecaster was an attractive blonde woman dressed as if she was going out on a date in a tight skirt, low-cut blouse, bright red lipstick and matching jacket. Archer wondered if the bodyguards were ever interested in the news and weather. He knew the answer. She had the room's full attention and promised no rain, blue skies and a cold wind from the North-east.

She smiled vacantly and started to go into more detail as the phone rang. All eyes jumped from the pretty weather forecaster on the big screen to the phone ringing on the desk.

Sinclair burst with energy. He pounced off the sofa towards the desk like a leopard focused on its prey. He grabbed the desk before pressing the speaker button on the second ring. He then paused briefly to calm himself before answering.

"Hello, Peter, where's my sister?"

"Oh Louise, it's you."

"Becky's not answering her phone – is she all right?"

"She's gone to the spa, she needed some space and alone time."

"But is she all right? You sound upset, is everything okay?"

"Yes, don't worry about her, she's fine. I'm just busy, that's all. Look, I haven't got time to stop and chat. I'll get her to call you when she comes back – could be a couple more days as the spa has a no-phone policy."

"Sounds a bit odd. Can I call the spa?"

"No, she's fine, Louise, she just needed a rest, that's all."

"Tell her I called from my hotel, and ask her to call me. I'm still due back Monday, there's a new seven star hotel opening in—"

Sinclair hit the phone off with a clenched fist. He was trembling with anger and leaning onto the desk to prop himself up.

"That stupid fucking skank of a woman. Why didn't they take her instead? I'd give them ten flasks of fucking diamonds to kill her."

The phone rang in front of him, but Sinclair just stared down at it like a zombie.

CHAPTER FOURTEEN

The phone rang seven times before Sinclair finally pressed the speaker button.

"Sinclair," he said, still staring straight ahead, slightly breathless.

"Do as we say and she won't get hurt." The mechanical voice boomed.

"Okay, so what do you want this time?" Straining, unable to hide his anger.

"Ten million Euros in various unmarked denominations in two waterproof canvas bags. Start driving around the park like before at exactly two p.m. and we'll call you on the mobile with more instructions. Keep the police away and we won't hurt her. Do anything stupid and she gets a bullet through the head."

The caller hung up. The dial tone purred loudly over the speaker.

Sinclair stood still like a dummy in a wax-works.

He looked stunned. No one spoke.

He sighed loudly, turned the speaker off and put his dark blazer on.

"I'll get the money in two hours. Clarke, come with me," he said, then looked at Jones. "Be ready with the car by two."

"Yes, sir," Jones said, obediently, as if addressing a general.

"I think we should get a speed boat on standby just in case," Haywood said.

"What for?"

"They asked for two waterproof canvas bags? I'll get them from Selfridges. They may be planning to use the river to get away."

"Get a boat from that charter company we used for last year's booze cruise." Sinclair flinched. In a rare moment of confession, he surprised Archer by saying: "They're not going to dump her body at sea, are they? Drowning gives me nightmares."

"What about placing trackers in the bags this time?" Haywood said.

"No trackers. If they find them they'll kill her."

"We need a car following us this time, tracking us. This will probably be the last ransom drop-off," Archer said.

"It's too risky – if they spot it, they might kill her." Sinclair's voice started to rise.

"What if they don't? What if they kill her anyway?"

Sinclair glared at Archer. His fists clenched tightly at his sides. He was simmering, a volcano close to eruption. He walked slowly up to Archer. His body stiff.

"I don't want any cock-ups, young man." Sinclair prodded him several times in the shoulder with his left index finger.

"There won't be any, trust me." Archer struggled to keep his cool but somehow managed. The prods were firm. They didn't hurt as much as they emphasised disrespect. He gritted his teeth, but kept his tongue in check.

"If anything happens to Becky because of this, I'll hold you responsible. Best, follow them in the Land Rover."

He prodded Archer one last time and scowled before turning his back on them.

Sinclair and Clarke left without saying another word. Archer saw a renewed sense of urgency in their eyes and in their step. They all knew that time was running out. Reality had sunk in and the finality of what could happen to Becky if they failed hung over them like a dark cloud. Their fears were unspoken, but tension was written over their faces and bodies.

Haywood confirmed he'd just organised a launch on standby down-river. Best and Jones left to prepare the cars. Archer followed them to the garage in Adams Row.

They checked the cars over for fluids and air. Jones topped up the screen wash. The cars were already clean and polished. They drove to a small garage near Park Lane and filled them both up on Sinclair's account. Then they drove back to Adams Row where they set the satellite navigation in the Land Rover Discovery to follow the Mercedes via the mobile phone. Jones put bottled water in the cars.

"I'm off for some food – anyone coming?" Jones said.

"I'll come. Mr Sinclair won't allow food in the cars. It could be a long old wait," Best said.

"I'm fine," Archer said. "I'll watch the cars, you two go."

Archer sat alone in the Land Rover. Contemplating what the kidnappers' next move might be. They had to start driving around the park by two p.m. Then there would be a call with instructions to go somewhere. The first drop had been in the park, South Carriage Drive. The second was at the Hilton Hotel on Park Lane. They didn't venture too far off the given circuit. So the next drop could be Kensington or Bayswater.

Archer looked in the glove box for a map. Sure enough, there was a mini *London A to Z* at hand. He opened it and flicked through the pages until he found Hyde Park on pages seventy-three and seventy-four. He followed the circuit on the map. It covered a large area. There were too many options to consider. The next drop-off could be anywhere. He went over the events again in his mind, searching for clues, but found nothing but more questions.

Who was the kidnappers' mastermind? What was their next move? Would they release Becky or would they kill her?

The nagging doubt of an inside job wasn't going away. But who could it be? If Becky just wanted to run away she had access to plenty of money. Taking on Sinclair was a dangerous game. The kidnappers were either brave or stupid. Most likely an organised gang of hardened criminals with plenty of muscle behind them. The odds of saving her were already slim and rapidly diminishing. They had to take a risk.

CHAPTER FIFTEEN

At ten minutes to two Archer saw Clarke and Haywood walk across South Audley Street with expressionless faces and purposeful long strides. They wore dark grey suits, shirts without ties and dark sunglasses. They walked with an air of confidence and calm that was silently threatening. Violent mercenaries constantly ready to unleash mayhem wherever they went.

The two men carried identical light-grey canvas sailing bags over their shoulders. Each filled with five million Euros and weighing in at twenty kilos. Despite the obvious weight of the bags they walked normal and treated them casually. They placed them in the boot of the Mercedes and walked straight back to the penthouse without speaking. Jones watched them walk across the road and then pressed the remote to close the boot.

Archer climbed in the front of the S Class with Jones. Best flashed the lights from the Discovery, signalling that he was ready to follow. Jones turned the radio on, but kept the volume down low. As the two o'clock news started on Radio Two they drove down Upper Grosvenor Street towards Park Lane.

The traffic was slower than the previous ransom drop. It took them just under an hour to make three laps as a long trench of roadworks on Kensington Gore slowed them down.

Archer was staring aimlessly at the window display in a book shop when the phone rang on the fourth lap while they waited to turn right from Kensington Church Street before heading east down the Bayswater Road. The voice modulator sounded eerie over the sixteen speakers but broke the silent tension inside the car.

"Turn left down Westbourne Terrace, towards Cleveland Terrace and look for the private car park on the left-hand side and valet park the car. Leave it there until six p.m. Understood?"

"Yes."

"Do not return to the car until six p.m. otherwise she dies."

They hung up and the radio automatically returned to the sound system.

Jones turned left and slowed down as he looked for the garage. Archer spotted a blue neon sign and pointed at it. The car park entrance was down a side street with just enough space off the road to stop and let the valet take over. Jones parked the car in the designated spot off the road and waited until a friendly-looking valet appeared.

Jones and Archer got out and a young eastern European valet wearing a royal blue jacket and broad smile took the key card and parked the car. Archer saw Best in the Land Rover, looking around for a parking space on the road nearby. Jones and Archer went into the office to pay, but had to wait until the valet had parked the car.

The valet returned with the key card and put it in a small cubby hole. Jones paid the minimum fee of sixty pounds for one day despite arguing that he would return for it at six p.m. As they walked out of the office and onto the street they saw Best drive past and cross Westbourne Terrace. He made a skilful U-turn and parked on the road in sight of the car park. He got out and looked around like a typical bodyguard before he casually fed the meter.

The area was busy with more people than usual and fewer cars. Several police vans were parked at the Bayswater end. Inside, armed police sat talking in a relaxed manner.

More armed police walked down the street wearing Kevlar vests and blue riot helmets. In the distance the unmistakeable sound of horses drawing nearer was getting louder.

Archer felt the air was charged with an electric tension as people in the street warily scrutinised each other. Some looked afraid and apprehensive. Archer asked a Lebanese shopkeeper standing outside his bazaar-style store what was happening.

"Supposed to be a student protest. Supposed to be peaceful. But the rioters have come instead. Many gate crashers wanting trouble. Wanting to fight the police."

"Where are the students?"

"They left already. It's just the anarchists now and the looters. But I have a baseball bat and my sons are ready to fight."

"Why don't you close the shutter and go home?"

"No. We stay and fight."

"Good luck."

"Filthy scum." He spat on the floor in disgust.

Archer and Jones crossed the street and got into the Land Rover with Best.

"Looks like we're in the middle of a war zone."

"We'll never spot the kidnappers now."

CHAPTER SIXTEEN

Jones sat in the front of the Land Rover and immediately retuned the radio. He kept the volume down and seemed to be weary of Best, who remained as stiff as a mannequin in the driver's seat. Nobody spoke as they kept watch on the car park. Best and Jones had brought small field binoculars and used them intermittently. Jones hesitantly turned the volume up to listen to the traffic news. He told them that he often texted in as "Spitfire Man" with tips on how to avoid the ever-changing bottlenecks. Nobody responded.

Dropouts with dirty clothes and matted hair walked past the car in small groups. Some threatened to rock the car and others took out keys as if they were going to scratch the paintwork, but they soon backed away from the silent threat of its inhabitants.

The rioters were mostly in pairs by now, trying to disguise their true nature, but they stood out. Some of them stopped and looked agitated. They were not causing enough trouble and the armed police kept them moving. The riot police owned all the nearby streets, including the one where Archer sat waiting as the tension evaporated.

At first the trouble-makers looked disgusted, then disappointed. They turned their attention from rebellion to drinking cans of cider and smoking weed. They soon slumped against the walls of the side streets in a dazed state. Sneering at the police and anyone they saw in smart clothes or cars. Dishing out slurred abuse as they stumbled and fell over themselves. One fell against the car by mistake. Best was out like a shot, taking the opportunity to vent his anger by threatening to break some bones.

When the *Drivetime* show started after the five o'clock news, Archer and Sinclair's men had been watching the car park for nearly two hours. Nothing had happened at the garage. No cars had gone in or out. Archer thought something was wrong. The garage was too quiet. They had not seen a single valet for over an hour. Was it because of the rioters or because of the kidnappers?

"Only another hour to go. *Drivetime*'s my favourite," said Jones.

"I'm not waiting any longer. I'm taking a closer look right now," said Archer.

"They specifically instructed us not to return until after six."

"I'm just taking a look, that's all."

"But they said they'd kill her if we went back early."

"Do you think they're still watching?"

"What do you mean?"

"Would you wait until six or would you take the money and run?"

"Obviously I'd take the money before. But no one apart from the valet has gone in or out of the office, and no one has taken the key from the cubbyhole yet."

"That's why I'm going to take a closer look. You two stay here and wait for my call."

"I don't think you should go back until six," Best said, loudly.

"Don't think, just wait here and watch."

Archer got out and walked towards the abandoned car park. The armed police were still milling around but the invisible electric charge in the air had disappeared from the collective mass of residents and shopkeepers out on the street.

The tired-looking garage was still and quiet. The valets' office had a glass door and floor-to-ceiling window facing the entrance. The messy office was empty. There was not a single valet in sight. Archer tried the office door but it was locked. The key of the Mercedes had been placed in cubbyhole number twenty-one, but he could see that it was now empty.

Archer looked inside the garage but there was no movement or sign of life. He shouted and waited, but there was no answer. He ducked under the red and white barrier, stepped over the yellow and black floor barrier and walked into the garage, following the lane up to the next floor and looking for bay twenty-one. The garage was only half-full of cars.

At the top of the incline he turned and saw the black Mercedes with the boot open. He jogged up to it and looked inside. The two canvas sailing bags full of cash were gone.

The key card had been left on top of the roof. Archer took it and noticed a staircase at the back of the garage with a bright green fire exit sign. He walked to the back of the long narrow car park to see where the fire exit led and peered over the handrail into a narrow lane. It had been a well-planned job. The bags would have been taken to the lane within twenty seconds. He walked down the stairs, pushed the bar and checked the lane. The alarm didn't go off. No cars in sight, just a few drunken rioters slumped against the walls. He went back inside the garage, closed the door and walked back through to the valet's office.

The street was still dead. Nothing interesting until he noticed a valet sitting in a coffee shop over the road, staring back at him in the window, sipping coffee and eating. Archer crossed the road and sat on the stool next to the smiling valet as he finished off a Danish pastry and washed it down with a large cappuccino.

"What are you so happy about?"

"Getting paid to sit here and wait until six o'clock."

"What happened?"

"Why should I tell you?"

Archer threw five twenties on the table. "Because, that's why."

The valet smiled again and purred under his breath. He looked pleased with himself.

"Okay, what a day this one is turning out to be. Better than birthday."

"What happened?"

"A man gave me five hundred pounds to close the office and return at six."

"Who?"

"Some stranger."

"Why?"

"He didn't say, I didn't argue, simple."

"But what about doing your job?"

"The boss called and said to close up until the trouble was over. We closed the barriers and left the office locked. No cars can get in or out."

"Tell me about the man with the five hundred."

"Early twenties, lean-looking, British."

"What else did he say?"

"He said that he had to collect something from the boot of the black Mercedes S600L. It was important, and he would leave the key on the roof. He seemed clean, not like the trouble-makers. And he couldn't steal the car with all the barriers, so I let him do it."

"What else did he say?"

"He asked me to switch the alarm off the fire exit door. His van was waiting in the lane and he was in a hurry. He told me to come over here where another five hundred was waiting for me in an envelope."

"And was it?"

"Yep."

"So you're a grand up?"

"Not bad work if you can get it."

"You didn't think that it was strange?"

"No, man. I need money, job pays minimum wage."

"I'm going to get the car back now – will you open the barriers for me?"

"But you're supposed to return at six o'clock, then I go home."

"So you can take the rest of the day off in two minutes."

"Okay. Let's go."

Archer drove the car back down the ramp. The valet opened the barriers and Archer parked it outside the valets' office. Best flashed the lights and drove slow until he stopped in front of the garage.

Archer told Jones and Best what had just happened.

"Take the cars back and tell Sinclair what happened."

"What about you? You tell him."

"I'm paid to investigate, not run errands."

"You're afraid to tell him."

"Just go."

Jones and Best left, frowning, clearly dreading the task of telling Sinclair that they had failed to discover any leads. Archer walked back towards South Kensington through the park and called Julian Cavendish on his mobile. He answered it this time.

"Mr Cavendish, my name is Sean Archer. I'd like to meet you."

"How did you get my number?"

"My office found it. I need to speak to you urgently. About Peter Sinclair."

Pause.

"Why?"

"I can't talk over the phone, but it's very important. Can you spare me just twenty minutes tomorrow morning?"

"Very well then, come to my office at nine."

Finally a chance to get a break in a case that was seemingly still without leads.

CHAPTER SEVENTEEN

Archer decided to spend an hour in the basement gym followed by a long run to make sure he was tired enough to sleep. He fancied drinking himself into a coma, but decided to take the healthier option, so he ran to the river via Chelsea. He had been born and raised there and often ran past his grandparents' old house, where his eidetic memory began, at fourteen years old. And not a single memory before the day his parents were found killed by a psychopath.

As he turned the corner from Cheyne Walk to Flood Street he could see the lights were on. The house was detached on a corner plot. Two storeys plus a partial basement. The glossy white painted stucco on the ground floor was grooved to look like stonework. The first floor was London brick. White Georgian sash windows with plantation blinds throughout, just like his house in Walton Street. And a flat roof which had been used for sunbathing while reading stacks of true crime books in his teens. The front door on Flood Street was gloss black like 10 Downing Street and he had a similar one in South Ken. There was a black iron gate with a double parking bay before a double garage with a flat above it where he had spent a lot of time recovering from his trauma. Professor Miles Davenport had been good to him and his grandparents after his parents were killed. He had provided the best psychologists and tutors from his team to help Archer catch up and then get ahead of his peers.

As he ran through the alley to Cheyne Walk two masked men dressed in black stepped out in front of him. He turned around and saw a third man behind him, breathing hard through a black sub-zero balaclava and wearing gloves. Archer pulled out a telescopic baton from his running jacket and snapped it into action. He turned his back to the wall so that he could see all three men and tensed his arms and legs as he prepared to defend himself. The three men flashed knives and guns inside their jackets and closed in on him. His heart rate rocketed, but then his Krav Maga training kicked in and he calmly lowered the simple baton down to his side. The alpha dog stepped forward like a battle-hardened soldier.

"Put that away, Mr Archer," he said, with a broad Yorkshire accent.

Archer closed the baton and put it back inside his jacket pocket as a black Audi S8 came to a halt beside the kerb at the end of the alley.

"Good lad, now listen hard: stop investigating the Boathouse, otherwise you're a dead man. The next time you snoop around or talk to anyone about it, will be your last."

The other two men grabbed his arms and Yorkshire kicked him hard between his legs. It felt like his intestines had just been ripped out, making him nauseated.

"You're due a good kicking," Yorkshire said, nostrils flaring. At six foot four, Archer was a few inches taller and smiled briefly before his forehead crashed down onto Yorkshire's nose. Yorkshire stepped back clutching his face as Archer pulled his arms in fast, cracking together the heads of the two men either side of him, then punching them on the ear and jaw.

Two men were bent over and one hit the ground as Archer sprinted away from the car, back towards Flood Street. He exited the alley and turned his head to look, but nobody was following, so he slowed his pace and headed home – on autopilot.

At Walton Street the navy Ford was waiting for him across the road from his house. Lambert lowered the window and held out an envelope with cigarette in hand. "Take a good look at the photo and put two and two together, you dumb fuck."

"DS Lambert, wrong side of the river again, I see."

"Shut up, fuckwad. You're in deep shit. You're being set up by the big boys, you dickhead. Lucky for you I need some fast cash and I can fix it for you. You've got two days to get me a hundred grand in used twenties and I'll make it go away, otherwise you're nicked." He threw the envelope on the pavement at Archer's feet and drove off slowly, waving his cigarette in majestic circles out of the window.

Inside the envelope were two photographs. One of Archer entering the De Winton Lodge apartment building just off Ruislip High Street. The other was the dead woman in her running kit splayed on the bed with the Fairbairn Sykes knife in her neck. But this time he could see her face. It was Gillian King, journalist, and Alex's flatmate and best friend.

She'd been investigating the Boathouse for the past six months and had called him and asked to meet. He'd visited her last Wednesday evening at her flat in Ruislip around six p.m. where they talked for an hour about the Boathouse. She and Alex had shared the flat for over two years and worked together on foreign assignments in the Middle East and Africa. She'd recently found Alex's list of over twenty names titled 'The Boathouse: People of Interest'.

It was hidden inside Alex's old-fashioned writing desk. Gillian had given him a scanned copy of the list and they had agreed to meet again in two weeks; after he'd run some background checks.

Peter Sinclair was fifteenth on the list. Now Gillian was dead and he was being blackmailed and framed for her murder by a dirty detective.

CHAPTER EIGHTEEN

The next morning Archer caught the Circle Line to his appointment with Julian Cavendish. The law firm's office was a five-minute walk from Monument tube station and resembled an ornate cut-glass trophy. Beams of morning sunlight radiated off it, casting facets of light like a brilliant cut diamond ring. It was a superior-looking building for people who really thought they were superior. A crystal palace for wealthy clients to hire expensive lawyers, and Julian Cavendish was a partner who charged his clients five hundred and fifty pounds an hour.

The first floor reception was as large as a football pitch with spotless marble and glass surfaces to reinforce the impression of exclusivity. The high ceiling spared no expense to provide excellent views of the Lloyd's Building. Insurance was obviously an important sector for the firm and close proximity to Lloyd's was prestigious as well as strategic. The firm's outward illusion of elitism was carefully built into the structure and fabric of the building.

Archer had been there before. He wouldn't work for lawyers, but he had worked for underwriters on salvage cases. He informed one of the four stewardess lookalikes at reception of his nine a.m. appointment with Mr Cavendish and was asked politely to take a seat.

Red and black leather Barcelona chairs were in even-numbered clusters of twos, fours and sixes. Coffee tables made each cluster an odd number and therefore more aesthetically pleasing. The walls were covered in modern artwork alternating between colourful splashes of oil on canvas and monochrome contemporary photographs of London with one red image per piece. The modern art made the room colourful and interesting as a whole, but Archer thought that splashing and swirling colours around was not that difficult. If it did not have to have any form or meaning then it was just random patterns of colour where the price tag reflected the name tag. It was another reference to exclusivity. Archer loved art, but he didn't get random splodges of colour that looked like a four-year-old had been messing about.

Large screens showed satellite news and weather channels without sound. Ironed copies of that morning's *Financial Times* and yesterday's *Wall Street Journal* fanned the tables along with *The Economist* and *Forbes* magazines.

An attractive attendant wearing a black and gold mandarin suit and ballet pumps arrived silently as if from nowhere. She asked him if he wanted some tea or coffee. Within two minutes she brought coffee and biscuits. Archer knew lawyers well. He had visited most of the top firms in the City. Good décor in client areas, expensive biscuits, company pens, pencils and notepads and attractive staff scattered around as impressive eye candy.

But the masquerade of pleasant calmness in client areas was little more than a clever illusion of smoke and mirrors. The engine-room reality went on behind the scenes, on the work floors, where stressed-out juniors and associates shuffled papers into the small hours as they jostled and fought for promotion from the fat cats. The firm discarded eight out of ten of its graduates with its aggressively competitive promotion policy. It was up or out. The poor sods needed Sun Tzu and Machiavelli as much as instant case law and *Chambers Guide.*

After dropping out of university, Archer had worked as an IT contractor in the City. He'd lasted three weeks as an IT support assistant; his first week was in a bank, then an insurance company and finally a law firm. The corporate workplace was too regimental, claustrophobic and toxic for him. He'd hated every minute of it and never went back.

Cavendish was a managing partner, so he knew exactly how to pull in work for the firm. Zoe's report indicated that he was at ease with senior corporate clients and even had a reputation outside London, especially in New York, where he was known by his partners as a lush, schmoozer and serial womaniser. He was also fifteen minutes late. Archer thought that this must be in all the manuals at City law firms, along with instructions to never apologise for anything. Archer was frustrated by his tardiness, but decided not to say anything as he needed Cavendish on side.

Cavendish wore a navy pinstripe suit with red buttonhole and was groomed within an inch of his life. He formally introduced himself. They shook hands firmly and he escorted Archer up one floor via the lift to one of the client meeting rooms. Cavendish was a smooth operator. He glided his slim frame around effortlessly. His attire was expensive and impeccable. Prada eyeglasses the only brand name on show. His silver tie was perfectly knotted. The matching silk handkerchief in his breast pocket perfectly ruffled. He wasn't classically handsome or plain vanilla and his greying red hair was cut extremely short as it was balding from the front. Archer thought he looked like he had just been made up to shoot an office scene in a film or read the news; he exuded total self-confidence with a relaxed and disarming style.

Archer decided not to mention the art along the way. The Turner Prize-winning pieces, in prime locations, were clearly strategically placed ice breakers, there to prompt new clients and their lawyers to talk about something other than their case. He wondered how much money the firm had invested in the artwork, but consciously waited for Cavendish to steer the conversation. He needed him to remain positive.

The meeting room was well appointed with fresh fruit and drinks on show at one end and a floor-to-ceiling window at the other. A large oak meeting table dominated it, surrounded by modern leather boardroom chairs, original award-winning pictures and state-of-the-art multimedia gadgetry. All the typical attire that the managing partners perceived their demanding clients expected from them.

"Coffee, Mr Archer?"

"Black, no sugar, thanks." He hadn't finished the one downstairs.

Cavendish poured two coffees and brought them from the host area to the meeting table where another tray of exotic biscuits waited to be unwrapped from silver and gold foil.

"Help yourself," he said, and gestured towards the tray.

"Thanks." Archer just stirred the hot black coffee and took a small sip.

"So you want to talk about Peter Sinclair?"

"How much do you know about him?"

Cavendish flinched. Folded his arms. His body language guarded.

"Perhaps you can tell me a little bit about yourself and why you're here first."

"I'm a consultant profiler and investigator." He handed over a Londinium Lux Limited business card. "I've been hired by Peter Sinclair to find someone. But I'd like to know more about him first. I'm sorry to be so direct, but I understand that you believe he had something to do with your sister's death."

"Can you tell me who you're looking for, Mr Archer?"

He shook his head. "It's confidential, Mr Cavendish. I'm afraid I can't discuss it."

"Yet you want me to help you." He shrugged and looked bemused.

"Yes."

"Then you'll need to tell me, otherwise we have nothing else to discuss."

"Only if I have your word that it goes no further than this room."

An awkward silence as Cavendish took a bite of a chocolate biscuit as if it were beluga caviar. "Very well, you have my word."

"Sinclair's wife has been kidnapped. If he goes to the police they'll kill her."

"I should have warned her not to marry him."

"Do you know her?"

"Not really. We met briefly at some cocktail parties in the City several years ago, when she was marketing manager for an international property company."

"Do you know Peter Sinclair?"

"Not personally. How well do you know them?"

Archer considered how best to play the conversation.

"I don't know either of them. I was recommended by an associate to help find Mrs Sinclair. My loyalty here is not to Peter Sinclair. I want to find Becky Sinclair, and I need to know more about her husband in order to do that. I think you can help me."

"What do you want to know?"

"I know he was engaged to your sister and that she died in a car accident. I'm sorry to bring this up, but I'm investigating his background."

"Does he know you're here?"

"No, of course not, he only knows that I'm out looking for his wife. I want to make sure there are no nasty surprises further down the line. He would be extremely angry if he knew that I was here talking to you."

"You're not worried that he could find out you were here?"

"I'm trying to find his wife. He won't find out that I've been here from me."

"Am I not one of your suspects, Mr Archer?"

"No, not at all."

"Why not? I could be out for revenge, couldn't I?"

"I've done some homework on you, Mr Cavendish." Archer paused. "Let's just say that you're not a suspect."

"What do you know about me?"

"I know you like the company of attractive women."

In the silence, Cavendish looked around and scratched his nose. He looked nervous.

"I'm sure Jane was murdered by that despicable man."

"What makes you think that?"

"The car crash was made to look like an accident, but it wasn't."

"How do you know that for sure?"

"I'll tell you how, but first you need to understand how they met, because it will explain a lot in terms of how ruthless he can be."

CHAPTER NINETEEN

Julian Cavendish stood up straight and walked over to the window. He gazed momentarily towards the Lloyd's Building across the street and then bowed his head pensively before he turned back round. Failing to hide the pain that was written all over his face.

"Jane was a name at Lloyd's," he said with sentimental pride.

His voice started to crack and when his eyes watered he turned his back to Archer and wiped them with a white handkerchief. "She was a great underwriter, moved in good circles and then she married a wealthy businessman who unfortunately for her knew Peter Sinclair."

Cavendish turned back round, walked over to the host area, grabbed the coffee pot and raised it, along with his neatly trimmed eyebrows.

"More coffee?"

"No thanks." Typical lawyer, drinking strong coffee all day.

Cavendish poured himself another coffee, returned the pot and took a sip before sitting down at the table. He looked directly at Archer. His eyes were still moist.

"Jane met Sinclair several times at functions. It was obvious he was smitten by her. The next thing, wouldn't you know, within a matter of months, her husband was in financial trouble and as a result committed suicide, allowing Sinclair to swoop in and come to the rescue. The black knight masquerading as the white knight, as it were. He bought the flailing business and helped my sister avoid bankruptcy. And of course they soon became an item."

"How long were they together?"

"A couple of years. They were engaged, she had planned a huge society wedding. She wanted children, but he didn't. She thought she could change him and fell pregnant a few months before the wedding, and then she was killed in a car crash."

"So she told Sinclair about the baby and he was still opposed?"

"Yes."

"Why didn't she have an abortion?"

"She was against the idea. She decided she would leave him and have the child on her own."

"But that's not proof that he killed her."

"I'm not a fool, Mr Archer. I hired a private investigator and she found out all about Peter Sinclair and his nefarious private life. It seems that Jane was not the first to suffer his wrath, you see; he'd done it before with a girl called Christina."

"What happened to her?" Archer sat forward on the edge of his seat. "And why did the police think they were accidents?"

"He always uses professionals. There was a high-speed chase, they were seen to be trying to escape from another car. The driver had been drugged, there was forensic evidence that he'd been drinking. He was over the legal limit."

Archer thought it sounded too similar to the conspiracy theories surrounding Princess Diana's final hours in Paris. People in mourning trying to find answers. Was Cavendish just creating these theories to satisfy his grief or his morbid inquisitiveness? Was he looking to find the truth or to reinvent it?

"I'd like to meet your investigator."

Cavendish stroked his chin and nodded.

"Very well. I'll ask her if she'll meet with you."

"Who is she?"

"An ex-detective. She's very thorough and a hard nut to crack." Cavendish licked his top lip.

"Can she meet me now, today? Time is of the essence."

"I'll call her and let you know."

"Does she have any evidence?"

"Maybe. But it's best you speak to her face to face. She won't talk about it over the phone, but she owes me enough to meet you."

"Okay, thanks."

"I could have put a contract out on him, you know. I know people."

Archer dismissed the idea with a smile.

Cavendish frowned and was silent. He looked awkward and uncomfortable.

He finally lowered his head. "I'm just not cut out for that sort of thing. I believe in the justice system, obviously. Fear of being caught and put in jail. I'm afraid of being killed, I suppose. I'm a bit of a coward really." He dabbed his damp eyes with his handkerchief.

"Time's running out. For Becky, and maybe for Sinclair. It's time to act."

"Leave it with me, Mr Archer. I'll call your mobile later this morning."

CHAPTER TWENTY

Archer took the District Line to South Kensington and grabbed two Americanos from Le Bistrot on the way back to his Walton Street office. Zoe was sitting upright at her desk hard at work; wearing a black designer suit and high heels with her long dark hair flowing in waves.

"I thought the voice recordings from the ransom calls would have provided us with some leads by now," Archer sighed and handed over her coffee.

"Thanks. The voice modulator was set up by an expert. No discernible background sounds, no way to untangle the voice or to get any kind of read or fix on it. These guys are pros. We need to trace the call or find clues somewhere else." Zoe raised her eyebrows and pursed her lips accusingly at him before she put some music on over the main speakers.

"What are all these boxes for?"

"That's the FBI's latest smart board for sorting and presenting data. It's like a sheet of glass with 3D images you can hand swipe. There's also some voice control. They've asked us to make some improvements to the software. The techies are in tomorrow to set it up. I'm so excited," she beamed with pride.

Archer nodded his head and smiled with approval.

"Great, just don't let it get in the way of the kidnapping case. Keep working the list of people close to Sinclair and drill down deep into the top ten."

"Okay. Now get out of my way and do some work."

"I'm going back to Sinclair's, see if I can find something useful, see if there's a connection with this private investigator, Sarah Forsyth."

"Want me to find out about her?"

"Okay. Why not?"

He left Zoe listening to Muse playing loudly and cross-referencing facts on huge databases and profiles in order to rank the suspects on the multitude of screens around her. He walked to the Brompton Road and took a passing black cab to Park Lane, returning to the penthouse living room just before noon.

A formally dressed woman he had not seen before sat at the entrance hall desk looking at the bank of monitors. A cleaner in a grey tunic dusted and polished nearby. Adams and Best were sitting quietly in the living room watching the twenty-four hour news channel. Adams was manning the phone at the desk and Best was slouched against the arm of the sofa, slurping at his coffee and watching the young presenter like a lecherous sex addict. They each gave him a dismissive glare and then ignored him – charming.

"Where's Mr Sinclair?"

"He had to go to the office, he won't be gone long," said Best.

Archer walked through the living area towards the kitchen.

"Does anyone want some water?"

No response. He was an outcast. Tolerated for the moment, but not made welcome.

Archer checked out the kitchen, which was immaculate like a minimalist show house kitchen from *Architectural Digest*. The rear hall was deserted. It was a prime opportunity to look around while it was quiet.

He used the rear staircase to avoid the living room, tiptoed upstairs and snooped around the guest bedrooms, but found nothing interesting. Sinclair's office door was closed, so he looked around to check if he was still alone. Opening the door quietly he entered the inner sanctum and sat at Sinclair's desk where his laptop was hibernating. There were no visible security cameras so he extracted the USB spike from his jacket pocket and placed it in one of the side ports. The blue lights on the spike flickered into action and Archer took in the room before he closed his eyes and tried to imagine how Sinclair felt when he was here alone.

"Can I help you?"

Best stood in the doorway with his hands on his hips, staring at Archer leaning back in the boss's chair with his eyes still closed. Archer opened his eyes slowly and smiled as he nudged a copy of yesterday's *Financial Times* over the flashing stick.

"Please sit down."

Best frowned and gave him a dirty look, but walked in and sat down anyway.

"Mr Sinclair doesn't like anyone coming in here without him. You'd better go back downstairs before he finds out."

"What's he like?"

"He's all right. He's busy. He can seem a bit abrupt at times, but he's all right."

"I couldn't work for him."

"You are working for him."

"He's my client, not my boss."

"You don't think you're the only one he's hired to find her, do you?"

"What do you mean?"

"He's probably talking to other investigators right now. He's probably hired bigger and better firms than yours. Proper firms, not one-trick-pony side shows," Best sneered.

"So you don't just grunt then. Tell me, who do you think did it?"

"Look, we'd better get back downstairs. We're expecting another call."

"There won't be many more ransom calls."

"What about Mrs Sinclair?"

"There must be somebody on the inside. Who do you think it is?

"What?" Best folded his arms and tensed his face muscles. He looked uncomfortable.

"Has Sinclair fired anyone in the last six months?"

"Probably, he employs people all over the world."

"But has anyone really close to him, like someone in his innermost circle, been fired or left recently? Do you know anyone with a massive grudge against him?"

"You think all this is over a grudge?"

"Sinclair's no saint. I assume he has enemies."

"What? These people are after ransom money."

"Tell me what you really think about him."

"What's wrong with you?"

"Come on, man, I won't tell anyone."

"I'm not comfortable talking like this."

"Don't you want to help find Mrs Sinclair?"

"Of course I do."

"Okay, good. Let's go and get some fresh air in the park, shall we?"

Best got up and turned. As he headed for the door, Archer yanked the spike out while the lights were still flashing, unsure if he had managed to download anything useful.

CHAPTER TWENTY-ONE

I n less than five minutes Archer and Best were walking under gently rustling autumn trees in Hyde Park. The grass was bright green and a sea of sulphur, burnt orange and crimson leaves popped under the clear blue sky. Archer thought it was a hundred times better than any of the random paint splashes he'd seen in Cavendish's law office. Dried leaves and gravel crunched underfoot as they headed down the rolling footpath towards the Serpentine.

"It's just like New England in the fall, only better," Archer said, casually trying to draw Best in like a devious salesman.

"It is nice this time of year," Best answered awkwardly, as if he shouldn't be there.

"So who do you think the inside man is?"

"I don't know."

Best looked away. He was avoiding eye contact on purpose. He was lying.

"It has to be someone who knows about Sinclair's access to cash and diamonds."

"But he has hundreds of business associates."

"And employees."

"No chance, they'd be too afraid."

"So who has the biggest grudge against him?"

"There could be several people that fit the bill, but what exactly are you looking for?"

"Just think about it. Who is the most likely person to do this?"

They continued to walk in silence along the northern edge of the Serpentine as Best gazed ahead with the occasional frown as if thinking too hard would hurt his head. Archer kept quiet. He knew that it would eventually force Best to speak up. They walked side by side on the gently winding path, watching the ducks, geese and swans scavenge for crumbs.

Despite the cool wind, the blue sky had attracted many visitors to the capital's largest park. Archer waited patiently for a response as the October sunshine warmed his face.

"Stuart Hunter has the biggest grudge. I suppose."

"Who's he?"

"Old business associate."

"Where is he now?"

"Nobody knows."

They turned left and continued walking south over the road bridge towards the Serpentine Gallery.

"He sold his business and went into hiding," Best said, his voice quivering nervously.

"But why does Hunter have a grudge?"

"Because he thinks he was shafted by Mr Sinclair."

"Why?"

"Listen, Archer, I look after Mr Sinclair's safety, he doesn't come to me for business advice. If you want to know about Hunter, ask Mr Sinclair."

"How come no one knows where he is?"

"Jesus, you're relentless. I told you the guy went into hiding."

"Why?"

"He was afraid."

"Of what?"

There was a sudden chill as a lone cloud passed in front of the sun like a giant ball of cotton wool, casting a wide shadow over the lake.

"I heard one of his associates was killed and that put the wind up him."

"Who was killed?"

"Nick Carnell."

"Who was he?"

"This conversation is over. It has nothing to do with finding Mrs Sinclair." He glared at Archer. "This conversation never happened." Even Sinclair's bodyguards seemed afraid of him.

As they approached a fork in the path near the small green cafeteria between Rotten Row and the Serpentine, Archer's mobile phone rang. They stopped walking and Archer turned his back on Best. The north wind picked up into a sudden gust that shook the trees around them like a chorus of paper tambourines.

It was Julian Cavendish.

Archer agreed to an urgent meeting, then turned back to face Best.

"I need to go back into the City for an hour. Where's the nearest tube?" He looked across the park at Wellington Arch. "That'll do it. I can take the Piccadilly Line to Holborn. I'll see you back at the penthouse later."

"Oh right, okay then, I'll tell Mr Sinclair." Best's tone was dejected. He stopped walking and watched Archer, unable to disguise a scornful gaze.

Archer took the gravel path that forked off to the right. He walked with long strides towards Rotten Row. Best started to amble slowly along the parallel path nearer the Serpentine and played with his phone.

Archer knew Best was uncomfortable about their conversation and that he would probably follow him. He also knew Best didn't like him. None of the guards trusted him. As far as the guards were concerned, Archer was just a temporary meddling outsider. Clarke and Haywood looked like they wanted to kill him. But he had an instinct that Best was psychologically the weakest and therefore the easiest to pump for information.

Hunter was a good lead.

CHAPTER TWENTY-TWO

Archer walked through the park to Hyde Park Corner tube station. He'd spotted Best, who was hopping behind trees, by pretending to look up at a passing police helicopter, using his peripheral vision to confirm that he was being tailed. His private field training never failed him in situations like this. Always head off in the opposite direction first. Everyone knows it and it sounds simple, but he hadn't had much practice lately.

Archer used his Oyster card to get through the turnstile without missing a beat. Best would probably need to buy a ticket and then go east instead of west. Job done.

Archer felt the warm wind rush down the platform and heard the rumble of an approaching train from inside the tunnel. The rails sang like an old Space Invaders game and then snapped like steel whips being cracked by an invisible tunnel monster in a low budget horror movie. The rumble grew louder, and he felt the vibration rise up through him from the platform as the air whooshed past and the train entered the station.

Archer often had to control dark thoughts at times like this. He wasn't really suicidal; it was only in certain situations he felt an urge from deep inside that he did not fully understand. He put it down to the trauma of his past. He had learned over time to control his demons, but he was still wary of them. He told his legs not to move. His feet were planted firmly on the platform six feet from the edge. Heights and approaching trains sometimes made him feel an urge to jump and end it all right there and then. No more past. Game over. He'd stopped base jumping and walking close to cliffs when he was twenty.

With his legs cast in concrete, forbidden to move, his mind played tricks on him. Would the electric shock from the rails do it first or the mechanical impact of the train as it sliced and diced through flesh and bone like a massive meat mincer? He felt the adrenalin kicking into his system as his mind and body fought to survive. Two more seconds and he would be safe. Safe from his dark side.

Archer knew there would be no mercy or sympathy from any commuters if the train was held and delayed. They wouldn't care about the loss of his life. Just the inconvenience of a half-hour delay to their journey. "Bloody jumpers." He'd cursed them many times himself.

The tube driver passed by, looking up at the ceiling of his cab, chewing gum, completely bored. Archer felt a surge of relief. Safe until some other day.

Archer boarded the tired-looking westbound tube to Rayners Lane. He got off one stop later at Knightsbridge. The train and the escalators were dead quiet. A few shoppers and tourists. He waited at the pedestrian crossing outside the station, looking up at One Hyde Park, and crossed the road that had been part of the ransom drop circuit around the park. He walked from the tube station exit towards the red brick and stone majesty of the Mandarin Oriental Hotel.

He hurried past the doorman in his red coat and top hat, up the worn stone steps and through the pillared archway and tall doors leading into the lobby. Cavendish was not there so he found a quiet red leather armchair with a good view of the entrance and reception desk and waited for him to arrive.

Sinclair called him on his mobile phone, but he let it go to voicemail and switched it on silent. Well-heeled businessmen and well-dressed shoppers came and went in all directions as the lunch crowds assembled for liquid refreshment. The aperitifs flowed like storm water going down the drain in a monsoon.

Cavendish entered the hotel lobby with an air of confidence and arrogance befitting a successful managing partner in a major law firm. The pin-striped lawyer glanced around, spotted Archer and smiled, but before he could get to him a junior member of the hotel management had recognised him and politely asked him if he was lunching there today.

Cavendish shook hands with the man and gestured to his waiting guest. Archer heard him explain that he required a table for four, but only two would stay after aperitifs for lunch. Archer got up and shook Cavendish's hand. The dark-haired junior manager asked them to follow him and led them briskly towards the high-ceilinged dining room at the rear of the hotel, overlooking the park.

CHAPTER TWENTY-THREE

Cavendish had a prime table, next to one of the tall crystal-clear windows. They sat down as half a dozen Blues and Royals passed by, providing a chorus of clattering horseshoes. Beyond them the familiar sights of Rotten Row and the colourful oak trees around the Serpentine, where Archer had been walking with Best less than fifteen minutes ago.

Cavendish looked immaculate with his silver silk tie and matching handkerchief ruffled flamboyantly in his breast pocket. He gesticulated a lot as he ordered sparkling bottled water and a good bottle of white Burgundy on ice.

Archer politely declined.

"Sarah Forsyth, my favourite investigator, should be here any minute," Cavendish said with gusto and a smile.

"Thanks for doing this. Will she talk candidly?"

"I've asked her to share everything she found out with you."

"That's good of you. Thanks. What's she like?"

"Fearless."

"Is this her?"

An attractive woman in her early thirties wearing a dark business suit and carrying a laptop-sized briefcase walked towards them. She smiled confidently at them both. She was tall, slim and tanned. Wide-set brown eyes, pert nose and a generous lower lip that shimmered with lip gloss. Archer's first impression was that she wore too much make-up for a business meeting and revealed too much of her cleavage and thighs. Pouting more like a glamour model than a businesswoman, she seemed too overstated to be real.

"Oh no, she's my client, and my lunch appointment in fact," he said with delight as he clearly savoured the view of her young slinky body moving towards him.

He made polite introductions and his client seemed happy with his choice of wine. The wine waiter performed a brief uncorking ritual and theatrically poured two good-sized glasses. The lawyer and his client looked into each other's eyes, chinked their glasses and smiled at each other with an aura of over-familiarity. They clearly knew each other well. Archer doubted that she was a corporate client, but kept silent on the matter.

The sunlight from the window poured over her shoulders, bronzing her dark hair at the edges, which picked up the small bronze flecks in her brown eyes. While they sipped wine and glanced admiringly at each other, lingering a little longer than they should have, Archer noticed an athletic blonde woman in her late thirties or early forties approach the table with long strides and a scornful look on her face.

"Ah there she is, looking radiant as usual." Cavendish stood up and welcomed his third and most serious-looking guest.

"My dear Sarah, so good of you to come and meet us at such short notice. I'd like to introduce you to Sean Archer."

CHAPTER TWENTY-FOUR

Sarah Forsyth stood confidently at the table and shook hands, keeping good eye contact with Archer throughout the introductions. Despite her unfriendly glower she was smart and well presented. A classy woman with sparkling blue eyes, milky skin and bouncing blonde hair which made her appear to be fresh out of the salon. Wearing figure-hugging clothes and brown leather boots, she clearly spent a lot of time in the gym. Her skintight beige trousers, white lacy blouse and embroidered silver paisley jacket attracted attention from around the room. Cavendish's client pursed her lips as if she was sucking on a ridiculously sharp lemon.

"Please sit down. Would you like a drink?" Cavendish asked enthusiastically.

"No thanks. I have to get straight back to the office."

"But I thought you could spare some time to talk with Mr Archer."

"I can give him an hour, but he'll have to come back to my office."

"There you are, Mr Archer, she's all yours." Cavendish beamed with satisfaction.

Archer excused himself. He briefly shook hands with Cavendish and followed Sarah Forsyth, who was already hightailing it out towards the lobby. Cavendish was oblivious now to everyone except his hot young lunch date, who had regained her wide glossy smile.

By the time Archer caught up with Forsyth outside the main entrance she was on her mobile phone having a heated discussion, telling off one of her employees for taking liberties and too much time off.

"Don't give me all that crap again. You need to work eight hours a day and that means work, as in productive and helpful for me. Not surfing the internet, painting your nails or texting your stupid friends all day. You're on notice, Hannah. Take this as your final warning." She ended the call and put her phone away in her bag. She was feisty and forthright and Archer felt like he could do business with her.

They crossed the busy road opposite Harvey Nichols and walked back to her office, which she explained was further down Sloane Street on the right-hand side. Her strides were long and fast and Archer found himself trailing her by a few paces. He was drawn by her hypnotic movement and impressively sculpted body. Long muscular legs and a perfect rear end that looked close to bursting through the seams of her beige trousers, which must have been sprayed on.

Archer scolded himself for being distracted by her appearance and sped up to walk alongside her and talk. As he drew level with her shoulder he felt his mobile phone vibrate in his pocket. When he saw it was Sinclair he put it back and let it go to voicemail – again.

"My client can wait. You have my full and undivided attention."

"Don't try your pretty-boy looks and charms on me, Archer. I'm married."

CHAPTER TWENTY-FIVE

They turned right and entered a smart retro-looking office building with a funky reception area washed in purple and violet mood lighting. Ancient relics housed in modern museum-style glass cases. Oversized and ornate silver rococo furniture. The décor was more nightclub avant-garde than Knightsbridge old guard. Archer preferred his understated office with whitewashed brick walls just down the road in South Kensington. What sort of clients came to a place like this anyway? They had to be foreigners with new money.

They bypassed the anorexic receptionists without acknowledgement and took the glass lift to the second floor. He followed her across a glass-floored walkway to an open atrium balcony area where boutique-style offices on several floors jutted out at each other, dripping with garishly modern designer trappings.

"What is this place?"

"Various independent lifestyle services for discerning clients, all under one roof, for people willing and able to pay the premium," she answered sharply.

"Are you a divorce specialist or what?" Tabloid paparazzi came to mind.

"Don't be silly." She frowned dismissively.

They entered her office, walked past the empty reception and meeting room to the back office. She went straight to sit behind her messy desk. There were piles of papers all around the keyboard and monitor. His eyes drifted around the cluttered room, searching out clues to get an initial read on his new associate. Messy, disorganised and swamped with work. There was a stark contrast between the aesthetics of her office and the rest of the building.

"You'd like my business partner, she'd have you organised in no time."

"My dumbass personal assistant is still at lunch. I need to find a new one."

She sat down and looked at Archer. Her frown deepened as she saw a stack of bills.

Behind her were several framed photographs, all with a sporting theme.

She looked much happier in them. Show jumping, polo, climbing a glacier, skiing and sailing.

"Take a seat."

"Thanks."

"So what can I do you for, Mr Archer?"

"I'm not sure what Cavendish told you, but I'm looking for a man called Stuart Hunter."

"Ah, yes. Cavendish also told me that you're working for Peter Sinclair. So what's your relationship with him?"

"Terse at best. I met him for the first time this week."

She studied his face carefully as if looking for signs that he was being truthful.

"Are you working for him or not?"

"I'm investigating his background."

Forsyth glared back at him in disbelief and shook her head.

"But you're still working for him though, aren't you?"

"I work for myself. I'm looking for someone for him, yes. He's my client."

"I'm not helping you if it's going to help that old bastard do anything."

"Cavendish said you'd investigated him. I understood you'd level with me."

"Is that right. Well there's just one question burning a hole through my head right now, and it's the oldest question there is."

"What's that?"

"What's in it for me?" She folded her arms aggressively. "Tell me why on earth I should help you to help him."

"Hang on a minute. You agreed to meet. You knew it was about Sinclair. I'll pay you by the hour if that's what you want."

"I'm not some cheap tart, Mr Archer, I don't work for peasants or for peanuts."

"How much do you want?"

"I worked that case for months, it's worth a lot more than an hour's pay, I can tell you. Even at my top rate for rich listers, it's just not good enough. I want at least ten grand for it – the rent on this place alone is five grand a month."

"What? Cavendish never told me you were a ruthless charlatan."

Forsyth leaned back in her chair and smiled unashamedly. "Didn't he."

She looked him up and down like a rinser in a gin palace looking for her next wealthy companion to drain dry.

"Are you single?"

"What's that got to do with anything?"

"Just curious." She smiled provocatively. "Are you?"

"I suppose so, yes."

What happened to the married woman, who just told him not to charm her?

"What do you mean, you suppose so? Either you are or you aren't."

"It's complicated."

"Don't be an idiot, it's perfectly simple."

She glared back at him. Holding onto the silence like a tool. Her eyes were beautiful. Her understated lip gloss shone. The ridges of her lips concertinaed to perfection.

"All right then, ten grand it is, send the bill to my office." He threw his card down on top of a ruffled pile of papers on her desk. She smiled at him and nodded confidently.

"I want ten grand upfront."

"Give me your account and sort code and I'll have it wired later today."

"All right then, let's get on with it. There's a man called Stuart Hunter. He knows everything there is to know about Peter Sinclair, but he's gone off the radar. I met him once, and his wife twice. I taped him talking about a man called Nick Carnell. I'll look for the tapes, you can buy a copy later."

Archer winced.

"Carnell was Sinclair's assassin until Sinclair had him killed because he knew too much. He killed people that wouldn't sell their property to Sinclair. He may also have set some buildings on fire that killed people in their sleep. Sinclair has bought a few burned-out buildings in his time. A bit too convenient if you ask me. But there's no proof."

Sinclair has killed people who know too much and Becky knows too much. If she gets through this kidnapping ordeal, she could end up in a worse one, Archer realised.

"What did Hunter do for Sinclair?"

"He owned a security business and properties. Sinclair stitched him up and took over the properties, then sold the security business to an associate, leaving Hunter with the crumbs. Hunter went after Sinclair with a lawsuit until he was scared off. Now he's either in hiding or he's dead. If he's alive he has a serious grudge against Sinclair and knows how to get certain things done, if you know what I mean."

"I need to find Hunter, in order to find someone else."

"I won't help you find Hunter just for Sinclair to bump him off. Not that I liked him, but I liked his wife and I don't want her getting hurt."

"It's nothing like that."

"Who are you looking for?"

"His wife."

"Hunter's wife?"

"No, Sinclair's wife."

"What's happened?"

"Look, it's a sensitive issue. I need to find her, and fast. Can you help me with some background information?"

"Sinclair's seriously bad news. He's trouble. Are you sure you're not getting in over your head?"

Archer took offence at the question, but consciously tried not to show it. He hadn't expected her to be so difficult to deal with. It felt like they were sparring partners warming up for a formal cross-examination in court.

"I'm not really sure about anything at the moment," he replied levelly.

"What was your first impression of him?"

"Not good."

"So why help him?" The real reason was off-limits.

"His wife needs help. Look, I don't like him any more than you do, but I want to help his wife stay alive." He couldn't tell her about the Boathouse.

"Why? She's better off away from him. Has she run away? Can't say I blame her."

"She's in serious trouble."

Forsyth stared at him before shifting forward in her chair. She placed her elbows on the cluttered desk and rested her head gently on top of her slender and perfectly manicured hands. She smiled and her face looked warmer. No wedding or engagement rings, but a tennis bracelet worth a packet.

"All right then. I'll tell you all about Peter Sinclair."

She explained details of the car crash that killed Jane Cavendish and her driver. The subsequent inquest which blamed the driver for going too fast after drinking alcohol. The dead witness who believed the driver's drink had been spiked and that they had been chased by another car. She explained that she had a unique file on Sinclair thicker than a phone book.

Archer listened as Forsyth bombarded him with information about Sinclair and his associates. During her lengthy appraisal, the man himself tried to call Archer again. It all went to voicemail. She continued to summarise months of solid investigation work. The convenient suicide of Jane's first husband which had allowed Sinclair to move in and offer his support. And the post mortem. She'd been pregnant with Sinclair's child when she died.

Her account was almost identical to what Cavendish had told him earlier, except that it was made all the more chilling when viewed in conjunction with the suicide of Sinclair's pregnant girlfriend Christina several years before.

"Tell me about Becky Sinclair," she asked.

Archer studied Forsyth's face. She looked cautiously concerned, but sounded precise and calm. He would need her help to find Hunter. That was all. He had to tell her something. But how much would be enough to get her to help him?

"She's been kidnapped," he said, taking a risky punt.

Silence.

"Sinclair has many enemies. Do you think you can find her?"

"I'm trying to, but time is running out."

"Are you sure he hasn't bumped her off himself already?"

"He can't be that good an actor." Archer started to doubt himself. "Can he?"

"What's your plan, Archer?"

"It really depends on you. I want you to help me find Hunter and then her."

CHAPTER TWENTY-SIX

Sarah Forsyth left her chair and paraded slowly around the office, avoiding stacks of files and mounds of papers sprawled over the floor. The metal-tipped heels of her leather boots made rhythmic contact with the light oak floor like a metronome beating out time while she carefully considered his unexpected offer.

"I'm very busy, hectic in fact, and my admins keep letting me down."

She picked up a box, emptied some papers onto a chair and took it out to the front office, then left the empty box on her assistant's blue ergonomic chair.

"She'll have a shock when she gets back from lunch, won't she? I really need to spend more time on search and selection in future; or at least hire a better head hunter." She looked smug as she walked back to her desk.

Archer felt like asking if it was her or the admins to blame, but decided it was better left unsaid at this point.

"How can I help you afford to work the case?"

"Pay me a premium day rate. Four figures." She glanced sideways at him as she sat back down. "And a decent-sized bonus."

The phone on her desk rang. She picked it up and swivelled around, turning her back to Archer. He was able to stare at the outline of her long legs without getting caught.

"I can't talk now. I'm in a meeting. I'll call you back later."

She slammed the receiver down hard and spun the chair around to face Archer.

"Client chasing you?"

"No, that was my lawyer. I'm in the middle of getting divorced. It's not much fun, I can tell you that for nothing."

"Sorry. Didn't mean to pry."

"That's okay, you're a detective. Maybe you do divorce, one way or another. Sorry, that wasn't a sporting remark. Flywheel and Shyster's negotiating a settlement deal for me, but I won't get much out of it. I signed a stupid pre-nup. I believed all of the bullshit charm and now it's backfired on me."

She leant against the desk, dropped her head in her hand and sighed. "I'm downsizing from a fairy-tale mansion into a two-bed flat in Knightsbridge, which is fine by me. The contractor tells me it will be ready in a week. It has a rolltop bath and will soon have a fridge full of wine, but you know what's really upsetting about it all is the fact that our married friends have all taken sides with him and left me out in the cold."

"Why's that?" Archer thought he knew why, but asked anyway.

"He's the one with the money. That means the ability to do whatever he wants. They all know he can open privileged doors for them, from private parties to better jobs and good business deals. Me, I'm just an ex-copper snooping around other people's bins."

"Sounds like a fairly shallow bunch to me. Don't be so hard on yourself."

"But I miss them. It was a lot of fun – another world, far away from all this crummy stuff. All I do now is hang around people getting divorced, bent coppers and shifty criminals. Well, the ones that don't hate me or want to get me back for something. It was really nice to hang out with different people, even if they were shallow."

"What about kids?"

"We kept putting it off, until it was, well, too late, I suppose. We'd already drifted too far apart."

"Look, Sarah, help me find Becky. Just tell me exactly what you want from me."

"Tell me about the kidnapping."

"Very professional. Well planned. Well executed. Becky Sinclair was specifically targeted. It wasn't opportunistic. They're using an electronic voice modulator to distort the voice. It's been set to sound deeper and flatter. The lack of modulation also makes it sound unsettling, which is generally the desired effect. We can't untangle it. Believe me we've tried. We can't get a read on the voice or the background noise. Nothing whatsoever."

"Can't you trace it?"

"We're trying to, but it's being bounced all around the globe by illegal and powerful servers in Bulgaria. We haven't had enough time during the calls to get to the source yet."

"You have that kind of manpower in your operation?"

"Just a know-it-all resident hacker."

"What about the police?"

"She dies the minute they're called."

"So what are you going to do?"

"That's where you come in."

"Why me? What can I bring to the investigation?"

"You have unique background information that I don't."

"But I'm snowed under with work and I really need the money to get back on my feet. I can't afford to mess my clients about."

"Juggle, postpone, refer. Do anything – this has to be more important. We're talking about saving an innocent woman's life."

"I have priorities too, Archer. Why is this case more important than mine?"

"Because we're running out of time. This case is life-threatening."

"You're absolutely sure it's not Sinclair playing games? He isn't bumping her off?"

"No. It's far more complicated than that. She's been kidnapped by professionals. He's not acting. He's way too angry – in fact he's getting out of control. When he finds the people responsible, I'm sure he'll have them killed. The problem is, when he finds Becky, I think he'll have her killed too."

"What's the reason this time?"

"There was a pregnancy scare. He hit her. Seems to have grown tired of her."

"He's a real piece of work, isn't he? So you want to rescue Becky from a gang of ruthless kidnappers and then convince her not to go back to her wealthy husband, but to go into hiding instead. How will you manage that?"

"We'll cross that bridge when we come to it."

"We?"

"Yes. We."

"It'll cost you."

"I'll pay you and help you clear your cases. My business partner is very good."

"So, you'll pay me, you'll help me, and you'll owe me?"

"Owe you what exactly, what do you mean by that?" Archer was confused.

"Owe me a favour. As I'd be doing you one under such difficult circumstances."

"Whatever it takes to get you on board. How about I wire you twenty grand upfront?"

"Really, just like that. You know what you want and you go for it. I like that." She smiled at him. "Let me make some calls, give me an hour or so, then call me on this number and here's my bank details." She scribbled them down on the back of her card.

"Thanks. I'll call you in an hour. We can work the case from my office."

She handed him her card and he pointed at his lying on top of her desk.

They shook hands and looked each other in the eye before she went back to her desk and started making calls. Behind the titanium facade Archer saw a softer side, but thought he understood that her fragile situation required her defences to be on full alert.

Archer walked out and waited for the glass lift. He felt the phone vibrate in his pocket and took it out to see who was calling. It was Peter Sinclair again. He had called six times and left five voicemail messages, which Archer swiftly deleted without playing back.

He walked back slowly towards Sinclair's penthouse to give himself time to think about what Forsyth had just told him. He noticed Louise Palmer's travel agency as he walked down Sloane Street. On the off chance, he went in to see if she was back. He asked an assistant if he could talk with her, but was politely told that she was away on business and would not return until next week. Archer decided it was a blessing. The last thing he needed was an hysterical family member making it harder than it was already.

He crossed the road near the Mandarin Oriental Hotel and cut through Albert Gate to South Carriage Drive, where two private soldiers in camouflage outfits were picking up horse manure from the road and putting it in hessian sacks.

He noticed Julian Cavendish was still at lunch with his promiscuous-looking young client. They sat enthralled with each other in the hotel window. He strolled along Rotten Row, quietly mulling his thoughts over and over until he got to the end of the park, where he stood and stared across Park Lane towards Sinclair's mansion block and up at his huge penthouse.

It was time to confront him about Hunter. Face to face.

CHAPTER TWENTY-SEVEN

Archer entered the Penthouse living room, which was graveyard quiet. He could feel the unspoken tension between the six men before anyone even noticed he had returned. Sinclair's anxiety had tacitly transferred itself to the rest of the solemn-looking group of mercenaries.

Sinclair sat motionless at the desk with his head bowed and his eyes closed like a meditating monk. His driver and his guards were at the table with complementary blank faces and arms folded. Best was back from his fruitless trip. He faced Archer, but avoided eye contact, looking suitably embarrassed after being given the slip.

Archer just stood still and watched them until Sinclair stirred from his trance and spotted him. He jumped to his feet and shouted, "Where the bloody hell have you been, Archer?" His face flushed red with rage.

Archer walked up to him and looked down into his eyes as he thought about his next move. He decided to use the simple technique of calmness and politeness to defuse Sinclair's anger; temporarily putting him off balance with a false but friendly-looking smile.

"I'm back. I've been following up leads. Have I missed anything?"

"Shut it, Archer, before you get a slap. I ask the questions round here, okay? So whenever I'm talking, you stay quiet, and then when I ask a question and my lips stop moving, that's when you answer, and it better be good. Got it?"

Sinclair's temple pulsated and his bottom lip trembled with anger. His clipped public school accent was occasionally tinged with a hint of the East End thrown in, but in moments like this, whenever he lost control, his working-class roots were much more pronounced.

Archer stayed quiet, but his friendly smile naturally turned into a defensive glare.

"Answer your bloody phone when I call you why don't you. You're working for me now, not some nobody. Why haven't you answered my bloody calls?"

Archer could see the pulse beating faster at his temple. Sinclair was having trouble keeping the fury from his face, which was still flushed, both fists clenched, knuckles white.

"Battery died, had to recharge it." He shrugged his shoulders and showed his open palms in a gesture that said no big deal, these things happen. "Too many Apps."

"Where the hell have you been all day anyway?"

"In my office, working the electronic side of the case."

"I need you to be more responsive when I call you. When you work for me I want you on call twenty-four seven – got it?"

"Oh, do you?"

"I fire people for less."

Archer held up his phone and smiled. "Well you can phone me right now if you want a chat. It's fully charged."

"Don't be so fucking insubordinate." Sinclair screwed his face up like a madman.

"Let's get one thing straight, Sinclair. I don't work for you. Remember that."

"What did you say?"

"You heard me. You're my client. Not my employer."

"So where's my bloody wife then? You're a typical consultant – fucking useless."

They stared at each other for half a minute, until the silence became uncomfortable and Archer decided it was a good time to drop his bombshell to maximum effect.

"You haven't been upfront with me." Archer's ice-cold stare drilled into Sinclair's eyes with laser-sharp focus, like a merciless barrister going in for the kill. "Tell me about Stuart Hunter."

Sinclair glared back at him as if he had just mentioned the unmentionable. Unable to control his rage he thumped down fast and hard on top of the desk in a fit of anger that left him trembling from head to toe. He hurriedly yanked open the desk drawer and pulled out a heavy silver handgun.

Archer knew instantly that it was a Magnum, Desert Eagle.

"I'll tell you about Stuart bloody Hunter. He's a dead man when I find him. Whoever's done this to me, whoever's taken Becky away from me, and humiliated me, and made me look like a fool in front of my men, whoever's done this – is a dead man."

He was still trembling when he walked over to the table with the loaded gun at his side pointed down at the floor and looked at his men.

"I want to send the world a message. Heads must roll. Understood? We have to settle this quickly before it gets out, otherwise we'll be a laughing stock."

He turned and aimed the gun at Archer's chest, across the table. His men all ducked instinctively.

"You need to pull your finger out. Personally, I think you've been oversold. You're overrated. If money doesn't motivate you then perhaps this bloody gun will."

Sinclair walked around the desk and walked right up to Archer. He pressed the gun barrel hard up against Archer's forehead. If it was loaded he was in deep shit. Sinclair was out of control, but at least the safety was still on.

"Do you know who I am?"

Sinclair's rapid breathing rose above the edgy silence.

"Do you? I'm somebody. Got it? And you're nobody. I'm Peter Sinclair, and that means I'm somebody in this town."

He pulled the gun back, leaving a stinging sensation on Archer's temple.

"Don't threaten me, Sinclair. I couldn't give a shit who you are." This was purely a gut reaction with no conscious thought process behind it.

"I'll bloody shoot you for that." But the gun was pointing down at the floor and the safety catch was still on.

"Go on then, shoot me. Then go to jail for me." Relying purely on instinct and nerve.

Sinclair's face reddened into a crimson glow. His hand oscillated back and forth with unrestrained rage. He closed his eyes as he steadied himself with a deep breath.

"I should kill myself and be done with all of it."

"You haven't got the balls," Archer said aggressively.

"What did you say?"

"You haven't – got – the – balls."

Sinclair slowly inched closer until there was no gap between them. He screwed his face up again and looked completely insane; he was a maniac – a megalomaniac.

"Don't tempt me, boy. I'm literally itching to do it."

"Back off. Don't ever threaten me again. Just carry on boring me to death as usual, okay?"

"I've had enough of your lip."

Twenty years of Krav Maga training in various dark alleys and an old crypt in Chelsea kicked in instinctively as Archer snatched the gun from Sinclair's hand and stepped back in a split-second move that caused Sinclair's jaw to drop.

"Who the hell are you, Archer?"

The bodyguards shot out of their seats, un-holstered their weapons and aimed their guns at Archer's head.

Archer removed the clip and the bullet from the chamber. He put them in his pocket and put the gun down on the desk.

"You're going through a stressful ordeal. Emotions can get a bit raw."

The guards re-holstered their guns, but instinctively closed in around Sinclair.

"It's all right," Sinclair said. He raised his hand and lowered his head. "It was my fault, he's right. I needed to vent. I'll be all right. Leave him alone."

Jones led Sinclair back to his chair at the desk and talked him through some deep breaths, which softened his facial expression. He told Best to fetch some water while Sinclair sat with his elbows rested on the desktop and his fists clenched white-knuckle tight.

Sinclair continued to breathe deeply and slowly. After his breathing had returned to normal he unclenched his fists and drank some water.

A mobile phone rang with a loud fanfare. Sinclair removed it from his pocket and listened quietly until it fell from his hand. He seemed frozen in time, tears welling up in his eyes.

CHAPTER TWENTY-EIGHT

Sinclair sat hunched at the desk staring into space as the tears streamed down his face. Jones fetched a square box of tissues and placed them on the desk before he picked up the mobile phone and gave it back to his boss.

Sinclair clasped both the phone and Jones's hand. He stared at him and thanked him, dried his eyes, blew his nose and sat up straight, trying to regain some composure, but the desperate look on his face gave him away.

Archer walked back up to the desk and looked him straight in the eye.

"Who was that?" he said.

"My lawyer – says the police have just found the burned body of a thirty-something-year-old woman dumped in a disused warehouse in South London. It could be her."

"It could be anyone," Archer said.

"It's her. She's dead. And I look like a bloody fool."

He looked more embarrassed or ashamed than grief-stricken.

"You don't know it's her. She could still be alive."

"What are the odds?"

"Fifty per cent or better."

The resolve drained out of him. His face went pale. "I look like a bloody fool."

Archer was certain he was more concerned about himself, his loss of respect, being shamed. Becky would always come off second best until she was dead.

"I'm done. Just find out who took her. Then leave the rest to me."

Archer left him looking up at her portrait and went out onto the terrace to make a private call to Sarah Forsyth. Sinclair disgusted him. The man was genuinely upset about the kidnappers getting one over on him. He was moved to shed tears for himself and his reputation. But his logic was that of a psychopath. Archer felt certain he would blame Becky for getting herself kidnapped. Without her, there would be no kidnappers. Archer couldn't trust him, not even as a client. He was a selfish man. A master manipulator and a control freak. It was difficult to be civil, but his personal investigation demanded it. For Alex.

His mind flashed back to the day Alex had been killed. The pain he had felt at seeing her dead body on the steel gurney and the emptiness which had soon turned to guilt for not stopping her. He carried it around with him, even now as he continued to dial the same engaged number over and over on his mobile. Sinclair wasn't showing realistic signs of grief. He was feeling something else. Not grief like Archer, but a selfish fear of not being in control, compounded by being made to look foolish in front of his peers. A killer combination. Finally the phone started ringing and a female voice answered.

"Sarah, it's Sean Archer."

"Hi Sean. I was just about to call you. I've managed to re-schedule my diary. You've got me for a few days. I'll drive over to your office in Walton Street now, shall I?"

"Can you come and pick me up first?"

"Sure. Where are you?"

"Sinclair's place. Park Lane."

"I know it. I'll meet you at the back entrance on Park Street, give me say fifteen minutes. I also have some old case files you'll need to see."

"Can you send them to the email address on my card?"

"No problem. I'll do that first and then pick you up."

Archer returned to the living room as the phone rang. Sinclair stared at it for several rings before he pressed the speaker button and answered sharply: "Sinclair."

CHAPTER TWENTY-NINE

Sinclair stood ramrod straight next to the desk and stared at Becky's portrait. Archer stood opposite him and listened carefully to the voice-modulated call from the kidnappers.

"One final payment before it's all over and you can have her back."

"Where's my wife?"

"Your wife is still alive and she'll live if you do exactly as we say."

"I want to speak to her, put her on now."

"Not today, I'm afraid. She's in another building."

"How do I know she's still alive, how do I know you haven't murdered her already?"

"Do exactly as we say and you'll get her back on Saturday night."

"So what do you want this time?"

"Twenty million dollars wired to an offshore account and then we're done."

"Are you insane?" Sinclair scoffed. "I've paid you more than enough already. You know what, you can damn well keep her. I've had enough of you and I've had more than enough of her. I think I've paid you enough already. I'm coming after you."

Archer looked at him harshly and shook his head, then signalled to play along by nodding and rolling his right hand around in circles.

"Twenty million dollars. Or else you'll regret it."

"What do you mean?" Unable to hide the angry edge from his gravelly voice.

"If you pay us, then she'll be released out onto the street with a cab fare, unharmed. Nobody will ever know what happened to you or her. Your reputation will remain intact. If you fail, and you don't pay the last ransom, then your reputation will be in tatters. Her defiled body will be found and you'll be made to look like the old fool you are. Her tortured body will make you physically sick, but that's nothing. We've also planted explosives in one of your trophy buildings."

"What? Where?"

"Central London – obviously. If you don't pay us, then you'll lose a trophy wife and a trophy building and a lot of innocent people will die."

Archer pressed the mute button, and said, "Agree – play along." Then unmuted it.

"What exactly do you want me to do?"

"Check your work email account. The instructions are all there. You have until eight p.m. on Saturday night to pay up otherwise she's a dead woman. You'll be publicly humiliated. Your reputation destroyed."

The call went dead. Sinclair looked at Archer and pointed his finger at him.

"You have two days to find them, Archer. They'll kill her at eight p.m. on Saturday night. And blow up one of my buildings. You'd better find them before then."

"This kind of call is highly unusual. They're preparing to run. Probably abroad. Are you going to pay the ransom or what?"

"It's a lot of money. I honestly don't know. I'll have to think about it. We've got until eight p.m. on Saturday to decide. Just make sure I don't have to."

"We'll do everything we can," Archer said as his mobile phone vibrated.

"Two days, Archer. Saturday night is just over forty-eight hours away. You need to get your fucking act together. You'd better buck up – fast."

It was Zoe calling from the office. "Okay, okay, I'll find them, don't worry, now if you'll excuse me, I have to take this call." Archer walked out to the terrace and answered his phone.

"Hey, what's happening?"

"Breaking news," Zoe said, excitedly.

CHAPTER THIRTY

Archer bit down on his bottom lip in anticipation of Zoe's latest findings; hoping for some information that would lead him to the kidnappers before it was too late. They badly needed a break. He was starting to feel unnerved by Sinclair's attitude, desperate even. Forty-eight hours was nothing, even if they had a lead. Sinclair was rapidly going cold on paying the latest ransom demand and saving Becky. He seemed to be more concerned about protecting his property portfolio and exacting revenge, as if he'd already come to terms with losing her. Sinclair was only interested in himself. Archer knew he was being used, but still hadn't worked out exactly what Sinclair was using him for. But he was also using Sinclair.

"I just upgraded the tracker on Sinclair's phone line and it worked. We've got the kidnappers' phone number and address."

"Where are they?"

"It's a serviced flat in Marylebone. I'm texting you the address right now. They've just rung off and it's less than ten minutes' drive away from you, so get going."

"Great work, Zoe. Stay on the line."

Archer walked back into the living room, picked the Magnum up off the desk and stuck it in his jacket pocket.

"We've got a fresh lead. I need this."

Archer was gone before Sinclair could ask him any questions.

He returned to his phone call with Zoe as he waited for the lift doors to open.

"I need you to find out when the police identify a burned body at a warehouse in South London in case it's Becky."

The lift doors opened slowly and Archer got in.

"Okay, already onto it."

"And look out for any emails coming in from Sarah Forsyth. Use whatever you can to find the current whereabouts of Stuart Hunter. He's gone off the grid."

"Okay, the emails are already in. Hey and listen, this bomb threat – if you don't find them soon you need to make Sinclair pay."

"They're bluffing."

"But what if they're not? Could you live with that?"

"No pressure then."

"Just be careful."

"Don't worry."

"But you haven't got your gun."

Archer had already rung off. He walked out of the building and looked up and down Park Street. A pale blue convertible Mercedes E350 with the top down flashed its powerful xenon headlights at him as it approached. Sarah Forsyth pulled up to the kerb with a radiant smile, gleaming white teeth and a husky voice.

"Get in, handsome. I'm all yours until Sunday night."

Archer smiled. "Change of plan. Marylebone High Street. Put your foot down."

"All right, I'm game – let's see if we can get there in under five. Who's there?"

"The kidnappers."

They headed north on Park Street towards Oxford Street and Gloucester Place. Archer entered the postcode into the satnav system and the map on the screen displayed an upside down L-shaped gap closing between them as the purple route indicator got shorter and the red flashing dots moved closer together. Five minutes after the call had ended Forsyth was driving like a maniac towards the caller's address, weaving through traffic and ignoring the traffic lights. Two red light cameras and one speeding camera flashed as they drove past. Forsyth smiled and winked confidently as if she did it all the time. Archer could feel his adrenalin kicking in. They were about to confront the kidnappers red-handed.

CHAPTER THIRTY-ONE

orsyth's Merc stopped outside the red brick mansion block less than twelve minutes after the ransom call had ended. She parked on double yellow lines and pulled out a small blue flashing light on a curly lead from behind her seat, placed it on the dashboard and plugged it into the cigarette-lighter socket. She then placed a red and white metal sign on the dashboard next to it. It had a red cross and said "Doctor on Call". Archer was impressed with her resourcefulness and composure under pressure.

They got out and peered through the glass either side of the shiny black front door. There was no porter or receptionist inside so they pressed the entryphone buttons for every flat and responded affirmatively as a pizza delivery company to the first respondent, on the fifth floor, who dutifully buzzed them in.

Zoe's text stated that the kidnappers' flat was on the first floor, so they quietly took the staircase, while the lift remained empty on the ground floor.

A sign showing the flat numbers on the first floor pointed them towards the left. Flat number six was the last door at the end of the hall on the right.

"What fake IDs have you got with you?" Archer whispered.

"Doctor and Crown Prosecution Service."

"I've got a Customs badge. Let's pretend to go in as bailiffs collecting a debt."

"Okay, but what if they're armed?"

Archer took out the Magnum and replaced the clip before he knocked on the door and pressed his ear against it. He couldn't hear anything.

"Mr Smith, are you there?" he said. Smith being the first name to enter his head.

No response.

"Customs and Excise, Mr Smith. Open up, we've got this place surrounded."

Archer banged the door harder. Still no response.

He put his ear to the door again and listened. No sound at all.

"There's nobody in there," he said, frowning. "I don't understand."

"Let's break in then."

"Okay. I'll kick the door down."

"Hold on, cowboy."

Forsyth rummaged through her handbag and found a professional lock pick set. She held up two thin pieces of metal with hooked ends and smirked.

"Girl Scout," she said, proudly.

"Don't you mean Girl Guide?"

"Whatever."

She frowned at Archer and fiddled with the lock for a few seconds and pushed the door inwards. It opened to its full width, revealing the kidnappers' eerily silent apartment. They tiptoed quietly inside the dimly lit hall, Magnum first.

CHAPTER THIRTY-TWO

They moved cautiously from room to room. The flat was still and empty. The transparent cream curtains were drawn, but it was light enough to see. It was a basic space with cheap modern furniture neatly arranged. The walls were a stark shade of white with nothing hanging on them and there was not a sign of dust anywhere, as if all the surfaces had recently been cleaned. A strong smell of bleach lingered in the air along with stale cigarette smoke – the distinctive aroma of unfiltered Gauloises. It reminded Archer of a serial killer he had found by geographical and retail profiles and two purchases on a store loyalty card.

No one was inside and there was no sign that anyone had stayed there overnight. The beds were made and the sheets were clean. They opened wardrobes and drawers, but there were no personal effects to be found. It was an empty flat with no comfort or luxury.

"We must have just missed them – what if they come back?" she said.

"Hopefully they will."

"What if they have guns?"

"They will."

Forsyth followed Archer into the second bedroom.

"Here's the luggage from the drops," Archer whispered and pointed.

He searched the cases and canvas bags from the ransom drops, all neatly arranged on top of the flimsy-looking double bed with no headboard.

"All empty."

"The kidnappers must have used the flat to transfer the money into different bags."

Forsyth searched through the luggage more thoroughly, unzipping compartments, and found two pairs of chrome-plated handcuffs with keys. They smelled of bleach, as if they had been cleaned recently. She looked under the beds and behind the furniture. They did the same in the lounge. She put her hand down the side of a corduroy armchair and pulled out a pack of Trojans and a shiny bullet. "It's custom made – it's got a cross and a J.M.J. inscription on it: Jesus Mary and Joseph. A silver bullet for stupid vampire aficionados. We may be able to track them down with this bullet, but it will take more than two days, that's for sure."

"Keep hold of it. Let's check out the kitchen."

There was no food in the kitchen cupboards. Forsyth lifted a blue and white tea towel to reveal two closed laptops lying side by side on a small white breakfast bar. Both were plugged into the mains sockets on the wall and both were turned on. One was plugged into the telephone outlet in the wall. The other had a custom-made wireless communications device sticking out of it. Archer looked for booby traps but they were clean. He lifted up each laptop and looked underneath. There was a silver confederate flag sticker with a shop address on each chassis. "These two laptops are the best chance we've got."

"Why's that?"

"Both custom built and bought locally from a computer shop on the high street."

"How do you know that?"

"Look." He showed her one of the stickers.

"You think they made all the calls remotely?"

"Definitely."

"Shall we take these computers with us?"

"No. Zoe will be watching the flat and listening."

"So what now?"

"Let's try the building manager downstairs first, then the computer shop."

"Somehow I don't think they paid with credit cards. Not their own anyway."

The small sign on the door next to the lift on the ground floor said "Management". Zoe had texted that the flats were serviced short-term lets mostly for tourists, but affordable enough for some longer-term visitors who needed to stay in London for a week or more and wanted facilities to cook their own food. Archer knocked on the door and someone shouted back instantly.

"Hang on a minute!" And then muttered loudly, "It's like Clapham bleeding Junction round here. There's no peace for the wicked any more, is there, Kitty?"

Someone inside was hastily bashing pots and heavy-handedly clanking dishes around.

The door opened to reveal a short rotund man in his mid-sixties. He weighed at least twenty stone and looked like a walking Toby jug with oversized ears, sagging jowls of flesh either side of bloodshot eyes, small round nose and purple lips.

Holding half a pasty in his left hand with brown sauce slowly dripping onto the black and white tiled floor, he scratched his bald head, licked his lips and smiled.

"How can I help you, guv'nor?" he said in an East End accent.

"We're with Customs and the CPS."

They both flashed their fake badges at him, long enough to look the part, but not long enough for him to scrutinise them in detail.

"We need to speak with the people staying in Flat Six."

"Is that right," he said, slightly out of breath. "I haven't seen him around all that much lately. He was back and forth with luggage for a while, laundry probably. Then he took it all away in different bags, which was a bit odd, but he hasn't been in today."

"Does he stay here?"

"Like I said, I don't think he's stayed here for a few days. He's had a few different women in and out of here though, quite good lookers too, short skirts and tight tops like models, but top shelf ones if you know what I mean." Toby Jug chuckled.

His voice reminded Archer of Ray Winstone, but his body and face didn't fit the voice.

"How long is the place rented for?"

"He took it two weeks ago and paid in cash for four weeks."

"Who is he?"

"He told me his name was Gerald Grosvenor." Toby Jug screeched with childish laughter. "He paid cash, in advance like, plus a tip, lovely jubbly. I think he's a bit of a young toff playing about with fast women – expensive ladies of the night, if you know what I mean."

"What does he look like?"

"Nice-looking kid in his early twenties, a bit too skinny like, but no trouble."

"Does he wear a hoody?"

"All the time, yeah, with the hood up mostly. They all do that now though, don't they."

"Any forwarding address?"

"He used a Mayfair address, which I thought was a bit odd – Grosvenor House, he said, on Park Lane no less. Do you want me to find it for you?" He chuckled to himself and bit another large chunk out of his diminishing pasty.

"Don't bother. Was there anything else, anything strange about him?"

"Like what?" Toby Jug scratched his nose.

"Anything that stood out, you know, any distinguishing features?"

"Well as nice as he was, I thought I saw a glimpse of a gun one time, but not really sure. Bit scary that. I thought what's a nice kid like that doing with a gun."

"You'd better keep your distance from him in future. Thanks for the information."

They left Toby Jug to waddle off back into his office.

"How did you know who the kid was?" Forsyth asked impatiently.

"He fits the same description as the one picking up the ransom drops, but there could be several of them, a bloody gang of armed hoodies."

They left the car parked with its blue lights flashing on double yellow lines and walked towards the high street. Archer looked up and down it and noted the change in the street numbers to get his bearings on the shop's address.

"It's this way."

"But the kidnappers might come back any minute to clean out the flat."

"We can't hang around here all day on the off chance. Follow me, it can't be far."

They dodged the crowds of shoppers and glammed-up mothers with pushchairs.

"It's all coffee shops and hair salons for yummy mummies round here."

"There it is look."

"Where?"

"Across the road over there."

"Which one?"

"The Phreak Brothers' Computer Shop."

CHAPTER THIRTY-THREE

The Phreak Brothers' Computer Shop on Marylebone High Street had a window display crammed full of technical gadgetry and computer parts, along with fake skulls and figurines of bushy-haired rockers wearing dark glasses. The front door was covered with Dead Head stickers and Grateful Dead posters, which made it look more like the second-hand record shop Archer used in Fulham than a computer shop. To the right of the window display, just beneath the start of the raised roller shutter, a neon sign said "Open". It sparked on and off, as if the power was irregular and it was about to blow. Archer thought it was just another part of the shop's unique theatre.

"Weird-looking shop. Think I'll stick to Apple," Forsyth said in a superior manner.

"Me too."

"Strange name. What's all that about?"

"It refers to phone phreaking, which subsequently became computer hacking."

"I knew you were geeky."

"I'm not," Archer replied, a little over-defensively.

"Okay, don't freak out, keep your cool boots on, Chelsea boy."

"It's a play on words referring to the Freak Brothers comic books from the Seventies. The skinny figurines in the window give that away. Along with all the Dead Head stuff I would say we're looking at a shop owned by a wannabe West Coast hippie who's really into psychedelic comics, loud music and computers."

"Not too shabby, Sherlock. So, you're not geeky; just a bit of a smartarse then."

"Just let me do the talking – while you carry on practising the Barbie thing."

"Ouch! Mean boy. So, let's get our story straight first. What are we going to say?"

"You're really into this planning ahead lark, aren't you?"

"They might not want to talk to you about their customers."

"So – we'll have to find a way to make them talk."

"Okay, how will you do that?"

"Play it by ear."

"You mean wing it."

"Exactly, it's more fun."

"So what shall I do?"

"Just go along with it."

Archer's phone rang. It was Zoe.

"Hey, what's up?"

"Hold on. I'm calling your new BFF as well."

"Okay."

Forsyth's phone started ringing, and she answered it on speaker after two rings.

"Hello, this is Zoe from Londinium. I need to ask you some questions, but hold on."

"Okay." They were now in a three-way call.

Forsyth frowned at Archer and whispered. "Someone called Zoe from your office wants to ask me questions." He nodded calmly and pushed the door open, holding it for her as they walked into the darkness. Forsyth cut the speaker and held the phone to her ear before she introduced herself to Zoe inside the weirdest-looking shop she'd ever been in.

It was like the moody film set of a mad professor's laboratory. There were dark murky corners and spotlights focused on objects displayed to great effect. Heavy rock music played too quietly in the background. As they moved, the wooden floorboards creaked loudly, as if amplified like a corny effect in a low-budget horror movie.

A Harley Davidson Fat Boy motorcycle was parked in the centre of the shop beneath film studio spotlights. Its turquoise and white petrol tank and chromework glistened. The shop was stuffed full of computer parts and rock memorabilia. It was definitely wacky.

At the back, behind the counter, were several tables with desk lamps illuminating half-built customised computers. On the wall behind them was a huge, partly torn confederate flag with a black Gibson Les Paul guitar hanging next to it.

A surreal-looking man with wild bushy grey hair and a pale blue paisley bandana was working on a motherboard. A Jerry Garcia lookalike except for the beard. Instead, he wore a thick grey goatee, well trimmed and brushed. Despite the softness of his paunch he seemed tough enough to look after himself if he had to.

He looked up and waved. "Hang on. I'll be there in a minute now."

CHAPTER THIRTY-FOUR

Archer watched Forsyth continue her phone call with Zoe as she studied an elaborate piece of equipment in a glass case with an odd combination of valves and transistors which glowed and flashed intermittently. A metal sign stuck on the glass case said "Lie Detector". Archer paced slowly around the Harley Davidson, admiring the shiny pristine engine.

"How can I help you?" The voice was deep, gravelly, a hint of Welsh rubbed off in LA, like Tom Jones, only lower-pitched and rougher. The man stood like a rock at the counter and looked straight into Archer's eyes. Reading him.

"Hi there, I'm Sean. Great bike. Great shop."

"Thanks. I like it anyway."

"Are you the owner?" Archer walked towards the man and the counter.

"I am indeed, for all my sins. I'm Jonesy." Not another one.

Jonesy looked over at Forsyth. "What's your name, love?"

"Hi, I'm Sarah," she waved and went back to her call. "Sorry about that ..."

Jonesy's face was suntanned. Well lived in, with heavy bags under dark bulging eyes that were surrounded by lots of laughter lines. The man had no earrings, no visible tattoos, but liked his bling – diamond-studded pinkie rings, diamond-encrusted watch and a heavy gold neck chain. Various rock star bangles and hippie beads. Clean manicured hands, more used to tinkering with motherboards and keyboards than engines and bike chains. And a contented beer belly. He clearly liked eating and drinking.

This man obviously had more than enough money to indulge himself in a fantasy world, so he could not be bought.

The fake Customs badge in Archer's pocket would not scare him into submission because he probably paid his VAT and taxes like all sensible business people.

But his fantasy world was definitely anti-Establishment-oriented, so helping the authorities would not appeal to him either.

"I'll be completely honest with you. I'm not here to buy anything and I don't want to waste your time as I can see you have plenty to get on with, but I need your help."

The men just stared at each other for a while like two wary gunslingers. Muffled power chords and guitar bursts resonated too quietly in the background.

"What sort of help?"

"I need to find someone who's gone missing."

"Are you with the police?"

"No."

"Have you called the police?"

"No."

The owner frowned as he looked even harder at Archer, studying him closely.

"Who are you trying to help?"

"A young woman."

"And how can I help you?"

"I need to find someone who can help me find her and he bought some specialist equipment from you."

"What kind of equipment?"

"Two silver laptops with your silver confederate sticker and shop name and address on the chassis. One wired to the internet. The other with a wireless device in a side port."

The owner's phone rang. He answered it and then laughed out loud and hung up.

"That was the lovely Zoe de la Croix. The only hacker in London better than me. She's the most devious social engineer I know, she's amazing. She says she works with you. So that's fine by me. We can talk. Okay, I remember the young lad that picked those laptops up. It was a few weeks ago. Cash in hand. No receipts."

"Did he leave an address?"

"I don't have any contact details for him. In fact he paid a premium to have those built in a week. He paid upfront. No questions asked. Job done."

"Any idea where I might find him?"

"None whatsoever."

"Did he talk much?"

"He told me he was making a film. He wanted to make the next low-budget movie to hit the big time. He wanted realistic equipment for the ransom calls as the film was about a kidnapping. That's exactly what he said. Voice distortion software just like the movies – he asked me to set it up to sound like the deep mechanical voices they use in Hollywood films when they do ransom scenes. He wanted to make the calls remotely from up to fifty miles away and for the calls to be untraceable. He wanted it all to be completely genuine so he could explain it in the film. So I gave him the real thing."

"And?"

"I also gave him some disposable mobile phones built just to call the wireless device. One laptop receives the call from the mobile. That's then networked to the other one wirelessly, which is connected to the internet and accesses a server in Bulgaria which bounces the call all over the world to make it untraceable in under two minutes."

Archer couldn't hide his disappointment at finding another dead end.

"If you can think of anything that could help find him, or if he gets in contact with you again, would you mind letting Zoe know straight away?"

"No problem. For Zoe. I'll help you find him."

"Thank you. Hey, is the bike just for show or what?"

"No way. I live in Highgate, right by the Flask actually. I ride it here on dry days and park it right there, under the spotlight." He smiled, looking completely satisfied.

"You've got a good thing going here."

"You'd better believe it."

CHAPTER THIRTY-FIVE

They left the computer shop, crossed the street, and headed back towards the car.

"So now we know how they made the ransom calls like pros," he said, exasperated.

"They paid a professional geek in cash and we just drew a blank."

"But we're getting closer. We're on the right track. Let's stay positive."

"What do we do now? Put a BOLO out for horny hoodies?"

"We focus on finding Hunter. He's our best lead."

"What about staking the flat out? They have to come back."

"Do they? Maybe later if we can't find Hunter, but we'll find him – we have to. He's the key to sorting this mess out before Saturday night."

"But he's off the grid. It's impossible to find him in two days."

"If anyone can do it Zoe can. What did she want anyway?"

"She was asking lots of questions about Hunter and his old associates. He's probably using a false identity. He could be anywhere. I don't think she'll be able to find him in two weeks let alone two days."

"But you said he likes London and Italy."

"Yes, he does, but they're pretty big places."

"Well his taste for culture may be his downfall. We'll run a GRID profile on him, back at the office."

"What's that?"

"Specialist software – I'll explain later."

They turned the corner to the side street. Archer spotted the policeman first and looked at Forsyth. She just smiled back at him without any obvious concern. Her car was still illegally parked with its flashing blue light. It was being studied up close by a young-looking copper with his notebook and radio out.

"Hello officer, everything all right?"

"You shouldn't park here, doctor – have you got any identification?"

Forsyth looked in her bag for her purse and showed him her fake Ministry of Defence doctor's badge. The young policeman looked at it quickly and handed it back.

"Is everything all right? Do you need any assistance?"

"Luckily it was a false alarm. But thank you, officer."

A dark red BMW M3 stopped in the middle of the road, blocking traffic in both directions. A grey-haired policeman wearing armoured diplomatic protection gear and carrying a light machine gun got out of the passenger side.

"Well, well, well. Sarah Forsyth. Up to her old tricks again. You've got some nerve."

"Hello, Newman," she said, with a cold dismissive tone.

"Can't stop to chat. Just make sure you give her a ticket, officer, otherwise you'll be walking the beat down in Brixton this time tomorrow."

"Yes, sir," the young policeman went red and duly filled out a ticket. He handed it to Forsyth before the red BMW moved on. Archer opened the door and got in the passenger seat.

Forsyth got in the car and handed the ticket to Archer. She started the engine, indicated left and headed towards Regent's Park and then turned left down Marylebone Road. Gently cruising west in heavy traffic towards South Kensington, via Hyde Park.

"Put it in the glove box with the others," she said calmly.

He opened it and saw it was stuffed full of old parking and speeding tickets.

"Do you always get special police treatment like that?" Archer asked.

"A few cops out there don't like me, but they're mostly knuckleheads. It's the criminals you really need to worry about."

"Why did you leave the Met?"

"Long story. I'll tell you sometime."

They turned left off Brompton Road and then into the narrow cobbled lane off Walton Road. Forsyth parked in the designated bay marked private and Archer led the way to the back of the building, up the stairs, and into the open-plan office area.

Zoe was busy giving orders to two men in khaki overalls who were setting up a large clear glass screen near her work area.

"Wow, this place is great, lots of screens and space," Forsyth said a little too eagerly.

"Sarah this is Zoe. Zoe – Sarah."

"Pleased to meet you, Zoe, nice office." They shook hands firmly and checked each other out blatantly, up and down, like cold-hearted gladiators about to do battle.

"Likewise, we're just setting the FBI's new smartboard up."

Zoe went back to her technicians and Archer showed Forsyth around.

"So what do you think?"

"It's huge. How many people work here?"

"Just me and Zoe. We like plenty of space."

"So those offices over there are what?"

"Meeting rooms."

Archer visualised the cogs moving into gear inside Forsyth's head.

"Hmm. Nice digs."

Zoe told the techies to take a coffee break over the road. Once they'd left the office she brought up volumes of information flashing and scrolling on multiple screens. Files and photographs of Hunter and his wife appeared and disappeared all over the place.

"Here's that spike from Sinclair's computer." Archer put it down on Zoe's desk.

"How come I've never heard of you guys? Don't you advertise?"

"No, we're busy enough with our existing clients and referrals. Our neighbours around here think we're software developers."

"So what's this GRID thing?"

"It stands for Geographical, Retail, Internet and Digital; it's tracking and profiling software that we developed and use as digital profiling consultants. The Met and the FBI just love acronyms. We use multiple inputs, GPS, phone, credit cards, point-of-sale, loyalty cards, internet, CCTV, ANPR, plus we fully integrate forensic profiling and psychological profiling and then cross-reference all relevant databases."

"So you just press a button to run it and that's it?"

"No. You need to drive it. Big data trawling can take weeks to run, months even, so the right information needs to be found and analysed and then we apply search algorithms and filters to save time. It's complicated, but it works."

"So give me an example."

"Okay, serial killers buy a lot of bleach to clean their crime scenes. They use multiple stores and always pay with cash. We helped find the Midwest Motel Murderer. We used all the available data to narrow down the search and found someone had used a store loyalty card with two cash transactions for bleach inside the target area. Point-of-sale, then CCTV footage and then GPS phone tracks. Busted."

"Sounds impressive."

"Hey Sarah, that plastic surgeon from Paris we talked about," Zoe said. "Well, he has a new name, new credentials all round in fact, and a new London address. He's operating from Harley Street now and he's as bent as a butcher's hook."

"Greasy frigging frog," Forsyth muttered. "Sorry, you're not French, are you?"

"Luxembourgeoise."

"Oui, très bon. He did some work for Hunter a few years ago, then he got into trouble over dodging his taxes and I couldn't find out where he went after that. Probably left the country. Did you manage to get any leverage on him?"

"Plenty: photo, address, client list, price list, tax returns, fake qualifications, fake passport, new wife, and wait for it, estranged wife, because he's not yet divorced."

"Then it's time for a private consultation with the tax-dodging bigamist."

CHAPTER THIRTY-SIX

Forsyth drove as fast as traffic conditions allowed, but clearly not fast enough to suit her lead-footed need for speed. She tapped the steering wheel impatiently in jams and used the horn far too frequently. The stop-start ride was uncomfortable as the gravitational forces on the body kept changing without warning.

"Well this feels like déjà vu. Are you always this much fun to work with?"

She smiled and winked at him. Her confidence was infectious.

"You must have plenty of points on your licence by now?"

"Clean as a whistle." She laughed and casually flicked her hair.

"Impossible."

"I might explain how it works later. If you're lucky."

"You drive too fast."

"Police-trained."

"For what? The Dakar Rally or the Secret Policeman's Ball?"

She gambled more red lights without any cameras flashing and got them parked on a meter outside the Harley Street address in less than ten minutes.

Two glammed-up middle-aged women sat in the waiting room quietly reading glossy fashion magazines. One wore dark sunglasses. She looked like Marilyn Monroe nursing a hangover. The other looked anorexic, with a face like a puffed-up trout. A butch short-haired receptionist with long dangly earrings stared and pursed her lips at them when they stopped and stood directly in front of her. The phoney doctor appeared to be busy consulting wealthy patients.

"How may I help you," she said, with a guttural German accent.

They both flashed fake badges.

"We're evacuating the building," Archer said. "There's a siege taking place upstairs in five minutes. You need to get out now, quickly and quietly. Who else is on this floor?"

The two well-dressed women stopped reading their magazines, looked at each other and left without saying a word.

"There's a client in with Doctor Azeez. He can't be disturbed."

"Call him and tell him he'll have to reschedule."

"I can't. He's doing an, er … examination."

Archer leaned over and pressed the speed dial for Doctor A. It started ringing on speaker, but there was no answer. Archer opened the nearest door and found a dimly lit narrow hallway with two more doors. The ageing paint was peeling off the woodwork more like that of a back street address than a prestigious one. He knocked on the door with the doctor's name on it. There was no answer, so he tried to open it, but it was locked from the inside.

"Doctor Azeez, it's urgent, please open the door."

"Go away. I'm with a client."

"We're evacuating the building, open the door right now, this is the police."

"Two minutes please."

Archer and Forsyth waited in the dark hallway. They could hear muffled voices.

The door opened and a skinny dishevelled woman in her twenties walked out doing up her sheer black blouse. She had a pale expressionless face and drunken swagger, as if she was high on drugs. Archer led the way into the examination room. When Azeez saw Forsyth he frowned and said, "Don't I know you?"

"You have a good memory, Doctor Azeez. Or should I say Benoir Fache."

"Who are you?" He continued to stare intently, but seemed to have forgotten her name.

"Nice little set-up, Monsieur Fache. Drug the patient, turn the lights out. And in such glamorous surroundings too. What do you think, Sean? Should I bring my mother-in-law to be treated by this snake oil salesman?"

"No, I think this dark cesspit has seen its fair share of venomous old cobras."

"What do you want? I have important patients waiting."

"Where's Stuart Hunter?" Forsyth said.

"Go to hell. *Putain.* I know who you are now. *Merde.* You're the mercenary bitch who falsified all that evidence against me."

"And here's some more false evidence…"

Forsyth held up a manila folder and took out a wad of documents which she threw down one at a time on his desk. His confidence drained away as he saw the files.

"Fake passport, fake qualifications, new marriage certificate, old marriage certificate. Impersonating a doctor. Bigamy. Taxes. Need we say more?"

He shook his head, mute as a mannequin, expensive white porcelain teeth gritted and slowly grinding together.

Archer stepped into his personal space. "Where's Hunter?"

Azeez stepped back and held his hands up in the air.

"Puh," he shrugged warily. "Nobody knows."

Forsyth picked up the documents, waved them in his face then slipped them back into the folder.

"Once these get around town, no one will know where you are either. Not where you're going. It'll be sausage and beans all day long for you, cowboy."

"All right," he snarled. "Let me think."

"No," said Archer. "Don't think. Talk."

"I don't know where he is. The driver does."

"Who's the driver?"

"He collects the medicines and treatments. Then he delivers them to the Hunters."

"Call him."

"But I don't have another delivery scheduled for two weeks."

"Call him. Tell him you have a small package for urgent delivery. Make something up, you're good at that. Just make it sound important. If you don't, you're going down."

"*Très bien*. I'll tell him they need some important medication. That will make it sound more urgent." The phoney doctor made a call then informed his uninvited guests that the driver would pick up the package within the hour.

They left quietly and waited in the open-top car. After half an hour, a black BMW Seven Series with tinted windows double parked in front of the address, blocking them in. They pretended to ignore the driver and acted like a couple saying goodbye. A shaven-headed thick-set man got out, wearing a long black leather coat and dark sunglasses. Archer saw a neck tattoo peeking out from above his collar. He looked like a Hollywood hit man. Two minutes later he returned clutching a small white paper bag with a green cross on it.

CHAPTER THIRTY-SEVEN

They followed the black Seven Series to Docklands without being spotted. Forsyth parked the convertible Merc in one of the empty parking bays at South Quay House, across the dark green water from Canary Wharf. The BMW was parked in a disabled space next to the main entrance. The driver waited outside it until a well-dressed young woman opened it and collected the package from him. He left without saying a single word to her, lit a cigarette and drove off. She went back inside and took the lift, but Archer could not make out where it had stopped.

He called Zoe and told her where they were. He read out the name and address of the building. Within five minutes she called him back and delivered her findings. She'd searched the information on all the tenants and found that the most likely property was owned by a shell company in the Caymans and rented out to a retired widow who was living off a trust fund allowance from Liechtenstein. She had a French live-in housekeeper and a British live-in boyfriend slightly older then her. The widow's name was Samantha Knight, but it was a false identity for Samantha Hunter. She was living in apartment 12A, one of two apartments on the top floor of South Quay House. Her "boyfriend", Hunter, might be hiding from Sinclair, but this was still an extravagant five-thousand-square-foot apartment.

"Do you think he could be armed?" Forsyth asked as she got out of the car.

"Possibly, but he's not used to using guns himself, is he? Zoe said he doesn't have a gun licence, so if he's got a gun it's unregistered."

"Aren't you concerned that we're about to rumble him and he's probably armed?"

"Not really. Hunter wouldn't get his hands dirty. He'd hire contractors."

"He could have contractors in there guarding him right now."

"I don't think so."

"Do you think Becky's in there?"

"I think Hunter's potentially behind the kidnapping, but I don't think he'd

121

use his own hiding place to keep her prisoner. Actually, I'm not expecting to find anyone in there apart from the Hunters and their housekeeper."

"Are we going to wing this one as well then?"

"I think we will. You ready?"

"You go from hero to zero in less than two minutes."

Archer frowned at her and pressed the shiny silver button for apartment 12A.

A soft female voice answered, "Hello?"

"Hello, Mrs Knight? I'd like to talk to you about Peter Sinclair if you can spare some time. He's looking for you and I want to help you stay alive."

No response.

"Mrs Knight, please open the door."

No response.

Archer pressed the buzzer again for ten seconds. He knew how to annoy. He smiled vacantly at the lens above the buzzer. "Mrs Knight. I have some vital information for you. You're in great danger."

CHAPTER THIRTY-EIGHT

Archer was directly in front of the video entry system camera. Forsyth stayed out of sight as she leaned back casually against the wall next to the camera with her arms folded and watched her accomplice attempt to get in.

"Who are you?" a female voice said.

"I have to talk to Mrs Knight."

"Mrs Knight is not here."

"Who are you?"

"I'm the housekeeper. What is your name?"

"My name is Sean Archer."

"I'll tell her you called. Goodbye, Mr Archer."

"I need to speak with her now. She's in great danger."

No response. The voice had vanished.

"That went well," Forsyth smirked, as if she'd enjoyed watching him fail.

"Thanks, I put a lot of thought and effort into it. It's all about detailed planning and flawless execution. You should take notes."

"I'm glad you're not perfect. But right now we look like a pair of door-to-door salesmen trying to flog Armageddon to Jehovahs. Hold on, someone's coming."

The door opened and a young couple walked out holding hands. Before they made it to their bright yellow Porsche, the uninvited visitors had quietly slipped inside the lobby and walked towards the open lift.

"I'm not taking the stairs to the twelfth floor."

"Nor me," he smiled and gestured with his right hand to let her go in first. Taking the opportunity to have a good look down at her perfectly sculptured body and then realising she'd clocked him in the mirror. He felt his face flush, but faced the door and stayed silent.

They took the lift to the top floor and got out onto an extra-wide hallway. The floor was covered with large dark slate tiles. The walls were covered with lighter stone tiles. The slightest sound echoed like the inside of an old church. There were two console tables with oversized glass sculptures and table lamps and a window at the far end with a clear view of the O2 Arena. The door on the left was labelled 12A and the one on the right 12B.

"The property developer wasted a lot of space on this hallway; these apartments must have cost mega-millions. I'd say Hunter still has plenty of money."

"He probably doesn't see it that way. He doesn't see what he has, but what he's lost."

"Shall we knock on the door?"

"Wait."

"Listen, did you hear that?"

"What?"

"Voices – arguing inside."

They tiptoed across the slate floor to the extra-wide light oak door with shiny decals stating 12A above a small peephole. Archer's left ear touched the polished oak and Forsyth listened with her right. Their faces were only a few inches apart. They could feel each other's breath; hers smelled minty fresh.

Inside, a man and a woman argued. The sound was muffled by the door and they couldn't make out exactly what was being said. From the tone and the raised voices they could tell there was an element of alarm.

After a couple of minutes the argument fizzled out. A moment's silence was followed by accomplished piano music and the distinctive sound of pool balls crashing into each other as they were hit hard and fast by a cue ball.

Forsyth touched Archer's shoulder. "Leave this to me," she whispered confidently.

"It's all yours."

He stepped back and watched. Forsyth clenched her right fist and knocked on the door assertively with the middle knuckles of her fingers.

"Mrs Hunter, it's Sarah Forsyth."

The professional piano playing continued without pause.

Forsyth hammered on the door with her clenched fist half a dozen times. Then they listened with their ears pressed up against the door again. They heard stiletto heels getting nearer as they clipped out a measured rhythm against the hard floor.

"Go away," a soft female voice said. "I'm calling the police."

There was a small lens built into the door and Sarah stood in front of it a good yard back to avoid any menacing distortion from the peephole view.

"We know who you are. If you don't open this door in twenty seconds I'm calling Peter Sinclair and within an hour you'll be in the boot of a limo driven by four of his thugs."

The heels clipped off again. The piano playing stopped. There was more muffled debate, but this time with three voices. One male and two female. It had to be them. Then the piano started playing again and the heels clipped back towards the door.

"Where did you last meet Mrs Hunter?" the soft female voice asked.

"We had tea at the Ritz; in the Palm Room. You've got three seconds."

The door opened slowly. A slim woman in her early thirties looked at them with a stern expression. She wore a black skirt, black seamed stockings and black stilettos with a white blouse. Her jet-black hair was scrunched up into a bun. Her accent was French, but her almond-shaped eyes looked Asian. Her unblemished face was white and her lips were painted bright red. She had a small beauty spot on her left cheek which made her look like a classic movie star from the monochrome Forties or Fifties. She looked like Zoe's sister, except far too short.

"You'd better come in then." She offered her hand. "I'm Madeleine, the Knights' housekeeper. I look after Mr and Mrs Knight."

"You mean Hunter," Forsyth corrected.

CHAPTER THIRTY-NINE

The apartment was huge with an open-plan reception area that looked straight across the quay to Canary Wharf. The towering mirrored glass skyscrapers were more in keeping with Manhattan than London, but the views were formidable by any standard.

The layout was open and uncluttered, although not sparsely furnished. It had a minimalist art gallery feel to it with fine art pieces, sculptures and paintings positioned for maximum effect. A life-sized copy of the Venus de Milo in dull white marble greeted visitors upon entry.

Steel-tipped heels echoed on the polished mahogany floor as they walked towards the massive sofas near the window. The polished black grand piano with the lid down had centre stage in front of the window. Next to it was a large red baize and light oak pool table with a game unfinished, but no players in sight.

"Wait there," Madeleine said harshly.

She walked to the kitchen area then out of sight around the corner. When she returned she was followed by a tall white-haired and suntanned man in his early sixties. He was informally dressed in a light linen jacket, pink polo shirt and beige chinos. Navy moccasins and no socks. The Glock in his right hand was aimed squarely between Archer's eyes.

"What the hell do you mean by threatening us with Peter Sinclair?"

"His wife's been kidnapped."

"So bloody what."

Hunter was a thin and gaunt-looking man. He had a red weathered face like a yachtsman, but there was something hard about his appearance. His nose was straight, but vertical like a boxer's. He looked like he'd been putting in the hours on the shooting range too. He wasn't going to miss at this quarter, no matter what. Archer calmly rolled his eyes at Forsyth.

"I know," she said. "He looks so accustomed to it, doesn't he."

"Shut up, Forsyth," Hunter said. "I know who you are. How did you find me?"

"We're private investigators," Archer said calmly. "It's what we do."

An elegant looking silver-haired woman in a cream suit walked into the kitchen area and then headed straight towards Hunter. She nodded curtly at Forsyth before resting her hand gently on Hunter's shoulder.

"So, Sean Archer, what the hell do you want?"

"Put the gun down and I'll tell you."

"Do you really think I'm that foolish? This gun is all I've got left between our life and nosy little busy-bodies like you two."

"Pardon the pun but you've jumped the gun a bit, I'm afraid," Forsyth said. "The fact is that we're all that's between your life and Sinclair. He thinks you've kidnapped his wife."

"Then you're bigger damned fools than I already thought. Sinclair's probably behind the kidnapping himself." He cocked his nose mockingly at his intruders. "It's what he does."

Madeleine clipped across the room, extending one foot exaggeratedly in front of the other like a catwalk model emphasising her swagger for maximum effect and attention. She barely glanced at the gun in Hunter's hand, treating it as if it were the most natural thing in the world. No one had asked her to, but she brought a freshly made cafetière of strong-smelling coffee on a tray with four bone china mugs. She poured, left the four mugs on the table then turned around and clipped back off towards the kitchen. The soles of her stilettos were as red as her lips. She might have been working as a simple housekeeper, but she was dressed more expensively than both of her employers.

"Tell us about Sinclair while we drink our coffee," Archer said, ignoring the gun himself and sitting down. Forsyth followed suit.

"You two have got some balls, I'll give you that."

Forsyth rolled her eyes back at Archer and faked a yawn. "I'll be on to my union rep in the morning. Sexual harassment in the workplace during my afternoon coffee break; erroneous gender-specific remarks about my private parts."

"What is society coming to? Hosts just don't treat their guests politely any more."

"But you're not my bloody guests though, are you?" Hunter said. "You're fast-talking intruders in a private home. Unwelcome hustlers bullying decent people like us around. I've got a good mind to shoot you both. I've a hermetically sealed room downstairs where I can dump your bodies for ever without any inconvenience to either me, my wife or the housekeeper. Do you understand?"

"Not really, no," Archer said. "Is that where Becky is?"

"Who the hell is Becky?"

"Sinclair's wife."

"For the love of God, why the hell would I want to kidnap Sinclair's wife and have every goon in the country after me, when all I want is to stay alive peacefully?"

Archer could sense that Hunter's façade was starting to crack.

"Then tell us everything you know about Sinclair."

"What good will that do?"

"It might save your life. If we can find you then so can he."

"How did you find us? We've been hiding in peace for years." Hunter's voice had cracked and his eyes welled up. He went pale and began sobbing like a spoiled brat.

Samantha put her arm around her husband to console him. "Are you feeling all right, dear?" She rubbed his shoulder affectionately. He looked like a helpless child.

"No. I'm not all right. I can't do this any more." Hunter started to tremble and the gun looked unsteady in his right hand. "Let me take that off you, dear." He tugged it back.

"No, leave me alone." Hunter threw the gun away. It crashed to the wooden floor without going off and slid along until it hit the skirting board. Luckily the safety catch was on. Hunter cried like a coward and buried his head into his wife's shoulder.

"If we don't find Becky Sinclair while she's still alive," Forsyth said, unperturbed by Hunter's melodramatic performance, "Sinclair will probably go on a spree and kill everyone he doesn't like. And you're top of the list."

"Talk to them, Stuart," Samantha Hunter said. "It may help us."

Samantha continued to console her husband by stroking his shoulder. His shivering eventually stopped and he dried his eyes with the backs of his hands, but still looked tense.

"Sinclair's an insane megalomaniac. He cheated me and other people I know out of vast sums of money. He has people killed. He wants me dead."

"How do you know he has people killed?"

"How did you find me?"

"My partner is good at doing things like that. She uncovered your wife's fake identity as the widow Samantha Knight."

"But there's no link between the Knights and the Hunters. Not on any database."

128

"She's very resourceful. We've found you, and Sinclair's still looking for you, so I think you should show us a bit more respect."

Madeleine returned with a tray of finger snacks and pastries. She placed it on the coffee table without saying a word. Passed around four small plates and napkins and then walked back to the kitchen with an accentuated sway of the hips. She left the gun lying where it was, up against the skirting board.

Hunter was nervously tapping the floor with his foot. His face was flushed. He was shaking and looked like he needed something stronger than a mug of black coffee.

"I haven't got the will or the energy to change identities again. Sinclair has a contract out on me. He'll have one out on you by now. Just because you work for him."

"Look, pull yourself together, man," Archer said. "He doesn't know where you are. He won't get anything from us. We're only interested in finding Becky, and then getting enough evidence to put Sinclair away."

"He killed Jane and her husband and Christina before her. He won't care about Becky – he's probably behind it all anyway. It's probably just another one of his smoke and mirror tactics to get rid of her. Then he'll find another one, a similar but younger model obviously and then carry on regardless. It's the way he's operated for years."

"What makes you so certain he killed them?"

"I know because I know who did it."

"Who?"

"Nick Carnell."

"Who's he?"

"Who was he, you mean."

"All right, who was he then?"

"He used to work for me."

"What happened?"

"Sinclair had him killed because he knew too much. He became a liability. The problem was Carnell told me everything before he was killed and Sinclair knows he told me. That's why Sinclair put a contract out on me."

This backed up what Sarah and Cavendish had said. If it was true then Becky would be bumped off if she survived. The contract hits might even stretch to annoying investigators.

"Who's after you, his bodyguards?"

"No. They're just stupid overpaid grunts that look after him. He's so paranoid about being killed that he protects himself with a number of highly trained, highly paid goons. But his dirty work is done by teams of hired professionals. Again, all highly paid. You get the picture, I'm sure. He has friends who own private armies."

"So if he trusted Carnell to do his dirtiest work, why would he then turn on him and kill him? What else did he know that was so important?"

"Good question."

"I'm listening."

CHAPTER FORTY

Hunter was regaining his composure. Samantha gave him a small pill, which he took without question. The tension rapidly evaporated from his face and the stiffness was instantly removed from his body. Gone was the hysterical anger, as he continued to drone in an upper-class monotone, far more subdued.

"Carnell worked for me. I had absolutely no idea that he was moonlighting for Sinclair until it was too late to stop him. If he'd told anyone what he had done for Sinclair it would have put them both away for life. Sinclair didn't trust him, but I never found out why."

"What was Carnell's official role in your company?"

"Weapons and tactics expert. Faultless at planning and cautious about the execution. He did excellent work for the government and for several private companies. He was a highly sought-after individual."

"You must have used him as well though. He did work for you after all?"

"Obviously. Clients paid well for his work."

"What happened to your company?"

"Sinclair's associates damaged the company by blackmailing some of my employees to spy for him. Industrial espionage is rampant these days, as I'm sure you're both aware. They then devalued it with leaks and lies, creating highly compromising misinformation. His American allies bought the company and cheated me out of tens of millions of pounds. I was forced to sell it in order to pay short-term debts that were being pulled by the banks. My clients were walking away in droves. I was lucky to have personal savings, otherwise we would have been left destitute."

"Do you still have a grudge against him?" Archer asked.

"Yes of course. He ruined me and now he's taken my liberty by forcing me to hide. But he's a powerful man and I have no plans for revenge. I'm simply trying to enjoy my retirement without getting myself killed. We enjoy the arts. We go to the theatre, concerts, museums, galleries and the like. Elegant and cultured behaviour. While his associates get away with murder and daylight robbery."

"Have you got anything at all to do with Becky's abduction?"

"Don't be absurd."

"You have motive."

"I'm hiding from him, not going after him. We're in a terrible predicament."

"Seems like you still have a high-quality lifestyle to me, Hunter." Archer already disliked the man as much as he disliked Sinclair. As far as he was concerned they were from the same mould, but Sinclair had got the upper hand in their pathetic relationship.

"Quality compared to your life maybe. So what. It's still only a flat, even if it is superior to your crummy little bedsit in Acton or wherever the hell you're from. But he forced us to change our names, have cosmetic surgery and fear people like you knocking on the door. If you tell him where we are he'll send a contractor straight over here to kill us. You don't stand a chance against him."

"You were a shit judge of character with Carnell, and you're an even worse lifestyle critic. I'd rather hear about Sinclair, if you don't mind," Archer snapped.

"Watch it, Archer. I've got a room full of loaded guns downstairs. Anyway, if he comes for me I'll take him down with me. Why should I tell you anything?"

"Because you don't want a shootout with him and we know where you live."

Forsyth casually walked across the room, picked up the gun, sat down, checked it was loaded, clicked off the safety catch and aimed it at Hunter's head.

"Don't threaten me, woman," Hunter said, visibly shaken.

"I'm not. You've forgotten your lines and I'm the prompt."

"Oh help them, Stuart, for Christ's sake!" Samantha screeched. "You got us into this goddamned mess and the minute someone wants to help get you out of it you throw one of your pathetic little hissy fits, pretending to have morals. You were happy enough to change your identity in some ways. Now you tell everyone you went to Eton whereas you really went to a grammar school in Swindon."

Hunter looked as if he'd have gladly shot her if Forsyth hadn't held the gun, but he was beaten. He'd reinvented himself once already. Now it was obvious that he had no energy to do it again. The thought of Sinclair coming for him was more than enough leverage.

"Very well, Archer. I'll tell you, then you leave us alone afterwards."

"Start talking Hunter. She's trigger happy."

"Sinclair helped his American associates take over several security companies and merged them into existing defence contractors. They employ all sorts of people including lobbyists, surveillance experts, spies and assassins. He's a very dangerous man. Way above your league. You'll just get sucked in by his fake charms and then one day you'll get a bullet in the back of the head for thanks."

"I didn't ask you to read my tea leaves. What sort of companies did they buy?"

"Oakland Security to look legitimate, but behind the façade he was covering up this terrible place he'd built. I don't know exactly where it is, not many people do, but it's an underground facility where they torture and kill people – you know, like insurgents or terrorist suspects or anyone they want and then dump their bodies out at sea. It enables MI6 and the CIA to have deniable access to a privately operated Guantanamo-style facility on UK soil."

Archer was stunned by this candid revelation. A shock of electricity jolted through his body, causing him to stiffen awkwardly. The rumours and suspicions were true. There was a facility called the Boathouse. And Sinclair was definitely connected to it.

"We can put Sinclair away. But we're going to need help putting together the evidence. More specifically, we'll need your help, Hunter."

"You mean you want me to testify against him as a witness?"

"No. That would be the very last resort. We need to get enough evidence together, then we can spare you the inconvenience of ever leaving your silver spoon existence."

"You want us to risk our lives, even more than now?"

"We can put Sinclair away for life. Why wouldn't you want to help us do that?"

"Why should we risk our lives?"

"You know very well why. He has to be stopped, put away. Until then you're risking your lives every second of every day. Talk it over with your wife. We'll sit here and admire your opulent emptiness while you do."

The Hunters looked at each other then got up and huddled together at the window overlooking the O2 Arena. For a minute they were engrossed in intense discussion.

"All right, Archer. Guarantee our anonymity and we'll help you, but remember, Sinclair has people everywhere. Eyes and ears in all sorts of places.

People in his pocket in the corridors of power in London and Washington, D.C. I just can't see how you could pull it off. Sinclair and his partners are too powerful. He's untouchable."

"There must be records of what goes on in these secret facilities."

"The records used to be kept on an encrypted laptop."

"I want you to write everything down. Use this Hotmail account and password." Archer started to write on the back of a business card. "Save it as a draft."

Hunter nodded.

Archer walked up to him.

"Okay. Here's my card. I want it all, every detail. Names, dates, numbers. You got that?" Hunter nodded silently and looked at his wife for approval.

"Well done, dear. Perhaps we can use our real names again one day."

Archer was disturbed. Hunter was the kind of man already planning his own way out. He didn't trust him and decided it was time to leave and find a fresh lead on Becky. At least he wasn't wasting his time investigating Sinclair. Hunter had confirmed that Sinclair was linked to a facility like the Boathouse. It had to be the same one. So once he found Becky he could spend more time investigating Sinclair.

CHAPTER FORTY-ONE

Archer and Forsyth crossed the road to a modern-looking Italian café full of polished chrome and black leather. They sat on high stools at the window bar looking out at Hunter's apartment building with the main entrance in good view. They ordered a black coffee and a cappuccino, which came in extra-large cups and saucers with small amaretti biscuits.

"We can take Sinclair down with enough evidence from Hunter," Forsyth said.

Archer simply wanted to take him down with a gun. He still had Sinclair's Magnum Desert Eagle in his pocket. He could make it look like suicide. His heart rate increased.

"Hunter won't risk his life to get back at Sinclair. There's something not right about him. I don't know what it is exactly, but he's too shifty. He's just as bad as Sinclair."

"I know what you mean. He creeps me out too – like Sinclair, only less successful. I don't trust him either, so where's that leave Becky?"

She sipped her cappuccino with both hands around the cup.

"We need Hunter's evidence, but he can't help us find Becky. I guess we need to move on and find her before Saturday night."

"Carnell worked for Hunter and look what he did for a living."

"Exactly, but I can't see his wife being involved in anything like that though."

"No, she never had anything to do with his business when I investigated them."

"Do you still think he's involved in the kidnapping?"

"No, but he definitely acted odd."

"We have to find Becky now. We can't be everywhere at once. Perhaps it's time to split up and see if one of us can find another lead. You could go help Zoe."

"Sean, look. That's Hunter leaving the building. What's he up to?"

Hunter wore a cream overcoat and hat. He had the collar up, the trilby pulled down and he wore large dark glasses. He looked conspicuous by his obvious attempt to disguise himself.

"Better tail him. Come on, let's go." Archer left enough cash for the coffee plus tip and they let Hunter get a head start. They followed him in the autumn sunshine to Canary Wharf where he stopped off at a trendy-looking but completely empty bar for a stiff gin and tonic. He took a long swig and then made a phone call using the phone behind the bar. The barman walked away to give his only customer some privacy.

Forsyth took a small radio from her bag and extended the aerial.

"Hardly a good time to catch up on the cricket scores down under."

"Watch this then, matey." She placed a small earpiece in her left ear and offered Archer the second. He accepted the bud and placed it in his ear. She then pointed the aerial through the window towards Hunter and started to tune in the device.

"You should never talk in public, especially in pubs, as there are nosy people like me around who can listen in." Archer smiled to himself. He had the newer model, but kept quiet.

They huddled together to listen, their faces almost touching. They could only hear Hunter's side of the conversation, but it was enough to get the gist of what he was up to. He was after a team of mercenaries to protect him. He asked for four men immediately and argued that tomorrow was too late. They were left unsure as to exactly what was agreed, but knew that two men would show up in the park near his apartment at six p.m. Hunter drank his gin dry and ordered another.

They left Hunter alone in the bar to wallow in his tall glass of Bombay Sapphire and walked back towards the car in the sunshine.

"I'll go back to the penthouse for a while. See if I can find something new to help us out from that angle."

"Are you going to tell Sinclair about Hunter?"

"No way. We need to stay one step ahead of him. We need Hunter to tell us all he knows, and then we can take Sinclair down. He's used to playing people, but he's not in control of the situation. I need to make the most of that leverage."

"I'll drive past the flat in Marylebone and check it out on the way to your office."

Forsyth's car still had the top down as they headed back to Sinclair's penthouse in Mayfair. She drove fast, accelerating and breaking hard with the radio on, singing along to Coldplay. She was badly out of tune, but seemed to be enjoying herself.

She dropped Archer off outside the rear entrance of Sinclair's building and waved at him as she took a hands-free phone call.

Archer entered the lobby and texted Zoe:

We must have missed something. Dig deeper into Becky's sister Louise Palmer and the driver Steve Jones as the prime insider suspects and then the bodyguards Haywood, Adams, Best and Clarke.

CHAPTER FORTY-TWO

The penthouse door did not open automatically and Archer pressed the small silver button next to it. After a two-minute wait the door opened and an expressionless Clarke waited at the console desk to close it behind him. Clarke measured Archer up and down like a warrior.

"Everyone's out. I'm manning the phone."

"Where's Sinclair?"

"He had to go back to the office."

"What about the others?"

"They had to go out as well."

Archer thought this was strange. The kidnapping was the priority. Wasn't it?

"I thought you were Sinclair's most trusted bodyguard?"

"I am. That's why he trusts me enough to man the phone alone."

Clarke walked back to the phone and sat quietly. Archer walked around the living room in silence, waiting to see if Clarke offered any additional information about Sinclair or his men. He didn't. He just sat vacantly by the phone like a robot on standby.

After several minutes Archer walked up to the desk and looked him straight in the eye.

"Where did they go?"

"Docklands," Clarke said matter-of-factly, looking bored.

"Why?"

"We have a lead on Stuart Hunter."

"What? Where is he?" Archer tried to hide his surprise.

"He made a call to someone he shouldn't have trusted. He thought he was being clever, but dialling 1-4-7-1 was all it took to find out that he was calling from a bar in Docklands. We've been waiting for him to make that call for some time. Something must have prompted it – probably because he's behind the kidnapping," Clarke sneered and made a fist as if he'd won some game.

"Which bar?"

"This one." He picked up a piece of paper and handed it to Archer. He read it and handed it back. "They're showing people his photo down there right now. They should find out where he's hiding in no time. He must be close by."

"Excellent. That's exactly what we needed. I'm going to help find him."

"They don't need your help, Archer. You've been worse than useless so far."

"Thanks for the pep talk. Unlike you I can't sit around all day doing nothing."

"Anytime you feel up for it, Archer. I'll be ready for you. Anytime you want."

"No point, you grunts are far too slow. You wouldn't even see me coming."

Archer left the penthouse in a hurry, not sure if he could make it back to Docklands in time to save Hunter. He'd wondered all along if Sinclair was surreptitiously using other resources to find people. Now he had confirmation that he was. He called Forsyth from the lift, but her phone was engaged.

Archer exited the lift on the ground floor and tried to call Forsyth again, but her phone was still engaged. As he left the building he could see that she was still parked right outside the rear entrance and was still on the phone talking about one of her cases.

Archer got back in the car and interrupted her call by pressing the red button.

"Call them back. We have to go. NOW."

Forsyth started the engine.

"Where?"

"Back to the Hunter's. Sinclair's men are on their way to get him."

"What?"

She floored the accelerator and raced up Park Street into a long gap in traffic that had been created between red lights.

"What's happening?"

"Whoever Hunter just called told Sinclair. The goon squad are on their way to that bar to ask around. We need to get him out of there before they find him."

Archer tried to call Hunter en route, but the phone was engaged.

Forsyth drove as fast as the heavy traffic would allow. Archer grabbed the door and seat at one point as they accelerated around a sharp corner.

"Don't worry, I'm an advanced driver. I've got a racetrack licence. The works."

"Good for you," he said, bracing himself and exhaling after another near miss.

They came to an abrupt halt outside the entrance to Hunter's building. None of Sinclair's cars were there and none of his goons were anywhere in sight.

They took the lift straight back up to the top floor. As they exited the lift to get to apartment 12A Archer looked down at the car park and saw Sinclair's men arriving in a shiny black Land Rover Discovery, stopping right next to Forsyth's pale blue Merc.

Forsyth knocked sharply on the door and shouted for Samantha to open up. A shocked-looking Stuart Hunter opened the door. Archer and Forsyth walked in and sailed straight past him without being asked and he shut the door with his mouth still open. He turned around and followed them into the living area where his wife sat talking to a friend on the phone.

"What's going on?" Hunter asked angrily.

"Sinclair's men are coming for you."

"What? I hope you're bloody well joking."

"I'm not bloody well joking. They're right outside."

The blood drained instantly from his face.

"How is that possible?"

"You made a call to a contractor from a bar and whoever you called told Sinclair where to find you."

"But I didn't tell him my location. I was just about to wire him some money."

"Never mind all that, they figured that part out for themselves. They're outside right now. We need you and your wife to hide and your housekeeper will have to act as a cover. I'll try and fob them off."

"Shit, we're like sitting bloody ducks."

Hunter's orange tan had gone pale.

"Quick, go, take Sarah, I'll prep the housekeeper." He turned to Madeleine. "You need to pretend the Hunters have just gone away for the winter season."

The knock on the door startled everyone inside the flat. Archer looked through the peephole and saw Haywood.

"They're here, go and hide, now," Archer whispered.

"Like where, under the bed?" Forsyth replied.

"Just go downstairs."

"Follow me," Hunter said, as he led the way down.

CHAPTER FORTY-THREE

Archer gave the terrified-looking housekeeper some last words of encouragement. He told her to breathe deeply, relax her tense body and leave all the talking to him. She stared at him silently and looked like she was on the verge of tears.

"If they ask you a direct question, just respond in French. Make out you don't understand English very well." She nodded silently, clearly petrified.

The knock at the door was much harder this time and Haywood shouted aggressively.

"Hunter, answer the door before we bash it down. We know you're in there."

Archer opened the door.

Haywood, Best and Adams stared back at him, with perplexed and angry expressions.

"What are you doing here, Archer?" Haywood snarled aggressively and pushed Archer backwards.

"Clarke told me what happened. Looks like I'm just better at finding people than you are."

"Where's Hunter?"

"He's not here. They've just gone travelling and won't be back before Easter. The housekeeper's here alone. She doesn't know where they've gone."

"Who are you?"

"She only speaks French."

"Stay out of our way, Archer."

"They're not here, dipshit."

"Back off, motherfucker, we're going to tear this place apart."

"I've just looked. There's nobody here."

"Yeah, well perhaps we're better at searching apartments than you are."

"You're wasting time. Typical grunts."

"We need to take her with us. Make sure she doesn't warn Hunter."

"No point. He has cameras everywhere, look." He pointed the cameras out.

"So he'll know already. He won't come back here again, so don't do anything stupid. You'll just get the police and media involved when her boyfriend calls her later from Paris. That won't go down well with your boss or the kidnappers, now will it?"

"Stay out of our way, Archer. We'll take great pleasure in restraining you."

"Be my guest. I'm fascinated to see what shit-for-brains looks like in action."

The goons ignored him and started to search the apartment roughly, leaving a trail of devastation like a tornado had just blown through it. Haywood went downstairs first, followed by Best. Adams wasn't satisfied until all the contents of all the cupboards upstairs were smashed and emptied out onto the floor.

Archer heard Haywood shout to Best. He went down to see what they were doing. Haywood had found a cupboard with a padlock on the outside. They prised it off with an old Cavalry sword that was hanging on the wall. The cupboard was full of old dusty files which Haywood threw onto the floor in a fit of rage.

"I told you. They've gone away for the winter."

After checking every room and cupboard, under every bed, and turning the apartment completely upside down, Haywood, Best and Adams left. Annoyed and irritated, they looked sheepishly worried about reporting the bad news back to Sinclair.

Archer watched them all get in the Land Rover with their heads down, but waited for them to drive away before he went down the stairs and shouted.

"Okay, they've gone."

As in many high-end apartments there was a compact space that had been planned as a panic room. The hidden door was in the dressing room, behind Stuart Hunter's conservative suits. These now lay strewn over the floor. The door looked like every other panel in the dressing room.

"You need to move," Archer said.

"No way, I'm staying put this time. I've got an arsenal down here and a team of mercenaries on their way."

"Suit yourself. We're out of here."

"Let me give you a lift home," Forsyth said with a cheeky smile.

"A simple lift, or another episode of *Top Gear*?"

"Speed limit and stopping at red lights. How does that sound?"

"Appetising. Let's go to my place and get something to eat."

CHAPTER FORTY-FOUR

Forsyth parked her car opposite Archer's white stucco house on Walton Street, SW3. He opened the gloss black front door and waited while she fetched her laptop from the boot, changed her jacket to a brown leather one and grabbed a pair of jeans from a suitcase before she closed the soft top and followed him. As she passed the threshold he looked up and down the street. There was no sign of DS Lambert's navy Ford Focus.

A lot had happened since they'd first met at the Mandarin. There was plenty to think about. Archer welcomed her to his house and locked them in with two deadlocks and the perimeter alarm before setting all external cameras on record.

"How about steak and salad?"

"Sounds good." She smiled and followed him through the modern open-plan living space towards the ultra-modern kitchen at the back where she placed her things on the island.

"Make yourself at home."

"Not a crummy bedsit in Acton after all. Shall we work on here?"

"Sure. Drink?"

"Some still water would be good. Thanks."

"Help yourself over there." Archer gestured towards the glass-fronted sub-zero fridge with plenty of bottled water stacked neatly on a shelf. Forsyth removed two half-litre bottles of Evian, placed one on the island for Archer, unscrewed the other and drank half of it.

They set their identical Apple laptops up on the island. Forsyth asked where the bathroom was and came back in a pair of faded old jeans. She still looked good in jeans, but it was a lot less distracting than before.

They started going over the facts as they currently knew them. Archer listed the relevant points and displayed them via a wireless connection on the large plasma screen on the wall. He quickly developed a timeline, but nothing obvious jumped out, so while they were thinking he got a huge marbled claret steak out of the fridge and seasoned it with pepper and paprika.

"Twenty-eight-day dry-aged Aberdeen Angus," he smiled with pride. "Organic. We'll share it."

He asked her to select a bottle of wine from the kitchen cellar, which was really just a tall fridge with two glass doors, one side for red and one set at a cooler temperature for white. She gravitated towards the reds. "Hey, there's some good stuff in here. Pétrus, no less. You clearly like your wine," she said.

Forsyth chose a ripe but still fruity Côtes du Rhône Villages Reserve from Les Dauphins. He gave her a Waiter's Friend corkscrew from the drawer. She swiftly uncorked it and poured out two equal measures into heavy lead crystal goblets.

"Good choice," he said.

He chopped some organic cucumber, sultan's jewel tomatoes, kalamata olives, jalapeño peppers, red onion and romaine lettuce. Added extra-virgin olive oil and balsamic vinegar and tossed it all in a teak serving bowl with large wooden spoons. He fried the thick steak on a griddle pan until medium-well and let it rest for five minutes. Dijon mustard was the only condiment placed on the island.

"Henckels steak knives and white linen napkins. How domesticated."

"Look, it's still juicy and tender, but no blood, exactly as promised," he beamed.

"Wow, Sean. It's amazing, cheers," she said, as they chinked glasses. "Taking Sinclair down won't be easy. Even if Hunter sings."

"I know, plus we still need to find Becky. If we do, maybe we can get her to help us."

"I hope we're not getting out of our depth here. It's getting complicated."

"We can get help taking Sinclair down. Time is running out for Becky, though. Less than forty-eight hours until the kidnappers' deadline. If we don't find her, or if Sinclair doesn't pay up, they said they'll kill her. The bomb threat's just a hoax."

"I don't want to even think about that. It can't be real, can it?"

"It doesn't make sense. This is about ransom money or revenge, not bombs."

"We'd better get some rest tonight. The next two days will be hard going."

Archer's mobile phone rang and he reached for his pocket.

It was Zoe de la Croix.

"Hey, what's up?"

"There's no record of Becky's sister flying from Heathrow."

"Are you sure?"

"Positive. I just checked the airlines and immigration databases."

"Okay, see if you can find her. Damn it, she could be that burned body they found in South London. Find the DNA report on her teeth. And keep an eye on the flat in Marylebone with a local camera."

"I'm doing that already, all night if I have to. I'll call you if anyone goes back in there, and I'll keep searching for the sister. I must be missing something somewhere. Her mobile is still in her office and it's closed for business. Empty. But there has to be a way to find her."

He put the phone back in his pocket. Forsyth looked at him inquisitively.

"What's up?"

"That was Zoe. Louise Palmer never left the country."

"Really? Well that's not good news. It makes no sense at all."

"There are numerous angles now. She could be in on it or she could be being blackmailed, threatened, coerced, even kidnapped herself. Or she could be dead, but whichever way, she's our number one lead right now."

"What do you want me to do?"

"Nothing yet, Zoe's still working on it."

"Whether she's in on it or not, it's not good news, is it?"

"Yeah, I've got a bad feeling about this."

Archer noticed how the mood in the kitchen had turned sombre. They both looked pensively up at the screen. Archer updated it and then put some music on his digital hi-fi system to help soothe their spirits. Clapton played the blues effortlessly in the background, bending the blue notes on his Stratocaster with melancholic passion and feeling. It fitted the moment perfectly.

"That was a great supper thanks," she said and smiled at him affectionately.

"Least I could do."

"Fancy a short break? I'm getting tired."

"Let's go and sit in the living room. Coffee?"

"Sure. I'll bring the rest of the wine as well."

Archer made two black coffees and they wandered into the living area holding their wine and coffee. It was a large open space with artwork on the walls.

Archer sat on the leather sofa, but Forsyth walked around the room admiring the paintings. Somehow she completely ignored the large insightful vinyl record collection and gravitated towards a bright painting of cypress trees and swirling clouds in Provence.

"Great artwork, I really like it. Are they copies of Van Goghs?"

"Yes, oil on canvas – hand-made copies."

"Where did you get them?"

"I had them done in Saint-Rémy-de-Provence."

"I love Provence. I'd like to live there one day."

"Yes, it's perfect." Archer's mind wandered.

"I'd love to live in a vineyard or in a villa close to the Rhône. I definitely want my own place down there one day, to cook and paint – that's my dream."

They finished walking around the room and sat on the sofa facing another large flat screen with lots of DVDs beneath it, mostly action and crime-related movies and his two favourite TV series: *Justified* and *Dexter*.

Forsyth raised her glass of red wine and they chinked glasses again.

"To finding Becky." They both took a sip of wine. "I feel a bit guilty enjoying myself like this while she's in danger," she said softly and bowed her head.

"We did everything we could today, the best we could. Now we're temporarily out of leads to chase down and we need to get some rest. Zoe will find something eventually and when she does we need to be ready to go. Like firemen."

"You're right, but it still feels wrong to relax like this."

"Don't beat yourself up too much, there's still enough time – we'll find her before the deadline. We always find something."

Archer could smell her now that she was closer. She smelled like fresh cotton in spring. She took her boots off and crossed one perfectly pedicured foot over another.

"Tell me about Zoe."

She flicked her hair and smiled flirtatiously. Her eyes were sparkling in the light, her smile disarming, her radiance captivating. She fascinated him.

"Tell me what you think first."

"Striking, strong and intelligent."

"We go back a long way. She's a really good friend. Hold on."

Archer's phone rang and he took it out of his pocket. The caller ID showed that it was from a tenaciously impatient caller with a reputation for being a cruel control freak.

"It's Sinclair, he's relentless. I'd better see what he wants."

CHAPTER FORTY-FIVE

Archer braced himself to talk to the man his gut was telling him ran the Boathouse.

"Where are you?" Sinclair asked.

"Back at my place."

"What are you doing?"

"Working your case."

"Any luck?"

"Not yet."

"It's not Hunter then?"

"No it's not."

"I thought it was him too. What happens now?"

"We're exploring other avenues; other associates of yours."

"Like who?"

"There's a long list. I'm sure you're familiar with all the names."

"Business is business. Some people take it personally. I don't know why."

"It takes all sorts." Archer winced at having to be polite to him.

"Well they're either brave or stupid. Whoever kidnapped her will regret it, whatever happens. I'm sure you're aware by now that if anything happens to her it will end badly. The reckless idiots that have done this to me must know what's coming to them."

Archer sensed that Sinclair was getting himself worked up again. He cringed at the idea that Sinclair had the ability to back up his death threats.

"Go to bed and get some rest. We've got another tough day ahead of us tomorrow. Don't sit by the phone all night, there's no point. They won't ring again."

"Don't tell me what to do, Archer. We've only got two more days before they vanish into thin air and make me look like a bloody fool."

"At least we've got two days."

"Find them, Archer."

"I'll do my best."

"You need to up your game, big time, you don't want to make a complete Horlicks out of it, otherwise your days are numbered too. Just remember that."

"I'd better get back to work then."

He had to find a way to take Sinclair down. Find Becky first, then find the Boathouse and Alex's killer, and then deal with Peter Sinclair.

Forsyth strolled back to the kitchen, shut her laptop down and put it back in its cinnamon-coloured soft leather case. She shared the rest of the wine out equally between the two glasses and handed one back over the island. They sat down on the kitchen stools with the lights dimmed.

"You didn't tell him about Louise, did you?"

"No, of course not."

"Do you think the sisters might be in on it somehow?"

"I did think so initially, yes. I thought that Becky might be running away from him. Who would blame her? But this whole thing is far too elaborate, and the sisters are too soft to do all this on their own. It's got to be someone fearless or powerful enough to take on Sinclair and his goons. I don't think it's just one person we're up against."

"So who do you think the insider is then – Louise?"

"It could be her."

"How would that work?"

"Well she's either in on it or she's being forced to do it."

"Or she's dead."

"Why would she be in on it though? It doesn't make sense," he said.

"No, she's not exactly short of money. She's got a lucrative business, I pass it every day. It's busy and she lives in Kensington. She's got to be worth a few million?"

"Her financial records show that her business is turning a healthy profit and her house alone is worth over two million, even in this climate – she can't be in money trouble."

"Okay, so let's say she's not in it for the money. And it's not jealousy as the sisters seem to spend a lot of time together. So she's either being forced to do it for some reason or she's been taken captive by the same kidnappers."

"Okay, let's say that they've taken her."

"But how and when?"

"Becky and her driver took her out to Heathrow for her business trip. She was last seen by them land-side at Heathrow Airport. We've checked Jones the driver out. Ex-soldier. Moonlights. Infatuated with Becky, but his digital footprint proves it's not him."

"How do you know that?"

"Never mind, but we're really good at it. And we know that she never made it air-side at Heathrow."

"So she was taken at the airport by the kidnappers."

"This has to have been planned ahead, but that doesn't explain how they knew about the money and the diamonds before they took her."

"Perhaps she was blackmailed or leveraged somehow."

"Hmm. Perhaps. We need to find out if she's involved, and, if she is, exactly how she's involved. That's how we'll find them. We'll sit with Zoe and search the Net first thing in the morning. Louise is still our best lead."

Archer sent an email to Zoe asking her to focus on the sister's digital footprint and to dig deep into her money trails. He closed his laptop down and switched the plasma screen off.

"We need to get some rest. The next two days will be tough."

"I'd better call a taxi. I've had too much wine to drive."

"You can stay here if you like. The spare room is comfortable."

"Oh, okay, thanks. Can I borrow a T-shirt to sleep in?" She smiled warmly and slowly looked him up and down suggestively.

"Sure, the spare room's that one over there." He pointed up the stairs. "Take a look. I'll get a fresh T-shirt."

Archer fetched a clean shirt and towel. She was admiring a full-size copy of Van Gogh's Sunflowers in a heavy wooden frame in the guest bedroom.

"That's just like the one in the National Gallery, isn't it?"

"Yes it is, here you go." Alex had bought it for him. He loved the picture, but recently felt sad whenever he saw it, so he had moved it into the spare room.

"Thanks."

Forsyth hugged him and kissed him softly on the cheek.

"Sleep well," he said, feeling uncomfortable with her intimate nature.

"You don't have to go so soon. Not on my account anyway."

"Sorry?" He'd only met her at lunchtime. That was less than twelve hours ago.

"You can stay with me tonight, if you like."

She started to unbutton her blouse, revealing her firm cleavage.

"I'm sorry, Sarah. I didn't mean to give you the wrong impression."

"Look, we're both grown-ups. We're both single. I'm nearly divorced, you seem lonely. Nobody needs to know about it. I won't tell anyone if you don't."

"I can't, I'm sorry. It's just that I'm, er ... goodnight, Sarah."

He left her casually undressing without showing the slightest hint of embarrassment. He went to his room with mixed feelings. He thought about her as he brushed his teeth and washed his face. Part of him wanted to go back.

He lay on top of the king-size bed in his boxer shorts. He always had problems getting to sleep without running or alcohol. He ran regularly to stop himself from being an alcoholic. He thought about his close encounter with Sarah Forsyth. She was attractive and intelligent. But her forward approach had taken him by surprise and left him unsettled.

He closed his eyes and went over the case. Sinclair. The Boathouse. He switched the light off. As soon as his head hit the pillow he was haunted by dark thoughts of Alex.

The image of her pale dead body flashed vividly inside his head. He had identified her only two hours after she had been shot at close range. He was going to ask her to move in with him; in their favourite bistro in Kensington later that evening.

The morgue had been cold and smelled of formaldehyde and bleach. The lifeless body on the steel gurney familiar, but also different. She'd looked the same, but her soul had gone. She used to wear her heart on her sleeve, but her pale body looked empty, as if she had left it behind. Her skin had lost its lustre. It looked waxy. Almost transparent. There were small holes in her head and chest. It was hard to believe he had spoken to her only three hours earlier. She was always so full of life. But her life was over. They should have been celebrating their future together, not facing the abrupt ending of it. The sheer grief had pulled him down into the ground stronger than gravity ever could. His knees had gone weak as it started to sink in. Time shifted gears into a vivid slow motion. The sterile walls oscillated in and out with each breath as the light faded into a narrowing tunnel and everywhere turned pink with a high-pitched sound. He had nearly blacked out, but had caught himself as he was falling towards her body on the gurney. He'd looked at her remains and realised that grief was the price we paid for love. But he could not accept that he would never see her smile again. Never hear her voice talking to him or feel her touching him with her soft hands. He would never be able to make her feel happy ever again. He'd felt completely empty inside, except for the overwhelming pain of loss. He had felt weak and lightheaded, until a surge of anger welled up inside him like an erupting volcano. Then he'd felt completely driven by the powerful internal force of revenge.

It had been a brutal murder by a professional hit man. Alex must have seen her killer coming. But had she recognised him or was he masked? Had she felt any pain? Did she know why anyone would want to kill her? He could never make it right, but he had vowed to himself, in that moment, that he would find and kill the people responsible.

His dark thoughts often kept him going, but they also kept him lying awake at night. Had Sinclair given the order to kill her?

He needed to run, to keep his mind away from his demons and the painful memories.

Wide awake now, he jumped off the bed and decided to go for a reassuring late-night run along the cool banks of the river to Westminster Bridge and back.

CHAPTER FORTY-SIX

Archer felt as cold as ice. He had absolutely no idea where he was. The place was completely dark, but sounded huge. He took a deep breath and tried to move, but he couldn't feel his arms or his legs. He was so cold – he was numb. The large space stank of diesel and musty decay. He turned his head left then right, letting his eyes adjust to the total darkness. He felt weightless and disorientated, like he was floating in deep water in the pitch black of night.

He remembered that he had been running away from four men dressed in black, wearing balaclavas. He'd been running south over the river at Westminster Bridge, but had blacked out and woken up in this hellhole.

His neck stiffened as he strained to listen to a slow rhythmic thud coming from above. Then he heard heavy footsteps echoing on the hard floor. Getting louder with each step. Dragging something metallic like a heavy wrecking bar scraping against a concrete floor.

Someone was coming directly towards him. His heart rate increased as he felt the presence of someone standing right in front of him. He felt their rancid breath wafting over his face. Nicotine, caffeine and halitosis. It was suffocating. He caught his breath as someone touched him on the top of his shoulder with a large calloused hand and then started to squeeze it like a powerful steel pincer with five sharp talons. As more pressure was exerted a bright strobe light flickered on and off rapidly. He saw a masked man standing before him. He tried to step back, but he couldn't move. He looked down. His entire body was trapped inside a bath-sized block of ice from his chest down to the ground. Panic and shock set in. He couldn't feel anything except his trapezius being crushed and his heart pounding like a drum against his ribcage as the strobe light flashed and his mind started spinning out of control.

Was this it?

Was this the final moment?

He held onto his breath. He wanted to die right there and then.

The sudden burst of sound made him jump as the bedside phone rang at twenty to seven. It woke him up from the depths of his recurring nightmare. It was still dark outside.

Archer grabbed the phone from the bedside cabinet and answered it with his head still covered by the duvet.

"Hey, it's me. I've found Becky's sister," Zoe said.

"Jesus, Zoe, what time is it? You've done what? Where is she?"

He put the bedside light on and sat up against the padded leather headboard.

"Oh sorry, did I wake you? Good morning, this is your friendly wakeup call from down the road in head office, where some of us are still working and haven't been home or had a chance to sleep yet. Anyway, that's enough about me. I've found something useful: Louise has a shell company that has rented a flat in Oxford. It's in easy reach of London, the M40, the A40, which of course provides direct access to the flat in Marylebone."

"Excellent – thanks, Zoe. Send me the address and we'll go and check it out."

"It's already on its way. So, I see you had female company round last night, didn't you? Is the wicked *Mrs* Forsyth up yet? And please note, I said wicked *Mrs* Forsyth as opposed to wicked *Miss* Forsyth. Subtle but poignant difference, don't you think?"

"We worked late in the kitchen and she stayed in the guest room. No hanky-panky."

"Hmm, now listen to Mummy, Sean, there's a good boy. I'm watching out for you as your best friend, looking after your best interests. She's got a murky past, so you better watch out with her. You're bad enough in fast cars; you don't need to get involved with fast women – you'll lose more than your licence with this one."

"Thanks, Zoe, but I think I can take care of myself. And just for the record, I knew she was married. She's separated. Getting divorced."

"Oh, is that right? Well the jury's still out on her at this end, so we'll have to wait and see. Actions speak louder than words. Oh, and I also found out that Louise is friendly with a dodgy Ukrainian businessman; he's a bit of an oil oligarch, I suppose. He uses her travel company and she goes round his mansion in Belgravia for regular meetings. I'm looking into it now, and I'll let you know if there's any links to Sinclair."

"Thanks, Zoe, keep me posted."

Archer got out of bed in boxer shorts, still half asleep. He went downstairs and put some strong filter coffee into the machine in the kitchen and turned the radio on to politely let his guest know it was morning, as it was still dark outside. He walked back up to his bedroom on autopilot. Took his shorts off and threw them in the basket. He turned the shower on and brushed his teeth before getting in. The hot power shower soon woke him up. He let it flow over his head and down his back to soothe out the crick in his neck. He must have slept awkwardly thanks to his nightmare, but he didn't have time to use the steam room.

He turned the shower up as hot as he could stand it, then straight back down, staying under the freezing cold water until it took his breath away. He wrapped a white bath towel around his waist and shaved. He had a good feeling about today: the flat in Oxford would help them track down Louise and lead them to Becky. Then they could concentrate on Hunter's information, find the Boathouse and Alex's killer and finally take Sinclair out.

He poured two mugs from the freshly made pot and knocked on the guest-room door, still in his towel. "Coffee?" There was no answer so he opened it and saw that the bed was empty. He heard the shower stop and the shower door open.

"Morning, Sarah. There's a fresh mug of coffee for you on the bedside cabinet."

The bathroom door opened and she peered out, wearing only a white towel wrapped around the top of her head. "Can I use this bathrobe on the back of the door?"

"Of course." Archer coughed as he caught himself staring at her naked body like a star-struck teenager. He looked away quickly, embarrassed at being caught gawping.

She looked incredible. She was like a *Playboy* centrefold, only better because she was all natural. What was wrong with him? How could he possibly have turned her down? He felt a rush of guilt hit him as he thought about Alex.

She tied the white bathrobe around her waist and picked up her mug of coffee. She smiled, winked and then gave him a playful peck on the cheek. Was she teasing him or just being friendly? Maybe Zoe was right after all.

"Morning, Sean. Thanks for the coffee."

"No problem. Anything else I can get for you?"

"Do you have a hair dryer I can borrow?"

"There should be one in the drawer, plugged in and ready to go."

"I slept like a log – how about you? Nice power shower, by the way."

"Thanks. Zoe has just found a fresh lead on Louise. We're off to Oxford. There's some fruit juice and toast in the kitchen. I'll let you get dressed. Need anything else?"

"I'm good thanks, although—" she looked at his body – "if your butt is half as firm as your abs look, then we definitely need to get to know each other better." She looked him up and down slowly, without shame. Smirked wickedly and winked at him again. He closed the door on his way out, still unsure if she was teasing or being serious.

There was something about her that fascinated him. She was attractive and intelligent. She was confident and flirtatious. But there was something else going on that he couldn't put his finger on and hadn't felt for a long time. Something in his gut told him he could trust her and his instinct told him that he would have to before the case was over.

CHAPTER FORTY-SEVEN

They left London with the sunrise washing the mackerel sky with soft metallic hues of pink and orange. Both of them wore jeans and leather jackets. Archer's black jacket was a present from Alex. It was the last thing she had bought for him. He also took his small combat rucksack, which was fully loaded with his customised Beretta. Instinct told him he would need it soon enough, as he expected a lot more trouble than yesterday.

Driving westward through the morning mist, against the heavy rush-hour traffic along the gridlocked A40 and M40, there was a comfortable silence. The air was a cool and damp six degrees outside, but a pleasant twenty degrees inside with the soft top up.

Archer reclined the back of his seat a little and tried to snooze while Forsyth listened to the breakfast show on Radio Two. She sang out of tune to all the songs being played and entered into lively discussion as if she was a guest on the show. It started off being more amusing than annoying, but impossible to ignore.

They arrived in Oxford at five to nine, just as Forsyth's strangled harmonies were making Archer want to reach for his Beretta. Luckily the GPS got them into the city centre without a problem and she stopped singing as she focused on carving up other drivers. The first car park they tried was full and they cruised around the second, looking for a space. A fat contented-looking woman was sitting in a tiny red Fiat bubble car stuffing down a cream doughnut and chocolate éclair. She polished them both off before leaving her parking space.

Forsyth jammed the Merc into the vacated spot and squeezed herself out of the small gap between the car and the door, then went to get change. Archer stayed next to the car and peered out from the car park. Out on the street people scurried about their business in a hurry. Most of the shops and offices opened at nine and plenty of people were clearly running late for work.

Forsyth returned, bought a ticket from a machine and displayed it on the dashboard.

"It must be that building over there, above those shops on Cornmarket Street." Archer pointed. One of his best programmers had lived in the next street so he knew Oxford city centre fairly well. Around the corner they saw a small sign over an old doorway, between a chemist and a phone shop.

"Agamemnon House – got it." Forsyth said. The name was new, but the building was old, traditional Headington Quarry limestone, with lead glass windows.

They tried the old wooden door and found it was unlocked. The corridor and worn stone stairs looked deserted, so they walked in and found the flat in question on the first floor.

Archer knocked and waited.

No answer. He knocked again.

Still no answer. He put his ear to the door.

"Listen," he whispered. "Sounds like someone's moving around inside."

Forsyth got the lock pick out of her bag and looked over her shoulder furtively before working on the door. It creaked open and the rummaging sound stopped. They stood in the doorway and took stock of the living room. Modern flatpack furniture rested on worn-out ancient floorboards. The white walls were adorned with black and white prints of waterscapes and New York skyscrapers, exported en masse all over the world from Sweden.

The room smelled of bleach and there was also a hint of Gauloises cigarette smoke, just like the flat in Marylebone. Surfaces in the room were bare as if it had recently been stripped of all personal belongings. They crept into the flat quietly as the floorboards creaked wearily underfoot. There was nobody in sight and it had gone quiet.

Archer was startled as a window slammed shut in the kitchen, followed by the sound of empty metal bins crashing around noisily outside. Forsyth ran to the kitchen while Archer raced back down the stone stairs, taking them two at a time, and ran straight out of the building.

Archer instinctively turned right and darted up Market Street. He glimpsed a man wearing a grey hoody and yellow rubber washing-up gloves sprinting away from him between the Covered Market and Jesus College. The hoody turned around to see if he was being followed. He looked a good ten years younger, but Archer was a natural runner. The hoody went out of sight briefly as the road bent to the right and then he disappeared again as he turned the corner and headed left down Turl Street. Despite his sturdy footwear Archer upped a gear and when he turned the corner he saw he had gained at least ten metres on him.

Archer swerved through crowds of students ambling to lectures on foot and side-stepped sleepy cyclists between the ancient walls of Jesus and Exeter Colleges. As the hoody turned left into Broad Street a distracted cyclist came out of Ship Street and crashed into Archer, knocking him off his feet and sent him flying into the fifteenth-century stone wall of Exeter College. Archer's right shoulder was numbed by the impact, but he could still run. The stunned cyclist shouted apologetically after him, but it was wasted breath as Archer ignored him and sprinted off.

Archer looked left on Broad Street and just caught sight of the hoody across the wide road, running through the stone arch entrance into Balliol College. He zigzagged across the road, causing traffic to brake hard and blast horns at him but he didn't stop.

He ran through the dark porters' lodge and out into the Balliol front quad, but couldn't see the hoody. He stopped and looked around. Where was he? Was he still running through the grounds up ahead towards Trinity College? Or had he gone upstairs and through the warren of corridors inside Balliol?

Archer decided to go back and check out the corridors just as he glimpsed a motorcyclist without a helmet in the darkened recess of the porters' lodge. It was the hoody pushing off and trying to start a trail bike.

Archer accelerated towards him as the hoody pressed the start button. Archer lunged at him, grabbing the back of his grey top with his right hand and causing a sharp pain to jolt through his numbed shoulder like an electric shock. The silver BMW motorbike roared to life and the hoody accelerated away, making Archer stumble and fall to the ground. He'd got away.

Archer got up, dusted himself down and returned to the flat crestfallen, nursing a sore shoulder and a bruised ego. Forsyth was sitting on a stool at the kitchen bar talking to Zoe on her mobile and emptying the hoody's sports bag.

The bag's contents were spread out over the breakfast bar for summary analysis. A full baton of ten packs of Gauloises cigarettes, more handcuffs, more Trojans, six different types of bullets ranging from a soft-point dumdum to a training blank. Plus an energy drink and a yellow Taser gun, fully charged. But no obvious prints on anything and nothing useful that would lead them to anyone specific anytime soon unless they could find fingerprints somewhere and then a match, but that would take too long without police help and the hoody might not even be in the system.

Forsyth rang off and recounted the call. Zoe had called and spoken to the estate agents for the flat twice, to no avail. Their databases were impossible to hack as they were currently offline. Their net had drawn a blank. Zoe had called the estate agents the "Barrow Boy" variety. She had a sliding scale of estate agents. They ranged from chartered surveyors to "Barrow Boys" and they were either posh or not. Apparently, these were not chartered surveyors and they were not posh.

They left the flat with their heads down and walked to the estate agents in the High Street. Archer knew it was the hoody and the trail bike from the ransom pick-up. They either had to find that bike or make the barrow boys talk.

Zoe was checking out the cameras. The bike was heading for Swindon, but Archer already knew the game the hoody would play. He would enter a car park somewhere and then in less than an hour the bike would disappear again into the back of a stolen van. It was another dead end.

They saw the estate agents' office across the road and checked out the window display. The flat was already back on the market as available to rent.

"So what do we do now?" Forsyth asked, looking disappointed.

"We're going to get all the information these estate agents have, one way or another. It's our last chance."

"That won't be easy. They wouldn't tell Zoe anything."

"We have to get it – physically; otherwise it's back to the drawing board."

"What's the plan?"

"Plan B."

"Oh, right of course. The famous Plan B. What's Plan B?"

"Plan B is to leave them without a clue as to what's going on."

"Oh, I see. You're trying it out on me first?"

"You got it. We need to change our appearances. Come on, we're going shopping."

CHAPTER FORTY-EIGHT

Twenty minutes later a man and a woman entered the High Street estate agents. There were two men sitting at their desks chatting casually in their matching navy pinstriped suits and no other customers inside. One agent was in his early forties with his feet up on the desk, the other in his late twenties, leaning back as far as he could in his chair. Both had thick dark hair gelled into random spikes of chaos and ridiculously large knots tied in their garish cyan and magenta company ties. It was exactly like Zoe had said, they were definitely at the "Barrow Boy" end of the spectrum.

The woman went up to the older estate agent, who threw his feet off the desk and leaned forward, smiling at her cockily. She wore a pale blue scarf over a dark wig with large Jackie Onassis-style sunglasses. She had unusually puffy cheeks like a chipmunk. The agent looked her up and down, visibly lusting after her taut body and undressing her from her brown leather jacket and skintight jeans.

"Morning, darling. You a celebrity or what?"

The man with her quietly closed the front door, pushed the deadlock button firmly until it clicked, turned the "Open" sign to "Closed" and casually closed the blinds. He was wearing a New York Yankees baseball cap and large sunglasses. He appeared chubby under his black leather jacket and also had unusually puffy cheeks. The younger agent slapped the desk, stood up and snarled at him aggressively.

"Hey pal, what the fuck you on?"

Archer and Forsyth simultaneously pulled guns from their jacket pockets and pointed them straight at the barrow boys. The young one sat back down as both faces drained to pale.

"Leave the computers open. Give us all the keys to the filing cabinets and tell us if we need any passwords to search the computers."

"Who the bloody hell do you think you are?" the older agent rasped.

"Don't you worry about who we are. Get up and move it. Over there."

The men were ushered to the back office, which had a table and four chairs for taking coffee and lunch breaks.

"Hands behind your backs. Quick."

Archer tied their hands together with grey duct tape.

"You just made a huge mistake, you mugs. Wait till you see the next customer."

"Shut it." Archer stuck rectangles of duct tape over their mouths, then taped their arms and bodies to the chairs. Forsyth went through the filing cabinets, and Archer started on the databases, looking for anything on Louise Palmer.

"Here's the company name she used for the flat," Forsyth said.

As she was pulling out the documents, the front door handle rattled and someone shouted loudly, "Open up!"

Forsyth walked to the window and looked through the blinds to see who was there.

"It's the local bobby in uniform," she whispered.

"Get rid of him."

She walked to the door and peered at him through a narrow slit in the blinds so that he couldn't see her face.

"Sorry, officer, but we're closed today," she shouted through the door.

"But I've got an appointment at ten."

"Come back tomorrow. No viewings today, they've all been cancelled."

"But I'm supposed to see some houses in Cowley."

"We're being audited, spot check from head office. Sorry for the inconvenience. Come back tomorrow."

"What about this afternoon?" he persisted.

"After four then, we may have finished the audit by then."

The fat-faced policeman waddled off, scratching his chin. Forsyth returned to rummaging through the packed filing cabinet while Archer tapped away at the computer.

"Here's the flat, back on the market. Shell company details, payment records and what have we got here then? You beauty, here it is. We've got them. Six months fully paid up on a thatched picture-postcard cottage with ample security in the Cotswolds."

"Take the address down and let's get out of here."

They took photos of the address using their smartphone cameras, leaving the agents taped up and the front door locked. Forsyth put the documents back, closed the filing cabinet and opened the back door into a narrow lane. "Come on, Sean, let's go."

She stepped outside and stopped. Archer ran into her back.

"What's up?"

"Clever old Dixon of Dock Green. He's rumbled us."

"Just run for it. He's a puffer."

Plod had looped round the back and was coming up the lane fifty metres behind them shouting "Stop!" and calling for back-up on his radio. Archer looked behind. They'd gained another fifty metres, so they took a corner and ran by three turnings before taking a fourth. The flatfoot was nowhere in sight. Archer knew his way around the lanes and back streets. He led Forsyth through a maze of alleyways, college quads and back entrances until they stopped at a rubbish bin in a dark corner of a Christ Church quadrangle and removed their hasty but effective disguises. With their jackets turned inside out and slung casually over their shoulders they strolled back through Corpus Christi and Oriel.

When they got back to the car park the Merc was clamped. A yellow triangle of metal was padlocked to a metal frame around the front passenger-side wheel and a ticket stuck on the windscreen. Forsyth calmly yanked the ticket off and opened the boot. She rummaged around and took out a heavy bolt cropper. Archer stood open-mouthed as she deftly snipped the padlock bolt and casually removed the wheel clamp. "I get clamped all the time in Knightsbridge," she said, as if it was an everyday occurrence.

Two burly men in greasy navy overalls appeared and walked briskly towards the car, scowling at Forsyth as she walked around to the boot. Archer rolled his eyes at her and got in the car. "Come on, let's go. Ignore those idiots."

"Don't touch that. You have to pay us first," said one of the clampers.

"Sod off, we're only twenty minutes late."

"We'll impound your car for that; you've just made a huge mistake, darling."

"Who do you two grease monkeys work for?"

"We work for ourselves. We're private contractors, clampers to you, right, and you owe us money or you're nicked."

"Pair of thugs, more like it. Now bugger off."

Forsyth put the bolt croppers back in the boot and opened her door to get in the car. One of the unshaven clampers slammed it shut and pushed her back against the car. "You're not going anywhere until you pay us, Lady Muck."

He folded his hairy arms and stood in front of her, baring his yellow teeth. He weighed somewhere over eighteen stone, but Forsyth didn't turn a hair. She even looked like she was enjoying the confrontation. Archer decided to see if she could handle it on her own. If she started to get out of her depth, then he'd intervene.

The clamper looked down at Forsyth. "Look, lady, just be a sweetie and pay up."

"No."

"Right, hand me the fucking keys or you'll get a slap."

Forsyth glanced over at his colleague then looked the alpha clamper in the eye.

"You really shouldn't threaten people like that."

"Oh yeah, what you gonna do – get your tits out?"

"What did you say?"

"You 'eard me, you stupid slag. Now pay up before this gets messy."

"I think we'll have a bit of messy first, wanker."

Forsyth kicked him fast and hard in the crotch with the toe of her right boot. He bent forward and yelled loudly. She swiftly turned to her left and kicked sideways and downwards on top of his knee with the outer sole of her right foot. His leg snapped backwards at the knee joint, cracking like a branch being ripped off a tree. The big man fell to the ground instantly and wriggled around screaming, as his smaller partner bolted.

CHAPTER FORTY-NINE

Forsyth ignored the injured clamper rolling around at her feet and got back in the car as casually as if she had just been out buying a newspaper. Archer decided not to comment on her brutally efficient self-defence skills and composure under pressure. He swiftly set the satnav destination for the country cottage. They drove smoothly and steadily along the gently undulating A40 to Burford and then followed the quieter A424 to Stow on the Wold, sticking strictly to the speed limits. The radio station played softly in the background, but the pensive passengers remained quiet, even during the daily pop quiz. Archer tried to make sense of what was happening, but he was not an impartial observer.

"Why has Louise Palmer rented a cottage in the Cotswolds for six months under the disguise of an anonymous offshore shell company?" he said finally, breaking the long silence with only five miles left to go.

"Maybe she's being forced to do it."

"Who's really behind it then?"

"Or, maybe she's in on it."

"To pull something off like this there has to be a team."

"So who are they?" Forsyth took her eyes off the road to look at Archer.

"Ukrainian muscle from her oligarch friend? They do all the dirty work, or they could be business partners."

"It doesn't make sense to me. She's a successful businesswoman in her own right."

"But is she? Perhaps she's in trouble. Perhaps she's in it for the money. Zoe thinks she's involved in offshore money transfers with the Ukrainian. Maybe she's cooking the books to look good in the economic downturn, or maybe the Ukrainians have some leverage over her. You know how ruthless they can be."

Archer's phone rang. It was Sinclair.

"Hello," he said abruptly.

"Where are you, Archer?"

"Oxford."

"Haven't you found anything yet?" Unable to hide the angry edge to his voice.

"We're following up a lead right now."

"Keep me posted. Time's running out, as is my bloody patience."

"We'll call you."

The drive to Stow on the Wold took them just over an hour. The satnav took them through narrow streets to the outskirts of the small peaceful village. The cottage was proudly set back on a ridge top, holding court above two to three acres of well-manicured land sprawling lazily around it. They stopped in a small unused picnic bay on a gradual hill, about ninety yards past the gated entrance. They turned the car around to face the cottage. Thick bushes between the lane and the lay-by hid the electric blue body of the car, but still allowed them a good vantage point from beneath the black soft top.

The honey-coloured stone cottage had been recently thatched with pale rushes stretching over a series of arches that swooped up smoothly around the small sash windows on the upper floor. The sash windows on the ground floor were larger, six over six panes, but the rooms were hidden from prying eyes by white blinds angled for privacy. The gravel drive swept up to a wide black and white Tudor barn on the left-hand side of the long picturesque cottage. The estate agent details showed that there were various smaller stone outbuildings behind it, including stables and a small paddock.

"Nice country retreat – wisteria, ivy, the works. Dare I ask what the plan is?" Forsyth turned her body to Archer and smiled at him warmly.

"Stake it out till we find out what's going on."

"Great. I love stakeouts. I've got all the gear." She leaned over and rested her upper body on his legs as she opened the glove box. There was a pair of Swarovski binoculars under piles of speeding tickets. He could feel her firm body resting on his lap. He couldn't believe she was unaware of what she was doing. She was either flirting again or teasing him.

"I'll take first watch." She reached behind the passenger seat with her left hand and grabbed a Nikon single lens reflex digital camera with a two-hundred-millimetre zoom and a listening device. "I've got night vision, the works."

Archer nodded and smiled. "You're well equipped. I'll give you that," he said, then blushed with embarrassment as he realised the double meaning.

Forsyth laughed and said, "Well thanks for noticing."

They settled in for the afternoon behind the tinted windows. For someone with such a messy office her car was kept in showroom condition, Archer reflected. The interior smelled new, like it had just been valeted. It was all black except for the aluminium trim, which meant it looked dark from the outside and they would not be seen spying on the cottage. The radio was still on, but the climate control had gone off with the engine. Archer lowered the electric window halfway and let the cool fresh air waft into the car. Memories of Alex drifted in with it, causing him to feel a pang of grief tinged with guilt. Not only because he was with an attractive woman he found fascinating, but remorseful because he hadn't stopped her investigating the Boathouse and she was dead. But she wouldn't have listened anyway. That's the way she was. Stubborn and independent. But now he was dragging someone else into this deadly pursuit. Someone he was starting to care about – after only twenty-four hours.

They sat watching the cottage for hours using Forsyth's powerful binoculars and zoom lens camera. Cooped up in a small space they managed to make it comfortable despite the lack of movement at the cottage and the lack of food in the car. They shared small bottles of Evian water and a small pot of extra minty chewing gum Forsyth had bought from the filling station. They had listened to the current affairs show and now the afternoon show was ending. The long wait had provided them with nothing. It seemed like they were wasting their time listening to the radio and playing an impromptu pop quiz.

"You won't get this one. What film soundtrack starts with *There She Goes* by the Boo Radleys and ends with The La's version?"

"*So I Married an Axe Murderer.*" She punched him on the arm and laughed.

"So tell me about all the parking tickets and speeding fines in the glove box. What's going on with all those?"

"Long story. And I've no idea why I'm telling you this, but I sometimes work for some shady characters and one of them paid me with this car. It's registered to one of his foreign companies. He foots the bill to keep it on the road and basically pays for everything except petrol. I don't have to worry about any tickets as he sorts them out. I don't know exactly how he does it, but apparently he has people in his pocket and connections all over the place. So there it is."

"An ex-copper driving a free car from a connected gangster."

"Hey, *Drivetime*'s on. It's all requests Friday, let's make a request."

"You won't get through, the show's started."

"I've got through before, and I've had a confession read out."

"What was it?"

"I think I've told you enough for one day."

"Were you absolved?"

"Split decision."

Archer laughed.

"It'll be getting dark soon. We can start snooping around the garden at least. We might see what's happening around the back. We need a clear view through a window, see what's on the inside."

"And then we can get some food. We can't fight on empty stomachs. I say recon first, then food, then hit them at three-thirty a.m. when they're at their lowest ebb. Just like special ops."

They each disappeared behind the hedge for two minutes, blaming too much water, and then waited until dusk to take a closer look. Archer led the way from the lay-by, but as they started to walk down the lane they saw bright headlights approaching.

They ducked into the hedgerow. The car stopped at the entrance. The gates started to open automatically and the SUV-shaped vehicle drove slowly up the gravel driveway and stopped in front of the barn.

"Looks like the new tenants have returned." Archer looked through the binoculars and saw a white Lexus SUV. The electrically operated tailgate opened slowly, revealing a luggage compartment full of bulging shopping bags from Waitrose.

Forsyth was looking through her camera zoom lens. "That's the hoody."

The hoody got out of the SUV and took the bags around the back. He then opened the barn door and parked the SUV inside. With the door open they could see a blue VW van and a silver motorbike parked inside.

"The hoody, the BMW trail bike and the blue Transporter van. This is it."

As he closed the barn door a dark grey Porsche Cayenne drove up the drive at speed, stopping with a cloud of dust rising from the tyres. Two massive men got out dressed in dark suits. Forsyth saw a tattoo on the neck and hand of one.

"They could be the Ukrainians," she whispered.

The hoody went out of sight while the two men stayed near their vehicle.

"This could be interesting," Archer said, staring through the binoculars.

A minute later the hoody returned with a heavy-looking sports bag and dropped it on the gravel driveway in front of the men.

"He's paying the Ukrainians off," Forsyth said, looking through the camera and taking pictures, including a close-up of the number plates. One of the men opened the sports bag and looked inside, but it was impossible to see the contents from the lane over sixty yards away. The two heavy suits got back in the Porsche Cayenne and reversed it out at speed, pulling a one-eighty-degree spin where the driveway widened. They accelerated away in a cloud of dust and the gates closed automatically behind them. Dusk had turned to darkness and the lights were on around the open parts of the grounds. Inside the house most of the rooms were lit.

"Time to climb over the wall and take a closer look."

"Yeah, and see exactly how many people we're up against."

Archer helped Forsyth up and over first. He sneaked a decent peak at her firm butt as she went over the wall and shook his head. She was incredible, but he needed to focus on the job. He chastised himself, then followed her over the wall. There were no obvious infra-red sensors and they stayed away from the visible security light sensors, keeping to the shadows, heading around the back and moving slowly to avoid crunching the fallen leaves.

They stopped behind one of the stone outbuildings thirty feet away. The wall was flanked by a tall bush that gave them cover for surveillance. They used the binoculars and camera to peer through the bush towards the rear windows. Most of the lights were on and the blinds were still open at the back. The listening device crackled like static interference. It was either broken or there was a jammer. They had eyes but not ears.

"The upstairs bathroom window's still open. There's a wall next to it. That looks like the best place to get inside."

"There's the hoody, watching telly in the lounge downstairs."

"There's someone else moving. Rear of the kitchen – hold on. There's two people in the kitchen."

"Unpacking the provisions."

"Two bloody women!"

"That one looks a bit like Louise from the side."

"You're right. I think it's her. We need her to turn around."

"Damn it. The hoody's closing the blinds in the living room."

"So, we've two athletic-looking women with ponytails. One blonde and one dark-haired, both dressed casually in jeans and sweaters. And the infamous hoody."

"They're preparing food. Look, one's chopping vegetables and the other's pouring two glasses of wine."

They continued watching the two women prepare food but couldn't get a good enough look at their faces to identify Louise. The hoody appeared at the back door and started smoking. The women laid the kitchen table with three place settings and candles. More wine was poured and they continued to fuss about preparing their supper.

The hoody lit a second cigarette and both of the women turned around and spoke to him harshly. One of them came out. Forsyth took a picture. "The dark-haired one is definitely Louise Palmer."

There was a small disagreement and the hoody walked away towards the barn. The brunette went back inside and the blonde woman came to the door and shouted at him to fetch some logs for the fire.

"Jesus Christ," Archer said. "It's Becky!"

He struggled to keep his voice down.

"No way! Hang on, bloody hell. It definitely looks like her picture."

Forsyth took a photo. Archer asked her to email the photos to Zoe for confirmation via facial recognition software. They stopped peering through the bushes and sat on the grass with their backs against the wall of the outbuilding, facing away from the cottage.

"What the hell are they doing here, Sean?"

"There *are* no kidnappers. It's all been a massive hoax."

Archer stretched his neck and looked up at the starry sky then rested his head back against the brick wall.

"You've got to be kidding me."

"I know. Unbelievable."

Forsyth bent her legs and put her head on her knees. "Why on earth would they want to have Sinclair come after them?" She raised her head slowly and looked at Sean.

"I don't know." He touched her hand and squeezed it gently. "They're conning Sinclair. This is going to get very messy. Come on, let's go."

"Sinclair will go completely ballistic."

"Let's get out of here. I need to think this through properly."

They left the same way they came and walked swiftly to the car. As they got back inside and closed the doors a text message arrived from Zoe. The facial recognition software had positively identified the three faces as Louise Palmer, Christopher Palmer and Becky Sinclair.

CHAPTER FIFTY

Forsyth confidently announced that she knew a good place to stay nearby and they drove in silence through narrow lanes with high hedgerows lit up by the powerful xenon headlights on full beam. They passed through the sleepy village of Slaughter and five minutes later they entered the private grounds of The Manor, where acres of landscaped gardens and rolling parkland boasted mature willows and oaks showcased by blue and green spotlights. The gravel driveway was highlighted by a series of low lamps and the hotel's weathered stone walls were washed with warm yellow lights. It looked like a rural oasis of five-star comfort.

They parked the car right in front of the hotel and entered the lobby where they were instantly welcomed by a blazing log fire and a smiling platinum blonde receptionist whose badge showed that she was from Estonia. Forsyth took charge of checking in at reception while Archer stood back and admired her sophistication and easy style amid the pleasant surroundings. She booked two luxury rooms on the first floor with four-poster beds and a table in the restaurant for dinner using her business charge card and a voucher, explaining that she would get double the points.

Looking extremely pleased with herself, she handed over his card key and he followed her upstairs to the first-floor bedrooms. She explained the maze-like layout and seemed to know her way around the place like a regular.

"Give me half an hour to freshen up."

"Why so long?"

"That's not long, that's fast. I'll meet you down in the bar. Seeing as we've found Becky in one piece, I think champagne's in order."

"Champagne, downstairs, half an hour."

Their bedrooms were next to each other. Archer's room was large and classically furnished, decorated in a spectrum of soft pastel shades. The four-poster bed was well presented with a super-soft duvet and a cascade of puffed-up pillows, all in white linen.

Archer noticed a wide connecting door to Forsyth's room and wondered if it had been requested as part of an alpha female's tenacious seduction plan, or if it was merely a coincidence. She had an uncanny knack of disarming him like that.

He hadn't brought much with him. Just essential combat gear in a small rucksack. Fortunately, the well-stocked bathroom had more designer toiletries on offer than he needed, so he washed his hands and face, brushed his teeth and ruffled his hair with wet hands.

He debated a second shave and shower, but decided to leave it. The throwaway razor could stay sharp for tackling his dark stubble in the morning.

Five minutes down and twenty-five to go.

What was she doing?

He lifted his top, sprayed some complimentary deodorant under his arms and slapped some spicy cologne onto his cheeks.

She must be showering again.

He sat down and put the news channel on the television. Nothing interesting or serious so he switched it off during a mind-numbing story about two backbench politicians overheard complaining about inadequate entertainment expenses while dining in the Savoy Grill. The media was trying to sensationalise everything, even the weather. He just didn't get it.

He sat back in the armchair and thought about the kidnapping case.

What were these gold-digging sisters up to? It could be an elaborate escape plan, Becky running away from Sinclair because she felt in danger of being bumped off.

But how were the Ukrainians involved? Perhaps her sister was behind it all, motivated by the ransom money and using the Ukrainians as business partners or paid protection.

Or the Ukrainians could be the masterminds and the sisters are just going along with it for a share of the ransom money and an assisted escape plan from Sinclair.

They couldn't tell Sinclair the truth without causing bloodshed, but it wouldn't be too long before Sinclair found out. Damage limitation would be vital.

Archer needed to find out what was going on. He could tell Sinclair a version of the truth to enable Becky to get away and after that she was on her own. That's if she would even talk to him when he paid her a surprise visit in the morning.

He stared pensively out of the window into the floodlit grounds and the darkness beyond. His mind was drifting off into the past, a vivid memory of staying in a similar country hotel near Oxford with Alex, when the phone rang in his pocket. It was Sinclair. He let it go to voicemail and a text came whooshing through straightaway.

Where are you, Archer?

Oxford. Busy.

He pictured Sinclair's irritation and felt a strange sense of satisfaction. Sinclair was corrupt; like a contagious virus contaminating his immediate surroundings. He was also self-centred and dangerous. No wonder Becky had run away from him.

He wanted to help her get away, but he needed an exit strategy that included finding the Boathouse. If Hunter's evidence failed to put Sinclair away, then Archer would have to take him down alone. He couldn't tell Forsyth everything without putting her life in danger. But to find the Boathouse, and Alex's killer, he still needed to stay onside with Sinclair. That thought alone sent a shiver down his spine colder than a midwinter mistral, abruptly ending his relaxed reverie. He bolted out of the chair and headed straight downstairs for a stiff drink.

CHAPTER FIFTY-ONE

Archer sat on a high stool, alone at the hotel bar sipping a tall Hendrick's gin with tonic over ice garnished with a longways slice of cucumber. A bottle of pink Moët was chilling in a silver ice bucket on the bar next to his left arm. He had been there for twenty minutes watching well-dressed middle-aged couples come and go from the bar to the dining room.

Forsyth was now ten minutes late, which totalled forty minutes just to freshen up, and he felt a strange sense of unexpected excitement. He was nervous, but in a good way, like a sportsman enjoying the sensation of butterflies in his stomach just before the game starts. He hadn't dated properly since he'd met Alex over four years ago. He'd had a few drinks and casual dinners, but nothing serious. Tonight it felt like he was out on a proper date.

Forsyth had made her intentions perfectly clear last night. It was Friday night and he was waiting for an attractive intelligent female dinner companion. He thought of Alex and quickly chastised himself. What was he thinking? He wasn't ready to start dating and Forsyth was clearly going through a messy divorce. His excitement rapidly turned to guilt. These mixed feelings suddenly made him feel empty and uncomfortable.

He heard loud footsteps approaching the bar from behind. Confident strides on the wooden floorboards getting closer until he could smell her familiar fresh fragrance.

"Guess who?" she said and giggled. Even her laughter was intoxicating.

She hugged him like he was an old friend and kissed him softly on the cheek. Her lips kept contact with his face just a moment longer than a friendly kiss should. Her hair fell in her face as she sat down on the stool next to him and she brushed it away casually, showing her wrists and then playing with her hair and smiling: all positive signs of attraction.

"So what exactly are we celebrating?" he said.

"Finding Becky, of course. Now you've had time to think, what will you tell Sinclair?"

"We'll visit her in the morning and find out what the hell is going on first."

"Well at least she's safe."

"I'm not so sure about that."

"We saw her – she was cooking supper with candles and wine, remember."

"Safe for tonight perhaps, but how long has she got before Sinclair finds her?"

Archer nodded at the barman to open the champagne.

"How do you think he'll take it?"

"He'll kill all three of them. Then Hunter, and then he'll probably come after us."

"Well let's just live for the moment then, shall we?" She touched his leg and smiled.

The barman popped the cork and poured two lively glasses of champagne. They raised their fizzing drinks to each other and simultaneously took their first sips.

"Here's to Becky staying alive and Sinclair going down."

She looked relaxed and happy, but he struggled not to make comparisons with Alex. He wished she was still alive and that they were here together. He was still uncomfortable about dating anyone seriously, as if being attracted to Sarah more than just physically was somehow cheating on Alex. Sarah smiled back at him confidently and gently brushed his thigh with her hand as if they were already an established couple.

"Do you think the sisters masterminded the whole thing on their own?" she said.

Archer paused as he thought about telling her about the Boathouse.

"It's too well planned. The Ukrainians must be involved, otherwise why would they show up and get paid?"

"And Louise Palmer's son, Christopher, is the infamous hoody."

"He's only twenty-one. Supposed to be on a gap year in South-East Asia."

"But why such a complicated and dangerous hoax? There must be a good reason for it, but I don't get it. It probably all boils down to money in the end – it always does."

"We'll find out tomorrow morning. I thought we were having the night off."

Their table was set for a romantic candlelit dinner. The mood continued to be light and cheerful until Forsyth pressed him to tell her about his family. He tried to change the subject several times, but she kept on until he told her.

"I lost my parents when I was fourteen."

"Oh I'm really sorry, Sean. What happened?"

He didn't want to tell her the truth and dodged explaining it by looking down at the table and using his old cover story. "There was a nasty accident. I try not to think about it. That's when I went to live with my grandparents in Flood Street."

"Small world. We used to live around the corner from each other. Tell me about your grandparents?"

"My grandfather was a criminal prosecutor and my grandmother had a jewellery shop on Brompton Road. She was a real character."

His smiled as he reminisced about his grandmother, who was the matriarch of the family, very protective. She'd had him trained in Krav Maga by ex-Mossad agents at age fifteen. He visualised the picture she'd taken of him with his parents, cycling along the Camel Trail in Cornwall, and he felt saddened by the fact that he couldn't remember them at all. It was painfully ironic that he could remember nothing before they died and absolutely everything ever since.

The waiter topped up their drinks and he was brought back to earth with another line of inquest.

"How come you're still single? You must have plenty of admirers."

She smiled and flicked her hair. Her body language was clear. She was flirting with him outrageously and he liked it, except for the fact that it reminded him of Alex.

"My girlfriend, Alex, died fourteen months ago."

Forsyth leaned forward, grabbed his hand and squeezed it compassionately.

"I'm so sorry, Sean. I wasn't thinking properly. It must be the champagne."

"What did she do?"

"Journalist. Mostly human rights-related assignments in foreign conflicts. Always rushing off to hotspots like Iraq, Chechnya, Afghanistan, Somalia, Syria."

"How did you meet her?"

She was relentless, but he could feel his stomach flutter at the thought of how he had met Alex. It was a great memory.

"We met at a Clapton concert. Both queuing for tickets outside the Albert Hall on the opening night; you know, for the standing area in the gallery."

"I've done that a few times myself." She smiled and looked receptive.

"Well, I was on a date, which didn't work out by the way, and this woman came up to me and said she couldn't go to the concert because her husband wasn't well and she had two stalls tickets in the second row to sell for cash. But I only had a tenner and my credit card, so this stranger, Alex, who was standing behind me, offered to pay for me. I asked her how she knew I'd pay her back and she said she just knew and gave me her number. The following day the *Evening Standard* said Clapton was slicker than Brylcreem."

"That's a classic."

"Tell me about your family," he said before she could interrogate him any further.

She regaled him with humorous tales of her extended family and he was glad to be out of the firing line. The final course was cheese and biscuits accompanied by vintage port. They talked about London and their work, and found plenty of common ground to keep the conversation light and flowing. They had both grown up in Chelsea, but the six-year age gap had kept them moving around in different circles, despite knowing the same families, particularly around Flood Street in Chelsea and the Little Boltons in South Kensington. They had both spent summer evenings drinking with friends outside the Anglesea Arms in around the same timeframe. They decided that they must have passed close to each other on more than one occasion, but it had taken them over twenty years to actually meet.

To finish the meal off they ordered a large glass of cognac and coffee.

Despite covering some sensitive issues, Archer felt that the evening had turned out to be a pleasant one. They were similar in several ways. They both worked as independent consultants and investigators. They both enjoyed helping others solve problems and tried to promote social justice. And they both despised Peter Sinclair with a passion.

Archer found it hard to believe that she was older than him. She looked more early thirties than early forties. She had good genes and judging by her smooth skin she used rich moisturisers and enjoyed a healthy diet and lifestyle. She looked radiant.

Occasionally throughout dinner he had felt her leg casually brushing against his. Initially, he thought it was accidental. When the coffee arrived she started to rub her calf against his and smiled at him provocatively. She touched his hand and gazed into his eyes.

"I've really enjoyed working with you," she said.

"Thanks for helping me out at short notice; somehow I knew you would."

Her face lit up. She drew herself up to the table and leant in towards him, smiling broadly as if they had just shared a special moment.

"Did you notice we have connecting doors?" she asked.

"I'd better keep my door locked, just in case I get lucky," he said, with a wink.

"I'd better keep mine unlocked, just in case I get lucky," she said and smiled back at him, gently flicking her hair.

They finished off their coffees. She ordered the cheque and signed for it on her room number. He said goodnight to her outside his bedroom door. She hugged him and kissed him on the cheek, keeping soft lip-gloss contact for several seconds.

"Goodnight," she whispered in his ear, then turned and left him standing alone outside his door. He watched her go into her room and she shut the door without looking back.

CHAPTER FIFTY-TWO

Archer splashed his face a few times and brushed his teeth. He got into bed naked and turned out the bedside light. He stared up at the ceiling, but couldn't see anything as it was pitch dark with the heavy curtains closed. The intimacy of the meal had reminded him of being out for dinner with Alex. He remembered the last time they'd had a meal in their favourite bistro in Kensington. She'd worn a simple black sweater and stonewashed jeans that showed off her athletic body shape. Her dark shoulder-length hair was tied back in a short ponytail and her green eyes sparkled; they were mesmerising and surrounded by the longest natural eyelashes he'd ever seen. They ate fresh rustic peasant food and drank red wine by candlelight. Her fair skin was still tanned from their holiday in the Luberon as they held hands and reminisced.

Then he saw her wounded expressionless face on the stainless-steel gurney. Her skin was as pale as candle wax. Her green eyes were closed for ever. There was a small dark hole in her forehead and two more in her chest. He fought the image and imagined her being there with him. Snuggled together naked in the four-poster bed surrounded by fresh Egyptian cotton.

The image of her dead body returned like a ghost watching over him. He stopped fighting it. He thought back to the bistro and it felt like they had just had dinner downstairs. He imagined he was talking to her as if she was lying there enjoying some pillow talk in the dark. The champagne helped him drift off as if he were still talking to her.

In the dream-fuelled darkness he vaguely heard a door close in the distance followed by some light footsteps on the carpet and then a bathrobe falling to the floor.

He was lying on his back and he felt the duvet shuffle a little before her warm body moved next to him. She was on her side. She stroked his chest with her fingernails and rubbed his leg with her thigh. He could feel her soft skin touching his, her minty breath on his face. They embraced and held each other tight as if they had been apart for too long. Her skin felt as smooth as porcelain. His was more rugged. They kissed slowly at first, but with the passion of long lost lovers that had been kept apart against their wishes. Their kissing intensified and Archer moved swiftly on top of her and kissed the nape of her neck. She wrapped her long muscular legs around his waist and rotated her hips upward, as he thrust his hips forward, savouring the act of penetration until they couldn't push their bodies any closer together.

He stroked her hair back from her forehead in the silent darkness.

"Alex."

"What did you say?"

Half asleep – he was still thinking about Alex.

"What's wrong?"

"Try Sarah!"

She pushed him off and to the side and jumped out of bed. He fumbled around and turned the bedside lamp on. She put her bathrobe back on and pulled the belt tight. He was dazed. He was still unsure about exactly what had just happened. The light was on a dim setting, but he could still see that she was glaring at him, unable to hide her anger, then her face reddened and she bowed her head.

"I'm sorry, Sean," she said. "It's my entire fault. I shouldn't have unpicked your locked door. I think I'd better go now before I make it worse."

"No, stay. Please stay and talk." He desperately wanted her to stay.

"Are you sure?

"I was dreaming about Alex. And then I was with her, but it was you."

He got out of bed and put his boxer shorts on with his back to her. "I was thinking about her and then we were in bed together." He turned around to face her. Her head was still bowed down – attempting to mask her embarrassment.

"I'm really sorry. Look, I was probably using you to help get over the thought of my divorce. It's left me feeling empty inside and quite frankly I feel unloved. I was looking for something to help me feel normal again," she confessed with a sad, strained smile.

"Do you want to talk about your husband?"

"No, not really, but – thanks."

"It may help you feel better."

"Hold on a second. I need another nightcap." She went to the minibar and took out two miniature bottles of Rémy Martin. She poured them into two small water glasses and handed him one. They got back under the duvet to keep warm, but stayed two feet apart.

They sipped the neat cognac slowly, both sitting up leaning against the pillows and the padded headboard. The awkwardness of the moment had started to subside. After the cognac warmed his stomach he felt more comfortable about what had just happened.

"I suppose you think I'm on the rebound," she said.

"I try not to sleep with my work colleagues."

"What are you afraid of? I'm not some nutty bunny-boiler."

He was afraid of losing people as everyone he'd ever loved had left him and he was afraid of falling in love again.

"Tell me about your marriage. Are you over it?" he said, looking concerned.

"No, not really. I still miss my husband in many ways, but he was spoilt and selfish and we drifted apart."

"What pushed you over the edge?"

"The bastard had an affair with a young American intern in his office."

"How do you know?"

"I found them in his office working late. I can still see them. I felt sick."

"Is he still seeing her?"

"No. He wants me back. Tell me, why can't you sleep properly?"

"It doesn't matter … I, um …"

"It does matter and I'm a good listener. Tell me what's bothering you."

She looked at him and smiled with genuine kindness. He felt incredibly comfortable with her. He bowed his head and sighed. Should he tell her? He wanted to.

"My girlfriend Alex was killed by a professional hit man and I'm looking for the people responsible."

"Oh Sean, I'm really sorry, but revenge is such a nasty business. What happened?"

"I don't talk about it. I don't want anyone else getting hurt."

"I'm an ex-copper. I know the risks. I won't tell anyone."

"Knowledge can be dangerous. You're better off not knowing. Not getting involved."

"I'm already involved. You can trust me. Really." She touched his hand and squeezed it. He felt he could trust her. There was something special about her.

"She was following up a dangerous lead about the CIA taking insurgents for torture and disposal to an off-grid facility. The disgruntled ex-agent who was left for dead took her from Syria to Yemen and then back here."

"Well that sounds ominous for a start."

"She was killed trying to find out who was behind it. She found out the codename of the place. It's called the Boathouse."

"What happened to her?"

"She was shot by an assassin on her way to meet me after work for dinner, walking from a meeting near Vauxhall Cross to a small bistro we liked in Kensington. They also killed her flatmate last week just after I spoke with her about it."

"Why haven't they tried to kill you?"

"I don't know. I've received threats, but nothing to worry about yet."

Apart from a dirty copper setting him up for murder and blackmailing him, while a car full of mercenaries chased after him dishing out death threats.

"You should stay well clear of it."

"I know, but I feel compelled to act. I've accepted what happened to her, but in order to move on, I need to finish it off – one way or another."

"Be careful, Sean," she said, then stroked his head and rested hers on his shoulder and stroked his chest. "I know this sounds insane, but I'm going to help you. No strings."

He turned to look at her as she put her arm around him and squeezed him tight. The kiss that followed felt perfectly natural and after he turned the light out their bodies fitted together without a hint of awkwardness.

CHAPTER FIFTY-THREE

Archer woke late on Saturday morning after it was already light outside. He remembered another episode of his recurring dream. He'd been followed by the four-man hit squad in black combat gear again, but this time he turned around and confronted them. As he got closer he could see that the leader was shorter than the rest of the team, with a clothing outline that revealed the curves of an athletic female body. He walked up to her without any fear and she told the team to holster their weapons and they did. She pulled off her sub-zero balaclava to reveal her identity. It was Alex.

She had told him to move on and forget about the Boathouse, and then kissed him passionately until he woke up. He tried to get back into the dream, to see her again and kiss her soft lips one last time, but it was impossible. He stayed awake and watched Forsyth sleep until she stirred, then she looked surprised when she realised where she was. He glanced at his watch on the bedside table. Ten past nine.

"Oh my God, my head has shrunk. I had too much champagne."

"Morning, Sarah."

"What the fuck am I doing here?" She looked startled.

"What?"

"I get frisky if I have too much bubbly." She slapped him on the shoulder. "I'm not even divorced yet, and now you've made me an adulteress."

"Sorry about that – I shouldn't have kept the door locked."

"You ordered pink champagne, which is my absolute favourite. Then you charmed me into your bed over dinner, like Casa-bloody-nova." She laughed out loud, then held her head and winced.

"It was a great evening, and thanks again for listening." He kissed her on the cheek.

Archer got up, walked to the bathroom and closed the door. His head felt heavy after all the drink. He shaved and showered. He stood for some time under the warm jets of water just to clear his head. When he returned with the towel wrapped around his waist Forsyth was gone. She had left a short note saying she had ordered a late breakfast for them both in her room and signed it with a big smiley face and three kisses.

He dressed and gazed lazily out of the window at the clear blue sky. Another calm sunny day in October. In the Cotswolds countryside with a beautiful woman who was great fun to be with. He had to admit to himself that the chemistry felt too good. He was miles away when his mobile phone rang. Without thinking he answered it – on hazy autopilot.

"What's going on, Archer?" Sinclair yelled.

"Can't really talk right now," he whispered.

"Why bloody not?"

"Stakeout."

"Where are you?"

"Near Oxford."

"Where exactly in bloody Oxford?"

"In the countryside just outside the city."

"Don't play dumb with me, sunshine. Whereabouts exactly?"

He needed to change the subject fast. Think of something to say. Quick.

"We're watching a remote cottage."

"Who's inside?"

"Louise."

"Louise? What the hell's going on?

"I'll call you back in half an hour. They're on the move again." Archer ended the call.

He felt uneasy as he walked through the connecting doors into Forsyth's room where a trolley full of food and coffee waited. He realised he'd just made a fatal mistake. He wasn't thinking properly. He should never have answered the phone. He shouldn't have mentioned the cottage or Louise. They had to move fast now as Sinclair's associates would soon dispatch a team after them.

CHAPTER FIFTY-FOUR

Archer and Forsyth skipped breakfast, checked out of the hotel and got into the car. Forsyth started the engine, dropped the soft top under the pale blue sky, wiped the dew off the shaded windscreen with one quick pass of the wipers and put the heater on.

The autumn sun warmed Archer's face as they drove down the meandering driveway. The gravel popped and crunched beneath the tyres and the birds sang in the trees. It felt more like spring than autumn.

Forsyth wore a red quilted gilet with jeans, boots and a red scarf. She looked as if she'd lived in the country all her life. Archer was still in his navy jeans and leather jacket. He was determined to get Becky to a safe place before Sinclair could find her.

Archer's phone went off loudly.

"Have you seen the news?" Zoe said, on speaker.

"No. What's happened?"

Forsyth stopped the car abruptly with a scrunch of gravel and a cloud of dust.

"Julian Cavendish and a woman were found dead in a hotel suite in the City."

"What?" Archer felt like he'd been punched in the chest.

"A cleaner found them and took photos with her phone. She's been sacked, but there are graphic pictures all over the Net. He was with a high-class escort. The pictures make it look like a cocaine and auto-erotic sex party gone wrong. They both suffocated to death."

"Are you saying it was an accident from sexual misadventure?"

"No accident, I'm afraid, because the Hunters are dead too. That's the big news story on all the main TV channels."

"What?"

"Their French housekeeper's dead too."

"How?"

"Burglars. They stole sculptures and paintings. Shot them all in their beds in the middle of the night while they were sleeping. And somebody has posted pictures on the Net."

"It has to be Sinclair."

"He's on the warpath. Be careful."

"We're on our way to see Becky now."

He hung up.

"Poor Julian," said Forsyth. "Hunter deserved it, but Julian was a lovely man, he was like an older version of Prince Harry."

"If we hadn't found Hunter, he wouldn't have made the call that killed him."

"It's not our fault he's dead. We're not responsible for Sinclair's actions."

"But why did he kill him? And all those innocent women."

"He never liked him, but something must have triggered it."

"It must be me. But how? I haven't been followed, my phone is clean."

Archer opened Forsyth's iPad and looked for the email from Zoe. He clicked on the links to see the websites.

"Pictures like this should never be allowed on these sites," he said.

The Hunters were shot in the head at close range while still in bed. The naked housekeeper Madeleine was spread-eagled on her back on top of the bed. Probably raped before half her face was blown off.

The bodies of Julian Cavendish and the young courtesan from lunchtime on Thursday were lying on top of their hotel bed with clear plastic bags over their heads.

Archer saw Forsyth's back straighten and her face tighten. She was a tough ex-copper, so she would be used to seeing images of violence, but clearly she was still human. Archer had also seen too much bloodshed. He was able to deal with death and even killing people if he felt it was deserved, but he could not accept innocent victims being tortured and then being murdered in cold blood. Whoever was responsible deserved the same fate.

Forsyth accelerated aggressively through the hotel gateway, her wing mirrors brushing leaves off hedges as she raced through the narrow lanes.

"Taking him down will be a lot harder now, without Hunter's help," she said.

"Let's get to Becky first. Then we'll take Sinclair down, don't you worry."

CHAPTER FIFTY-FIVE

Forsyth nearly crashed into the hedge as she skidded to a standstill leaving two lines of rubber behind them on the narrow tarmac lane. She slowly edged off the lane and inched up the recess towards the wrought-iron gate, nudging it softly with the Merc's bumper. Through it Archer could see the sisters and the hoody unloading cardboard boxes from the Transporter van and taking them into the house. Forsyth blasted the horn for a few seconds, causing three heads to turn around sharply.

Louise Palmer said something to the others and then walked straight towards the gate. She was Amazonian in stature and looked like the natural leader of the group. As she got nearer, Archer could see from her frown that she was really pissed off.

"I'll make the introductions. This could be tricky," Forsyth said, getting out of the car.

Louise stopped twenty yards away. She stood with her legs apart and her hands on her hips. "What do you want?" she shouted.

"Open the gate. We need to talk."

"Who the hell are you?"

"Private investigators. You're in deep shit unless you open up."

"I don't think so somehow. The gate stays closed, so fuck off."

"You'll need a new gate, then. I've just turned the airbags off."

"Right, I'm calling the police." She turned around and started to walk away.

"I don't think you'll do that, Mrs Palmer. Peter Sinclair didn't call the police. He's coming after you himself."

Louise froze on the spot. She was visibly shaking as she turned back round, all colour drained from her face. She looked like an aggressive middle-aged Goth.

"Shit, shit, shit. Why are you here?"

"We want to help you."

"Why? I don't even know you."

"Sinclair's on the warpath. He's close to finding you."

"Hold on."

She hurried over to Becky and they spoke for a minute with lots of head-shaking, posturing and arm-waving. Then Louise pointed the remote control at the electric gate and it opened slowly. Forsyth got back inside the car. The hoody gazed at her coolly, wearing large headphones, but continued to unload the van. The sisters stood with folded arms and watched the Merc drive up to them and park in front of the barn. Their faces looked suspicious. Their body language guarded. They looked set to bluff it out now and stared silently as the unwelcome visitors got out of the car.

"Morning," Forsyth said in a friendly tone.

"What the fuck's going on?" Louise said harshly, glaring back at her.

Forsyth smiled and extended her hand. Archer did the same. They were both refused.

"What the hell do you two fucking shitheads want?" Louise said.

"Can we go inside?" Archer said, gesturing towards the back door of the cottage.

"No. If you've got something to say, say it here," Becky said.

"Your husband's looking for you. It won't take him much longer. He's already killed Julian Cavendish and Stuart Hunter. Basically you're next."

This time their faces completely crumpled.

"You'd better come in then," Becky gestured for them to follow her.

At close quarters Becky was as beautiful as her portrait, but Louise was a hard-looking forty-something with sharp features smothered in too much make-up. Her figure was cosmetically enhanced and her hair dyed jet black. Her pale skin looked tired. As they entered the cottage Archer thought she looked better in softer lighting, but the daylight had already exposed her attempts to look younger and the black bags under her eyes were still puffy.

The country farmhouse kitchen was larger than Archer had thought, with a wood-fuelled Aga and long wooden table in the middle with bench seats either side. Becky poured fresh coffee into four Portmeirion mugs and threw four teaspoons on the table. There were no takers. The foursome sat awkwardly around the kitchen table with folded arms.

"He's a psychopath," Becky said, staring wildly at her steaming mug. Her eyes danced angrily, then glazed over as her rage broke and she looked frightened.

"He's nasty. Total control freak. Everything always has to be his way. He threatens to kill me if I don't do exactly what he wants. It's horrible." She stared harshly at Archer.

"Did you really think you could get away from him?"

"He was planning to kill me. He's got a younger woman lined up and he wants me out of the way so he can marry her."

"Why not get a divorce?"

"You obviously don't know him," Louise interjected bitterly, glaring at Archer.

"What about the Ukrainians? What's their involvement?"

"What's that got to do with you?"

"We saw the Ukrainians being paid off yesterday. What was that for?"

"None of your fucking business," Louise blurted as her face flushed red.

"You're not trying to take Sinclair out, are you?"

"Don't be ridiculous – don't you know anything?"

The sisters looked at each other nervously. "Anyone that tried to take him out wouldn't last a week. That's why he's so cocky."

"So what were the Ukrainians doing here?"

"All right, if you must know: Louise has a Ukrainian friend; she borrowed some money from him to keep her business going through the recession. We paid him back with interest."

"Who planned the kidnapping and ransom drops?"

"We did."

"What? All of it?"

"Every last detail. We couldn't kill him so we had to run. We wanted to start a new life down under. My sister and her two children in Sydney, me in Auckland. It's as far away as you can get and Peter has no interests down there."

"Why did you take so much money from him?"

"Shows how little you know. It's gonna take a lot to change identities and not get found. We had to make it look realistic. If we asked for too little he'd be sceptical and figure it out. It seemed more convincing this way."

"So you executed all the ransom drops yourselves?"

"Yep."

"No help from professionals? No Ukrainians?"

"Nope."

"How long did it take you to prepare for it?"

"Six months."

"Why rent this place? Why are you here and not in Australia?"

"We're waiting for my niece to finish college in Cheltenham. That's why we rented this cottage. It's close to her school. We thought nobody would ever find us here."

"But look how easily we found you. If we can do it, then he'll know other people who can. Didn't you think he'd come after you?"

"The Ukrainians are going to make it look like I'm dead. It's all planned and paid for. Then Peter can move on and forget about me and my family," Becky said, looking worried.

"What? When?"

"Next week. It will stop him from looking for me or thinking that Louise is involved. He'll think it was a real kidnapping, that it was all about the ransom money."

Archer didn't believe all he was hearing. He looked at Forsyth and could tell from her frown that she wasn't buying it either. The sisters had planned parts of the operation well but they'd also grossly underestimated Peter Sinclair.

Archer's phone rang. He pulled it out of his pocket.

"Shit. It's him."

CHAPTER FIFTY-SIX

Archer stared at his phone and let it ring six times before he answered. His voicemail kicked in after eight rings and he knew how persistent Sinclair could be. He held his hand up, signalling to the others to stop talking.

"Yes," Archer said, sternly.

"Haven't you found her yet?"

"No, not yet."

"I have people near Oxford that can back you up. Where exactly are you?"

"It wasn't her. We haven't found her yet. We're on the move, still looking."

"My patience has finally run out with you, Archer." Sinclair's tone was grim.

"There's still time."

"What good will that do? We're done." Sinclair hung up.

Archer put the phone back in his pocket. It was a huge relief that his civilised relationship with Sinclair was finally over. He knew that their next encounter would be very different.

"We need to get away from here. He has men near Oxford. They could be here in under an hour." Archer stood up from the kitchen table.

"Where do we go?"

"We all need to ditch our SIM cards and go. I know somewhere that's safe. Pack your essentials and be ready to leave in ten minutes."

"Ten minutes? But that's not enough time."

"Leave all the boxes, just bring some clothes. Follow us in your car. Put the van back in the barn, we need to shut this place down and leave. NOW."

The hoody swaggered into the kitchen. Headphones skewed around his neck. Cigarette hanging from his lip. Gun tucked into his jeans. Eyes glazed over.

"You old fuds are all shit-scared of him," he said, then leaned back and grabbed his gun, pointing it at the floor. "I'm not. I'm gonna kill the fucker."

Louise stood up and gently took the gun from his hand. "No you won't, darling, just go put the van back in the barn and get the Lexus out. Lock all the outbuildings. We're leaving. Hurry up."

He looked at her for a moment then lowered his head. As he closed the door behind him her mobile phone rang. She stared at it vacantly. Then her jaw dropped and her bottom lip fell.

"It's coming up as 'Peter's Private Number'," Louise said.

"What?" Becky said.

"He's calling my new mobile." The blood drained from the sisters' faces.

"What the fuck? How did he get this number? It's a bloody brand-new phone and I haven't used it to call him yet."

Louise Palmer stared at her mobile. It rang on until it went to voicemail. Two seconds later it rang again. She stared at it with her mouth open and let it go to voicemail again.

"Why's he calling me?"

A text message arrived with an old car horn sound.

Answer the next call if you ever want to see your daughter again.

Louise started to shake. First her hands, then her arms and finally her body. Her breathing became shallow and more rapid. She strained as if she was struggling to stay on her feet. She looked like she was starting to hyperventilate.

"Oh my God. He's got Amanda," she said.

She dropped the phone. It landed on the table and spun around face up. They stared at it as it lit up and rang again. They could all see on the screen that it was another call from Peter's private number. Louise braced herself, took a long deep breath and managed to control her breathing enough to pick up the phone and answer it. She pressed speaker with both of her hands still shaking.

"Morning, Louise," he said, as if they were old friends about to enjoy a pleasant chat. "I thought that last text message might get your full attention."

"What have you done with Amanda?" She was breathless.

"I've taken her as an insurance policy."

"You'd better not touch her, you bastard. Where is she?"

"Shut up and put Becky on the phone."

"What are you talking about? She's not with me. I'm on a business trip, you must know that. Where's Becky?"

"Don't lie to me, you stupid slag."

"Don't talk to me like that. Where's Amanda?"

"Shut the fuck up, you skank. I realise this must be a bit of a shock, but I've outplayed your pathetic little game. I figured out your little scam, you know. I've made moves so far ahead of you that your head would spin. Who did you think you were dealing with?"

"What are you talking about? Where's my daughter?"

"Listen very carefully, Louise. I'll tell you what we'll do."

"Leave Amanda alone and tell me where she is."

"Shut up, woman, for crying out loud. I'll give you ten minutes to think straight, get over the shock of what's happening to you and then I'll call you back. Becky had better answer the phone, otherwise Amanda dies."

"You dare touch her. I'll kill you."

"No, Louise, you won't. You've made a huge mistake doing this to me. Now I have Amanda, but I can only guarantee her safety if you do exactly as I say. Make sure that Becky answers the phone. Understood?"

"Don't you hurt her, you fucking bastard."

"If you talk to the police, she dies. If Becky fails to answer the call, she dies. If you don't do exactly as I tell you, she dies. Recognise these words, Louise?"

"Leave her alone."

"Becky answers the phone in ten minutes or Amanda dies." The phone went dead.

CHAPTER FIFTY-SEVEN

The mood around the kitchen table bombed as they all realised that Sinclair held the upper hand. Archer paced around the kitchen table with his head bowed down in deep thought. The sisters had no real choice. They had to do whatever Sinclair said, to save Amanda. He stopped and looked directly at Louise.

"I don't understand. How did he know I was involved?" Louise was still shaking.

Becky awkwardly put her arm around her sister to console her, then quickly pulled it away and looked nervous. It looked like they had been arguing about something.

Archer started to pace around the table again with Forsyth staring at him. He stopped and stared back as if he were questioning her loyalty, but immediately felt stupid. He'd been the one who had told Sinclair about Louise. Was that all it had taken for Sinclair to figure it all out? Or was there someone else keeping him informed?

"I'll have to answer it. I'll have to speak to him," Becky said, and her eyes gave away her fear. "What if he hurts Amanda?"

"He'll want you to go back with him," Archer said, looking directly at Becky.

"I'll have to do what he says. There's no alternative."

"No, there's not."

"Do as he says, agree to his terms. We'll have to figure out a way to get you out after the exchange."

"He'll probably kill me."

"As soon as we get Amanda back, we can call the police."

"What if he doesn't give her back?"

"He can't kill all of you without drawing serious attention to himself," Forsyth said.

"He'll probably mastermind a car accident for us all. He's done it all before."

"We'll figure something out. We'll get you out before then." Sean said, as confidently as he could, but knew it wouldn't be easy.

Ten minutes elapsed, faster than anyone expected. Louise jumped when her phone rang. She picked it up off the table and handed it to Becky as if it was contaminated.

Becky answered it after four rings and pressed speaker.

"Hello," she said quietly, placing it back on the kitchen table. The four of them hunched in closer, all staring down at the phone.

"Hello, Becky. I want you to come home."

"Where's Amanda?"

"She's being driven somewhere in the back of a car. She's safe enough for now."

"Don't you dare hurt her. You want me, not her, so let her go."

"She looks so pretty, all dressed up for her boyfriend."

"She doesn't have a boyfriend."

"Shows how much you know about her."

"Don't you dare touch her."

Archer saw Becky look sideways at her sister, who was crying and gasping for air, both hands covering her mouth. Her thick mascara running down her puffy white cheeks.

"She's a bit of a tease, you see, in her pleated tartan skirt and white blouse. She's filled out rather well too, hasn't she? A fit womanly figure, all grown up. Only she's in a spot of bother, I'm afraid. You see, she's wearing a blindfold and handcuffs."

"Don't you do anything to her, she's only seventeen."

"Have you got access to a car?"

"Yes."

"Then listen carefully and do exactly as I say. You and Louise get in the car right now and get to the M5 motorway. Head south towards Exeter and then take the A30 and A35 towards Poole. Repeat what I just said."

"South on the M5 towards Exeter then the A30 and A35 towards Poole."

"I'll call you with more specific directions en route. We'll make an exchange along the way. It's you for her. It's that simple. Okay?"

"Yes." Her bottom lip was trembling. She was a dead woman.

"Leave now and we'll make the exchange in a couple of hours. I'll call you on this phone number, so keep it handy."

"We're leaving now."

"And don't do anything stupid like call the police or anyone else. Okay?"

"Okay."

"Now, listen to me very carefully. Take a quick look in your Hotmail account before you leave and follow the link. You'll see a short video of Amanda that was taken ten minutes ago. That should stop you from doing anything stupid."

CHAPTER FIFTY-EIGHT

The email with the link was from an anonymous remailer. A YouTube video popped up and Becky hit play. The fluffy sound of a home-made video recording started. It was taken from the passenger seat inside a moving car. The dark interior looked like a Range Rover. It was being driven down a motorway on the inside lane. The camera shifted awkwardly towards the back seat. A young girl with jet-black hair in a ponytail was blindfolded and handcuffed, the cuffs visible in front of her. She was crying, calling out for her mother, screaming from the bottom of her gut with pure fear as two men held her. Their handling was rough and insensitive, one muscular thug wedged in either side of her. They both wore black sub-zero balaclavas.

The front passenger was filming with one hand, the gun in the other hand pointed at her head. Initially he pressed the gun against her forehead, then lowered the barrel down her nose. He put the last three inches inside her mouth.

The sisters were shaking uncontrollably, hysterical, making guttural noises and crying. Amanda wriggled around as her body trembled. Her high-pitched screams caused the driver to lose concentration. The camera jumped and the cameraman turned round to see what was happening. They were overtaking two duelling lorries in the first two lanes and the faster lorry had started nudging over, forcing them to the right of the outside lane. The tyres thrummed over the ridged white line, which sounded like a thunderstorm on the hand-held video.

The engine revved higher as the car accelerated, overtook the lorries and got back on the inside lane. Archer saw a blue and white road sign. They were on the M5 heading south. The gunman turned back and put the gun back inside Amanda's mouth. She wept and started to scream as best she could. He withdrew the gun from her mouth and she managed to slow her breathing down. They gave her some water from a plastic bottle and a small pill and then gagged her with a white silk scarf. She breathed noisily through her nose and begged them to stop in a weak muffled voice.

The two men either side pulled her legs wide apart and held her firm. She tried to fight back and started to hit them with her two cuffed fists, but one of the men used his left hand to snatch her arms up over her head. The other ripped her blouse open, popping all the buttons and revealing her white lacy bra. She moved around in the seat, but they were far too strong and held her legs uncomfortably wide apart. They moved her body forward so that she was almost lying down. Her knees touched the back of the front seat headrests. The gunman reached up her short tartan skirt and ripped her small white knickers off in one violent movement before throwing them down on the floor. She squealed from deep down in her gut as the handgun was pushed inside her.

"How d'ya like that, ya snotty-nosed little bitch?" he said, in a Yorkshire accent.

She screamed harder, but the sound soon vanished as her voice faded into submission. Mascara-drenched tears streamed down her face like diluted ink from beneath the damp blindfold. The video stopped. The file instantly disappeared from the website.

Becky stared at the computer screen, unable to move. Louise picked up the laptop from the kitchen table and threw it hard against the wall. The screen broke away from the keyboard and the two parts crashed down onto the terracotta-tiled floor. The four of them stared at the broken pieces in silence.

CHAPTER FIFTY-NINE

The pale and frightened-looking sisters set off in their white Lexus SUV towards the motorway. Forsyth closed the soft top of the Merc and followed. They'd changed their SIM cards and stuck their old ones onto an eighteen-wheel lorry from Glasgow waiting next to them at the traffic lights. If the phones were being triangulated or tracked by Sinclair's people it would throw them off and waste time.

Archer had told the sisters to keep a mobile phone switched on inside the car so that he and Forsyth could also hear any calls and communicate with them. He had also given Becky a spare mobile and taped it inside her long leather boot.

The mood inside the Merc was sombre. Archer couldn't imagine how much worse it was for the sisters. Forsyth had turned the radio off. The open line on the mobile phone was being transmitted over sixteen speakers inside the car. It was mostly breathing, sobbing and sighing. They tracked the sisters on the dashboard screen using the satnav. They had links to their phones and the car tracker, in case any of the signals were lost. They stayed at least a mile behind the Lexus, all the way down the motorway towards Exeter. Their own phone was on mute so that the sisters couldn't hear them talk.

"I don't like those two freeloaders," Forsyth said, tapping the steering wheel with her thumb in frustration. "They give hard-working women a bad name. They're a couple of selfish mercenary bitches. Some of us work really hard for a living to pay the bills and all that. Those two want it all and they don't want to work for it."

"I don't trust them either. Something's wrong. There's got to be more to it. They're not telling us the whole story."

"What are you thinking exactly?"

"I'm still trying to figure it out. But we can't leave them now."

They listened patiently to the inside of the gloomy SUV up ahead. As they passed the turn off for Cribbs Causeway near Bristol they heard a mobile ring inside the SUV. Becky was driving as Louise was too distraught. They heard Louise answer it on speaker.

"Hello," Louise said, her voice trembling.

"Where are you?" Sinclair said.

"We've just passed junction seventeen on the M5."

"Are you two alone?"

"Yes."

"When you get to Exeter just keep heading towards Poole." Sinclair hung up.

Forsyth followed using the satnav along the south coast road until they heard Becky's phone ring again.

"Where are you now?" Sinclair said.

"On the A35 towards Poole."

"Look for a hill with a single oak tree on top and a black Range Rover Vogue parked next to it. Then pull over and wait for a man to come to you."

"Where's Amanda?"

"Just do as he says." Sinclair hung up.

The single tree on top of the hill looked like an advertisement to attract people to the peace and quiet of the countryside. Forsyth maintained a safe distance behind the sisters' Lexus. They could hear them talking, their voices booming over the car's speaker system.

"Look, that's it there on the next hill," Becky said.

"What if they have guns?" Louise said.

"We have to do whatever they say until Amanda's safe."

"I should never have kept her in that stupid boarding school. It's all your fault."

"We didn't know this would happen. We had a good plan."

"I should never have listened to you. I knew something like this would happen."

"I thought we were doing what was best for Amanda."

"We could all be in Australia by now. Doing our own thing. Not cooped up together like this. She doesn't need an education with all the money we've got. This is unbelievable."

Becky was crying. Louise shouted random insults and expletives at her as the Lexus parked up behind the black Range Rover on top of the hill near the solitary oak. Forsyth parked her car behind a copse of trees with a view of the hill through some branches. The Range Rover had a vantage point for miles.

Archer watched both cars through the powerful binoculars and heard the sisters talking nervously and intermittently over the stereo.

"Do you think Amanda's in that Range Rover?" Forsyth said, turning towards Archer.

"I think so. There's a good chance it's come straight down from Cheltenham."

Becky continued to cry. Louise continued to rant. It was all Becky's fault; she never wanted to see her again. After a long five minutes the Range Rover doors opened and two thick-set men wearing black balaclavas got out.

CHAPTER SIXTY

Archer watched through the binoculars and Forsyth through the long lens camera as the men climbed out of the black Range Rover. One from the front passenger side and one from the back driver's side. They walked towards the white Lexus, opened the back doors and looked around before they entered it and slammed the doors shut. The open phone line boomed loudly over the speakers inside the Merc.

"Follow our instructions and nobody gets hurt. Follow the Range Rover and don't do anything stupid," Yorkshire said. Archer recognised the voice, the same one from the YouTube video. It was the alpha dog from Tuesday night's encounter in Chelsea. A link between Sinclair and the death threats. ·

"Where's my child?" Louise asked.

"Shut up. Search them," Yorkshire boomed at his burly accomplice.

The door opened. Two phones were thrown out and the car's factory-installed GPS device was ripped out and dumped. Archer switched the link over to follow the only remaining tracker. The spare mobile phone taped inside Becky's boot.

"Looks like there's no exchange taking place," Archer said.

"Not here anyway." Forsyth looked at him knowingly.

"There won't be one."

"Exactly."

The black Range Rover drove off slowly, the white Lexus glued on its tail.

Forsyth followed at least a mile behind. The boot phone was still working as a covert tracking device. But for how much longer?

Archer replayed the Yorkshire accent over and over in his head. A shiver ran down the back of his neck. The cops from the railway bridge on Monday night, DS Lambert and the four mercenaries in the Audi S8 must all be connected to Sinclair and the Boathouse.

They headed east along the south coast towards Poole, past a private airfield, and then turned off the main road and headed south. The roads got progressively narrower and the hedgerows higher as they went further off the beaten track.

Archer pictured the large map of Britain on his touch screen at home and the red dot that signified a potential location near Poole.

"Look, they've stopped again. Pull over," Archer said, tapping the satnav screen on the dashboard. Forsyth pulled over next to a five-bar gate. A herd of cows waited patiently to be milked. She dimmed the lights even though they were at least a mile behind the other cars.

"What's happening?" she said.

"Not sure."

"Shit. We can't see them and we can't hear them."

"Just keep watching the flashing red dot on the satnav."

"They're not going to kill them and dump them out here, are they?"

"Hold on, look, it's moving off to the right. Off the road, onto that shaded area. What does it say on the map? Hold on. It's a private estate – old ruins and disused buildings."

"How close are we to the sea?"

"Less than a mile from here, but the road doesn't exactly follow the coast."

The red flashing dot moved towards the coast and finally stopped next to the sea. Archer took a breath. "Let's go. I think they've just reached the end of the line."

The final destination was on the coast and near Poole. Archer's mouth went dry. The anticipation made his senses feel extra sharp. His heart rate increased, pumping adrenalin. This had to be the secret location of the Boathouse.

Forsyth drove slowly towards the private estate. She braked a few hundred yards from where Becky's tracker had stopped. There was a ten-foot high stone wall with shiny razor wire running along the top. Ahead was the outline of an old building with castellations. They moved forward slowly and saw it was an old stone gatehouse with ivy growing over it. A large stone plaque above the entrance archway was partially clear of ivy and said Tremont Hall. Archer had read about it. It was supposed to be a private old coastal estate in disrepair but the heavy black gates were electric and worked perfectly. Forsyth drove past it slowly, but they could not see anything inside.

She reverse parked the car into the woods, down a small dirt track opposite the estate, invisible from the road. Archer could see no obvious CCTVs in sight and no hint of any concealed security cameras. Forsyth opened the boot remotely and they both got out and walked around to the back of the car.

"I'm going to put some dark clothes on," Forsyth said, then tied her hair in a ponytail.

Archer nodded, took his black beanie hat out of his jacket pocket, put it on and reached inside the boot for his combat rucksack.

They both changed quietly into their own versions of black combat gear as an owl hooted above them in the trees. Forsyth's clothes were fitted and stylish. Archer's functional. He rummaged in the small rucksack for his most trusted pistol. A black Beretta with a customised grip and a shaved hammer to stop it snagging. It was completely untraceable. Its reliability never failed. It gave him the level of confidence he demanded in unknown situations like this. Sinclair's Magnum was also inside the bag with the safety on.

"Want some camouflage paint?" he asked, blackening his face.

"Not good for the skin. I'll watch out for the cameras." She adjusted her black Blade sunglasses and baseball cap, pulling the peak down, making sure it was on tight.

He put his leather jacket back on and slung a small bag across his shoulder. Underneath, he was in his full combat gear and more eager than ever to confront Sinclair.

They crossed the road and walked down the eastern perimeter wall, looking for the best place to get over.

"What about calling for backup?" Forsyth whispered.

"We don't have enough time. We have to go in now over the wall."

Away from the road the trees became thicker and the bushes denser.

"Look," Archer pointed up ahead. "There's an old log we can use to climb the wall."

They manoeuvred the heavy old branch towards the wall and rested it against the masonry at an angle. They climbed up and got a foothold, enough to reach the top of the wall, where a cast-iron sign said Private Property. It was one of many fixed to the wall every fifty yards or so.

"Private Property. We know what that really means now," Forsyth said.

"Shit, there's a car coming. Get down, quick." Archer jumped off the log, grabbed Forsyth and pulled her down into a squat position next to him.

"It's slowing down. Must be going inside."

They hid behind the bushes and heard the electric gates clank open. The black Audi S8 passed through the gatehouse into the estate. The windows were too dark to see who was inside. Despite the different numberplate, the sound of the twelve-cylinder engine gave it away. Archer knew it was the car from Tuesday night.

A text arrived from Zoe:

Just run GRID with GPS: Hunter was right!
Get out now! CIA torture facility!

CHAPTER SIXTY-ONE

The gates slammed shut and the powerful twelve-cylinder car sped off inside the dark estate. Archer felt the adrenalin surging through his body. He looked at Forsyth as she checked her own gun, a sturdy Glock 9 mm. She had been an unexpectedly good partner, but he couldn't let her risk her life for him, not now, not here.

"Let's go," she said.

"No. I can't allow you to take the risk."

"What are you talking about? It's my choice."

"Look, Sarah, I can't put anyone else's life at risk. Not for my own personal crusade."

"What about saving Becky and Louise?"

"There's more to it than that. It's about me and Sinclair and you know it."

"Okay. I know that. But those stupid sisters both knew what they were up against too. They're a pair of deadbeats, and I wouldn't risk my life for them, but you can't do this alone. I'm choosing to help you. So I'm coming with you whether you like it or not."

"No. Look, I'm touched. You've been amazing, but I'm sorry. I can't let you do it. I can't let anything happen to you like it did to Alex. Stay on this side of the wall. Walk the perimeter and see what's happening across the other side over there where the lights are coming from. But stay hidden and don't get caught. You may need to call the cavalry if anything goes wrong."

"What are you going to do?"

"Just recon, so don't worry. We'll meet back at the car, in exactly one hour."

"Okay, one hour. Keep me posted by text and be careful."

She kissed him on the lips and gave him a spontaneous hug, squeezing him tight like she didn't want to let him go. He climbed back up the old log and stood on top of it as the moon broke through the clouds. He took his leather jacket off and threw it over the spirals of shiny razor wire. He looked down and saw her watching him. There was no one else around inside or out and no cameras. The estate looked completely deserted except for a sodium glow about a mile away in the far corner.

He slowly pulled himself up, shimmied over the jacket on top of the wall, threw his feet over the edge and jumped onto the soft grass below, landing in a squat position. He took a breath and stood up slowly. He was on his own now. Inside the grounds without any proper backup or support, but he couldn't involve Forsyth any further. His jacket snagged on the razor wire and ripped as he pulled it down by a dangling arm. He cursed and put it back on but it was badly torn in the front. He didn't worry about material things and normally he would have just left it there, but it was special. It was his last present from Alex.

In the distance he could see the outline of an old country house. It looked to be in monumental disrepair. Between him and the house he could make out a wire security fence. He walked towards the fence, constantly looking around in all directions. There were no lights to be seen in this dark corner of the estate. It was cloudy, but the moonlight enabled him to see where he was going.

He tried to make sense of the situation, but couldn't focus on anything except Sinclair and the Boathouse. He headed for the old building across the long grass, avoiding thick clumps of tall spiky thistles. The ground was uneven with molehills and rabbit holes making it slow going. He could feel the wind on his face and hear the sea crashing against the rocks in the distance. The air was fresh and he could taste the salt from the sea.

He couldn't stop thinking about the Audi S8. Who had been in it just now? Why had they come here tonight? Archer's head was still spinning at the thought that Sinclair was the person he had spent fourteen months looking for.

The Boathouse had to be here somewhere. The reason Alex had been killed. The clandestine location about which people he had pursued were too afraid to talk.

The wire fence was six feet high with four parallel strands of barbed wire running above it. He took a small pair of snips from his bag. There was no sign of it being electrified. He touched it quickly to check it. No shock.

He cut the diamond shaped wires next to a galvanised metal post from the ground to about half way up and put the snips back in his bag. He crouched and crawled on all fours through the loosened corner of the fence. It must have rained earlier as the grass was still damp.

Once inside the first fence he had no idea about who or what to expect next.

He looked around, but there was nobody in sight, so he kept walking towards the large ruined building.

A dog barked in the distance, from near the cliff edge. It barked again. The sound was getting louder.

He grabbed his razor-sharp survival knife from its ankle holder. It felt familiar and comforting. His grandmother's ex-Mossad friend had spent days teaching him how to use it.

He crouched down on one knee and looked towards the approaching sound. The wind picked up, the cloud broke. A charging Rottweiler leapt towards his head, slobbering jaws wide open, ready to sink its sharp teeth into his neck.

Archer ducked to one side and drove the sharp serrated knife deep into its throat, still in mid-air. He twisted it ninety degrees and pulled it straight back out. The dog yelped at the initial impact of the blade before crashing into a dead heap on the ground with a dull lifeless thud. Archer wiped the knife on his thigh and slid it back into its holder. Normally he liked dogs, but not killer dogs, and especially not killer Rottweilers.

He looked around. No more dogs. No more sounds except the sea crashing tirelessly into the rocks, the wind lashing the coast and his heart pounding inside his ribcage. He took a deep breath to steel himself and carried on walking towards the large building until he heard shouting in the distance.

It was either the dog handler or a roving guard out looking for the dog on foot. Archer crouched down next to a tall thistle and waited. The shouts came closer. He fell flat on his stomach as the clouds broke and the direct moonlight threatened to expose him. He could hear the guard heading straight for him.

He sprang up and tackled the guard from the side, knocking him over and landing on top of his muscular thigh. The guard was quick. He had a gun out, pointed at Archer's head. It was a fight for survival. He moved and placed his boot against Archer's neck and told him to get up. Archer moved back slightly, putting both his hands up head high.

"It's not me you need to worry about, it's him," he said.

The guard flinched and looked sideways with his eyes. Archer kicked the gun out of the guard's hand and pulled out his survival knife. In one swift move he threw it quickly and confidently into the guard's neck. It pierced straight through the cartilage of his Adam's apple. Archer pulled his knife out, causing the guard's neck wound to gurgle with blood as the man's last breath escaped.

He wiped the warm blood off the knife onto his thigh and put it back in the ankle holder. He'd killed before, but never an innocent man. His senses sharpened, but he felt no remorse. It was too late to turn back now and he had no intention of doing so.

He explored the external wall of the old ruined building, which was boarded up. He put his ear to one of the boards and listened. No sound, not even bats. He walked towards the back and found a large metal tank next to a brick outbuilding with yellow warning signs: high voltage electricity. It reeked of diesel. It was the fuel tank for an emergency generator. He took out a plastic explosive charge and detonator from the bag on his back. It looked like a small tin of shoe polish and was magnetic. He stuck it on the tank next to the outlet manifold.

The outbuilding was a sub-station with a sturdy grey metal door which was locked. Next to it was a green metal fence surrounding heavy-duty electrical equipment. Inside the fence was a transformer the size of a garden shed. Humming away with a low-frequency electrical buzz.

He ripped a branch off one of the bushes planted to hide the fence. Wedged another charge into the branch, held it over the fence and lowered it gently onto the transformer, next to one of three large antennae sticking out of the top. He then went around the back of the building and saw bright lights and a dozen or more buildings four hundred yards away towards the west, next to the coast.

The buildings were a mixture of old green hangars and portable grey cabins inside a high-security fence, similar to the ones used at power stations. Archer noticed there were several cars and Land Rovers parked inside. The Audi S8 was there too. Off to the left just inside the compound was a track and a path that crossed it leading down towards the sea.

He stayed in the shadows away from the lights, which meant keeping close to the cliff edge. He hated walking near sheer drops in case his demons tempted him. As he got closer to the fence he could see that it was electric and well lit with cameras on tall metal posts.

He peered over the edge of the cliff and saw a ledge ten feet down. The ledge was narrow but constant. He climbed down and braced himself as he edged his way along with his back pressed hard against the rock face. He seemed to be moving in slow motion. His heart rate increased and his breathing became shallow. His vision narrowed and went black and white. He fought it. Now was not a good time to have a panic attack. If he blacked out now he was a dead man. If the fall didn't kill him then the waves would smash him to pieces. He took a deep breath and focused on staying alive.

Facing out to sea there was nothing to break the wind that hit him full in his face, which was starting to go numb. His lips tasted salty from the sea. The south-west wind was straight off the Atlantic. Only sea, wind and rain for thousands of miles until America.

The bay on his right-hand side had a deep scoop out of the high cliffs with a concrete road leading somewhere out of sight. He looked down and saw the surf crash and surge all around craggy black arms of volcanic rock. He felt himself being pulled towards the hypnotic draw of the sea. He caught himself just in time – instinctively pushing his shoulder bag and his back hard into the cliff.

He continued until he was past the electric fence. As he looked up he could see it overhanging the top of the cliff above him. He edged his way around a sharp rock and saw the steep rocky bay into which the sea was rolling and foaming. He climbed down to a narrow path and followed it around a slow bend. A Land Rover Defender was parked next to an old grey building. Archer headed towards it with purpose. Drawn to it like steel to a magnet.

This was it. A disused lifeboat station with a steep rusty-looking slipway going down into the stormy sea. He'd finally found the Boathouse.

All kinds of thoughts rushed around inside his head as he walked towards it, but all he wanted to do was break down and weep. This rusty old building housed the reason why Alex had been killed.

It began to rain. The Atlantic Ocean made its formidable presence known. The wind and rain lashed him as he continued to descend a succession of steep pathways until he reached the gun-metal grey Land Rover. There was not much room to pass between the cliff face on one side and the sheer drop on the other. The sea crashed against the rocks below and he decided to pass it on the safer side next to the rock. He squeezed through the gap and stood between the vehicle and the Boathouse. The door was ten feet in front of him. It opened slowly with the sound of rusty hinges creaking and a guard filling the doorframe.

For a moment that seemed to last for an age they simply stared at each other. Trying to figure out the next move. Tactically waiting for the other one to move first.

"Who are you?"

"I do spot checks for Mr Sinclair," Archer said confidently, despite feeling tense.

"Nobody told me."

"It's a test."

"I'll have to radio this in."

"I can't let you do that, I'm afraid."

As the guard walked up to him he pulled out his radio. Archer snatched it from his hand and threw it over the edge. The guard rushed at him and threw a slow punch, but Archer ducked and hit him in the stomach. The guard reeled at first, but then he bent forward and charged at Archer, headbutting him in the stomach and knocking the wind out of him.

He was pressed against the front of the solid Land Rover. The guard grabbed Archer around the neck and pushed him towards the cliff edge. Archer managed to turn, but the guard slipped. He grabbed at Archer, causing them both to fall to the ground. They wrestled and grappled at the edge of the cliff. Archer headbutted him and kicked him in the knee. The guard fell back and his legs dangled over the edge. He grabbed Archer's legs to save himself, but his momentum took the rest of his body over. Archer tried to kick him off, but the guard's grip was too strong. Archer felt himself falling forward as the man's whole bodyweight pulled him over the edge. Archer fell feet first and they both slid towards the sea over loose rocks.

The guard fell over fifty feet to the foaming sea and jagged rocks below. Archer fell ten feet and his shoulder landed hard on the narrow rocky ledge, then his head hit the rock.

CHAPTER SIXTY-TWO

He woke up on the ledge with the sea crashing hard against the black rocks below. He felt as cold as death, as cold as the icy wind battering him and fuelling the damp that had crawled inside his bones. A deep chill had crept along the back of his skull and down his spine. His ribs hurt. His ears rang. Even his eyelids ached. They felt as if they were made of lead. They opened slightly, but then clanked shut again from the sting of the salty sea air. For a moment he didn't know where he was or what had happened, but as the rain lashed into his face it all slowly came back to him like a bad dream.

The noise in his head still resonated like thunder, echoing around his brain. A dull ache throbbed inside his jaw. He clenched his teeth together to try and stop the pain, then tried to open his mouth, but it was too painful. His left cheek and his top lip were sore. He touched his face and felt a sliver of skin that had been ripped right off. The scar being washed clean by the rain.

His predicament threatened to crush him into submission. He was balancing precariously on the edge of a vertical cliff face. Teetering on a ledge with a sheer death drop beneath him. Down on the black ragged rocks below, the livid sea was frothing away like a boiling cauldron. Battering the dark cliffs with a thunderous fanfare that was already pounding a dead man into a bloody pulp.

But he had no urge to jump. He refused to give in. Breathing in slowly and calmly, he summoned up sufficient courage from somewhere deep inside. He consciously took a moment to find a reason to survive. Conscious of his past and what he still had to do. He dug deep and felt a powerful will to live – he wasn't going to give in now that he was so close. His adrenalin kicked in and gave him added strength.

He looked up and saw a sheer wet rock face. There was no doubt that it would be a perilous climb. His heart sank briefly, but he fought the dread and self-doubt.

With effort, he straightened back up and ignored the pain. He was physically shaken and his skin was scratched, but he was not seriously injured.

Everything still worked well enough to climb. There was an abseiling rope dangling from the old Boathouse, but he couldn't get to it. The cliff face between the ledge and the rope looked like a sheet of glass.

The only way to survive was to climb straight back up. Flashes of lightning lit the bay like a strobe light and thunder rumbled overhead.

Archer found a foothold in a crevice that seemed to run all the way to the top. He grabbed inside it and pushed himself up with one leg and pulled with one arm, then found another hold for his left leg on a nub of rock sticking out.

He fought and struggled for hand- and footholds, but slowly made progress with either a foot or a hand slipping occasionally, but managing to save himself with the other. Somehow he clawed his way back up the rock face to reach the edge. Once he pulled himself over the top he lay on his front for a moment of sheer relief before he got up and found his bag.

He was completely drenched to the skin. The rain was stinging his bruised and scarred face. He opened the creaky Boathouse door and went inside. His joints ached as he walked, but he fought back the only way he knew how: he simply kept moving forward.

The rain lashed hard against the metal walls and roof. Its volume grew louder until it sounded like a water cannon. Archer cleared his wet eyes with his fingers and saw a grey lifeboat facing a steep incline down to the sea below. It looked as if someone had been working on the boat as there were red tool chests on wheels and an assortment of spanners sprawled over the floor.

He walked to the back and found a sliding grey steel door. He pulled the metal lever towards him and slowly pulled the rusty door open just enough to look inside. It revealed a wide corridor carved into the rock and lit only by dim safety lighting at ground level. The corridor went deep into the cliff in the direction of the hangars. It felt cold and smelt of mouldy decay and damp. Archer guessed it must be the entrance to a tunnel that linked the Boathouse with the compound above. He went inside and the sprung door startled him as it slammed shut behind him.

The tunnel hummed with high-voltage electricity. He followed it for over a hundred yards and found another grey steel door with a long lever. He pushed the lever down, opening the door on to a dimly lit but even wider corridor. It looked empty so he continued. The corridor had dark murky holding cells on the right-hand side. Ten foot by ten foot squares with thick glass fronts. Each cell had an LED screen and a glass tank of coiled-up snakes.

The last cell had a light above it which created a mirror effect in the glass. Archer looked at himself in the reflection. He looked like hell. His face was dark, puffed with scars and sore with bruises. Dark dried blood was smeared all over the remains of the camouflage paint. He'd lost his beanie in the fall. His hair was thoroughly messed up. He looked away. However bad he looked it wasn't as bad as he felt.

At the end of the corridor there was another grey steel door with a vertical steel ladder fixed to the wall next to it. The door was locked. A small sign on it said Equipment Room. The ladder accessed a metal catwalk overhead. It seemed to provide maintenance access to all the exposed pipes and cables up above.

He climbed the ladder and walked along the catwalk towards a large air duct. He was directly above the equipment room. There was a grille in the ceiling beneath the catwalk. He lay flat on his stomach and could see inside. It was full of electronic equipment in tall racks: communications hardware, network servers and CCTV recorders. He dislodged the grille enough to get his hand through and dropped another shoe-polish-sized charge on top of the nearest rack.

He heard the faint sound of people talking. He got back up and walked towards a large air vent in the wall with slats angled away from him at forty-five degrees.

Somewhere on the other side of the wall a door slammed. The muffled voices grew louder. He looked through the slats into the space below. A droplet of sweat ran down his forehead and stung his left eye. He wiped it and took a deep breath.

There was a much larger room on the other side of the wall. It was like a warehouse with a ramp up to ground level inside what appeared to be one of the hangars. A dozen people were talking in one area and moving equipment on pallet trucks in another. There were cameras on tripods and huge portable lighting rigs on hydraulic arms and wheels.

A stocky bald man in a dark suit dished out orders like a sergeant major on parade.

"Five minutes, everybody out except the medics," he shouted.

Objects were wheeled around frantically. Lights flashed on and off and the area was chaotic until all but three of the men in sight went up the ramp and a noisy roller shutter door at the top descended slowly, shutting them all out.

As the area was being prepared Archer found he had a mobile phone signal and managed an exchange of texts with Forsyth. She was now inside the perimeter and more determined than ever to help him. He wasn't sure if she could manage it. But she had climbed and abseiled; he remembered the photo behind her desk of her climbing a glacier. The area suddenly went quiet. The lights were dimmed down to darkness. A large fan whirred somewhere on the other side of the air vent. There was a high-voltage hum and a pulsating vibration through the structure.

Archer felt hot and agitated. His mouth was dry and he sucked a lungful of air down fast as he'd subconsciously been holding his breath. It was the familiar onset of a panic attack. But what had triggered it? He thought about sitting in his steam room, meditating, controlling his breathing. It was helping. He closed his eyes and focused, taking long deep breaths and then breathing out slowly. It was working.

"Ready," the sergeant major shouted. "Three, two, one."

Spotlights lit up more glass-fronted cells. Each appeared to have different types of equipment inside. An old grey-haired man in a white coat walked into one of the cells. Inside was a large cylindrical metal tank painted grey. Archer watched him press a large red button on the side of the tank. The top lifted slowly to one side on hydraulic pistons. Two men in white coats appeared next to him. He whispered something and they leaned over the tank and reached down into it.

Becky Sinclair was pulled from inside the main body of the tank. Archer realised that it was a Sensory Deprivation Chamber. She wore an orange tracksuit without shoes and she was soaking wet. Her body was limp and she was beginning to regain consciousness. The men placed her in a wheelchair and walked out. The older man in the white coat wheeled her out of the cell. Her hair and tracksuit dripped a trail of water as he wheeled her to a large ugly-looking wooden chair beneath a bright spotlight, and then walked away. Two men in white coats lifted her from the wheelchair to the wooden chair and strapped her waist, ankles and wrists to the chair.

"I'll take it from here," a man out of view said. "You're sitting on an exact replica of Old Sparky."

Archer's hackles rose. He recognised the sinister tones before the speaker wandered into view. Peter Sinclair was inside the Boathouse.

One of the medics in white coats fastened a metal dome to Becky's head and another wheeled over a trolley with some sort of transformer unit on it. Another medic attached cables to the unit and then to the chair. He pulled a lever and the unit buzzed and lit up, revealing a large round dial and an analogue meter.

"So, my dear, you've experienced some of our facilities first-hand. A relaxing spell in the isolation chamber. Plenty of time to think, as it were. But before I ask you if you've made your decision, I want to show you something." He turned around and yelled. "Where's the bloody hangman?"

Muffled shouts. Then a man dressed in black with a sub-zero balaclava over his head appeared holding a wired-up winch control unit. Another spotlight went up left of the cells and the others slowly dimmed. A large mechanical rig appeared with two orange figures standing beneath it.

Louise and Amanda Palmer stood six feet apart with their heads bowed. Both wore orange tracksuits and white trainers. Their hands were tied behind their backs with rope. Dazed looks on their pale faces showed that they were not fully registering the situation.

Their raven hair still in tight ponytails. Slumped lifeless shoulders and weak legs bent at the knees. The pinstriped sergeant major stood next to them, unarmed, but there were now two men with guns standing four feet behind him.

Louise and Amanda each had a thick hangman's noose tied around their necks. The other end of the thick rope was tied to a yellow steel hook attached to a mechanical winch on a large yellow steel beam above. Archer couldn't believe what he was seeing. He felt sick.

"Pull the ropes tighter. One at a time," Sinclair barked.

The hangman operated the winch control. He pressed a button and the electric motor whirred as the noose slowly tightened around Louise's neck until she was on her tiptoes. Then the second winch did the same until Amanda was straining to stop from swinging.

"Shall we rape them first or simply hang them?" Sinclair said.

He laughed mockingly at Becky. His laughter echoed around the huge room.

"Let's hang them and be done with it," he said, with a harder edge.

Both winches tightened simultaneously. Both bodies left the ground until they started swinging from their necks, wriggling human pendulums. After several seconds he signalled to the hangman. The winches were reversed and the bodies dropped to the ground where they slumped into lifeless heaps.

Archer didn't like Louise, but she didn't deserve to be tortured, and her innocent daughter was only seventeen. The thought that people were being tortured on UK soil was hard to imagine, let alone believe, but here was the proof. It was disgusting.

Another yellow gantry rig moved into place above Becky and the hangman stood next to the wooden electric chair, taunting her with his noose. She spat in his face.

"Now, now," he said.

"Fuck you."

"Calm down, you old slag."

"Fuck off. You fucking twat."

Sinclair nodded and a medic slowly turned the electric dial. Becky started to shake and then convulse uncontrollably with a low guttural scream. When it stopped she slumped to one side. The medic unfastened the dome and straps and threw a bucket of water over her.

The hangman dropped the noose on the end of the winch. He carefully tightened the noose around her neck and pressed the winch controls until it took up all the slack in the rope. Sinclair nodded at him and he continued to raise the rope. Becky stood up as the rope slowly tightened until she was on tiptoes and it stopped abruptly with a loud clunk.

"Now then, my dear, what's your final answer? Yes or no?"

He looked at her like she was a piece of rotten meat.

"All right, you impotent prick. Yes."

Sinclair beamed.

"Let her down and bring her with me."

Sinclair casually strolled up the ramp like he was perusing around a museum on a Saturday afternoon, with Becky being dragged after him by two medics, a few paces behind.

"Put them back in the cell. You know what to do with them," Sergeant major said.

Louise and Amanda were untied, picked up and carried away, coughing and spluttering over the shoulders of two guards. Archer let out his breath. The steel door beneath him opened and he saw them being carried fireman-style towards the empty cells. They were both dumped in one and the glass door was locked. The guards smoked cigarettes and stared at them like morons at a zoo. They sounded like they were from Atlanta.

216

"What's happening with these two folks?" one said.

"We keep them down here for a couple days, do some psychological experiments on them, and then dump them at sea," the other replied, unfazed, as if completely bored by it all.

"How do you know all that?"

"Seen it all hundreds of times. You'll get used to it."

A deafening buzzer sounded around the public address system.

"Code red alert. Repeat, code red alert. All guards report to the command centre immediately. We have an intruder between the primary and the secondary fence. Two guards are down. The intruder may be armed. All guards report to the command centre."

"This intruder must be a real space cadet. There's over forty armed guards in here."

"What an idiot."

The guards ran through the steel door and up the ramp to the hangar compound, leaving the cell locked but the area unguarded. Archer knew the odds of escaping were against him. And decreasing as rapidly as the seconds ticking away on his Luminox watch.

CHAPTER SIXTY-THREE

Archer swiftly climbed down the vertical steel ladder and ran over to the cell holding Louise and Amanda. For a moment he simply stood still and stared through the thick glass wall. Two lifeless prisoners waiting to die on death row. Their bewildered look of hopelessness stared back at him, red raw rope burns visible around their necks. Their pale expressionless faces failed to acknowledge him. The life and soul had been completely drained out of them.

"Can you two walk?"

They stood up wearily and nodded. They looked cold and numb. He could tell they were still in shock. They could barely stand up. Amanda nearly passed out, but caught herself in time. At least they weren't hysterical, but they would be slower than normal.

"Stand back."

Louise and Amanda shifted awkwardly to the back of the cell and Archer shot the lock off with his Beretta. The thick glass door slowly swung open.

"Follow me. We have to move fast, we haven't got much time left." He spoke calmly, but fully aware that Sinclair's men could come back any second.

He led them back through the corridor. Back down the dimly lit tunnel towards the Boathouse and the waiting lifeboat. Their weak legs caused them to stumble and fall, but Archer kept picking them up and dragging them forward as they sobbed and choked. He fumbled in his bag and took out a small remote control device with four red buttons. He pressed the first button. No explosion would be heard from inside the tunnel. He just hoped it had worked. The diesel tank exploding would throw the guards off his tail for a short while, but he sensed it was only a fragile advantage. He needed to keep moving.

He pulled the lever, opened the heavy steel door and saw Forsyth waiting for him on the other side. She must have got down to the beach and climbed the abseil rope as planned.

"You got here then. Any problems?"

"My hair's a bit messy."

"Look after these two. I'll get the boat ready."

The two women were too weak to climb into the lifeboat. Archer and Forsyth had to lift them up into it one at a time. It wasted valuable seconds. Archer's injuries made him jolt with sharp bolts of pain. He rested on the stern for a second. His tired muscles burned. Forsyth took them down below deck and strapped them into their seats.

"You sure this tub still works? It looks completely knackered to me," Forsyth shouted from down below.

"We're about to find out. If it doesn't we'll call the coastguard."

Archer looked down below. Louise and Amanda held onto each other. They looked terrified. Forsyth climbed into the navigator's chair and strapped herself to it. Archer jumped down off the stern and opened the Boathouse doors wide enough for the boat to get through. He stumbled around the portable tool chests as he prepared to launch. He closed the grey steel door that led back into the tunnel and wedged the door lever shut with a rusty but sturdy-looking steel bar and yanked the handle to check – it felt secure.

He climbed up the wooden ladder into the boat and strapped himself into the helm. He took aim and shot the red launch button on the wall with his Beretta to save time, but nothing happened. He shot it again. Still nothing. He cursed to himself under his breath. The automatic release mechanism didn't work.

"You're a shit shot, Archer."

"I'll have to do it manually."

The grey steel door to the tunnel started shaking. He could hear muffled clanking and shouting on the other side. Automatic weapons started firing at the door. The noise was deafening, but the bullets didn't penetrate the thick steel plate.

Archer pressed two more red buttons on the remote. The first sounded like a firework exploding in the distance. The second much louder, causing the tunnel door to shake. Then the main lights went out, leaving only a dim glow from the battery-powered emergency lights.

Archer unstrapped himself and jumped out of the boat. He looked around for something heavy to release the catch holding the lifeboat in place.

A shadow appeared from the doorway leading back outside to the Land Rover.

"Hands up, Archer. You're meat." It had a Yorkshire accent.

Archer was partially behind the boat. He ducked behind it and out of the line of fire, pulling out his Beretta.

"Don't be stupid, Archer. You're outnumbered, we're way out of your league. Don't you realise where you are? You should have listened. We told you to back off on Tuesday. We killed your pretty girlfriend, Alex. I got to know her and fucked her a few times before I killed her. She was always gagging for it." The man's thin lips twitched before curling into an arrogant smile.

Archer quickly climbed onto the front of the boat. He saw a reflection on a shiny yellow oil drum. Someone was moving around the back of the boat. He stood up slowly, pointing his gun where he thought Yorkshire would be. As he gained height he could just see the top of somebody's head. If he didn't get the first shot right he was a dead man. He aimed instinctively, his body raised just enough to clear the cabin.

The bullet went in through Yorkshire's left ear. Blood sprayed instantly from the exit wound and splattered red arcs over the grey wall. Yorkshire's body slumped to the ground knocking over a small diesel jerry can. The can clanked hard against the concrete floor, spilling diesel towards six yellow oil drums.

Archer picked up a heavy sledgehammer leaning against a tool box and smashed the rusty steel hook holding the boat in position at the top of the slipway. He jumped back on the boat and held onto the rails as every muscle burned with the effort.

The lifeboat creaked and groaned loudly as it began to move. Archer searched the stern and found a box of flares. He fumbled around and took one out as the boat hit the slipway. He pulled the pin out and it lit up like a Roman candle.

He threw the flare back through the doorway at the diesel spill. The fuel vapour caught fire as the boat rapidly built up speed and glided noisily as it descended down the steep slipway and crashed into the raging sea. Louise and Amanda sobbed uncontrollably as the waves engulfed the boat in water. The boat popped back up and then rocked and rolled with the swell as the waves crashed over the deck.

Archer was drenched, but managed to get back to the helm and strap himself into the captain's seat. Forsyth was holding her head. She must have banged it when the boat hit the water. She was still holding on tight, but looked pale and worried.

Archer looked behind and saw the Boathouse engulfed in flames. He heard the familiar sound of automatic gunfire. A stream of bullets ripped into the front of the boat, tearing chunks out of the grey fibreglass nose. It bobbed around without propulsion like a dying duck about to be slaughtered.

The heavy rain and waves continued to bombard the windscreen, but the lightning had passed. The worst of the storm was over. He pressed the small red button which generated an electric starter motor, followed by a deep rumble as the twin Volvo diesel engines kicked in and spluttered to life first time. Finally some good luck.

"Thank God for that. I thought we were stuffed." Her face was white.

"Hold tight. Let's see what this rust bucket can do."

He pushed both throttles fully forward and grabbed the small wheel. The screw propellers generated enough thrust to make the boat stand up at forty degrees as they headed out towards open water, leaving a chevron-shaped wake of churned water behind them.

Archer looked back at the rocky bay. The guards had fled the growing flames. They stood behind the Land Rover, MP-5 machine guns pointed down at the ground. They had given up shooting. The boat was out of range for their automatic weapons. Archer prayed they didn't have any rocket launchers. He heard an explosion and hoped it wasn't a missile. He looked back at the Boathouse. It was a fireball, engulfing the Land Rover. One of the guards was on fire and jumped over the cliff as the Land Rover's diesel tank exploded and the flaming vehicle crashed down into the sea.

Archer kept cruising at full speed towards open water for two miles. Mindful that they might come after him with another boat. When the shore looked far enough away he reduced speed and cruised slowly towards the row of lights that he took to be Poole Harbour.

Forsyth went and explored below deck and found a couple of red blankets to wrap around Louise and Amanda's shoulders. She then did the same for Archer and herself at the helm. She also found a bottle of Martell brandy and poured some into four enamel mugs.

"Medicine," she told the silent recipients.

Archer left the helm set on autopilot and checked that Louise and Amanda were unharmed. They finished their brandies and he told them to lie down on the bunks until they found a safe place to dock. He returned to the cockpit and checked the sonar and radar. They had clear depth, no sand banks nearby and no other vessels in the area. They headed towards Poole Harbour, but needed to dock somewhere quieter to avoid any unnecessary attention. They checked the local charts and headed for an old, disused jetty.

In less than an hour they were tied off alongside the derelict jetty, which was even quieter than Archer had hoped. There was no sign of anyone. No boats. No fishermen or late-night dog walkers. The lights of the town began half a mile down the road. They had both worn gloves so there was no need to clean up any fingerprints. They disembarked in the moonlight. It was the ideal place to abandon the damaged boat without being spotted. Without the bilge pumps working the bullet holes would scuttle it before sunrise.

Archer told Louise to book into a local hotel and get some proper rest, but she had regained enough energy to get her headstrong personality back. She said she was going to find a taxi which would take them to Oxford. From there she would hire another taxi to return to the cottage in Stow on the Wold. Archer offered her some money but she wouldn't accept it. She told him to leave her alone and stay out of her way. She said that she could charge anything she wanted to her business accounts with one simple phone call.

Louise and Amanda stumbled off towards the lights of Poole in matching orange tracksuits and white trainers without saying goodbye.

"Ungrateful bitch. Not a word of thanks," Forsyth said.

"Let her go. She won't listen. She's heading for trouble. At least we don't have to babysit her now. She's not our problem any more."

"What about Becky?"

"We still have to get her out."

She touched his arm and looked him in the eye. "You're going back for her tonight?"

"I can do it alone. I don't want you getting hurt."

"Bit late to tell me that. I'm not leaving you now. If anything bad happens to me don't feel guilty about it."

"You don't have to come."

"I know. Look, I may need your help one day."

"Are you sure you know exactly where Sinclair's place is?"

"Of course. Come on, let's see if the ferry's still running, otherwise it's twenty-five miles to get around. What makes you so sure he'll be there?"

"He's taken Becky with him, but I don't think he would take her back to London. He'll take her somewhere quiet."

"Like his house on Sandbanks."

"Exactly."

CHAPTER SIXTY-FOUR

The storm had subsided into a breezy drizzle and the waves diminished into calmer wavelets. They caught the last ferry to Sandbanks with only two cars on board and a small group of foot passengers. The weary-looking couple attempted to blend into the background as some post-dinner revellers laughed and joked. But they stood out as their clothes were drenched and they were wounded. They told a concerned passenger that they had fallen while hiking and huddled together in the shadows, pretending to be on their way home.

Most nights around this time Archer was out pounding the streets alone next to the Thames trying to get tired enough to sleep. He had been running from his past as well as pursuing it for years. Tonight he had a strange feeling that somehow he was closer to unravelling it than ever before.

The ferry docked onto the Sandbanks peninsula with a soft bump after only four minutes. The two cars disembarked first and the other foot passengers headed off to the right. Forsyth struck out to the left away from the beach. The rain had stopped but the ground was still wet and the road was full of puddles.

"Property per square foot on here is more expensive than New York's Fifth Avenue."

"How do you know that?"

"My husband nearly bought a place here but chose Jersey instead."

"Tax benefits?"

"Exactly."

The leaves rustled in the breeze. The lane was deserted. The houses were set back in large pristine gardens. Most houses were dark, but some still had lights on upstairs. Forsyth pointed towards the house at the end of the road. It was a mansion lit up like Las Vegas.

"You sure that's the one? It's not a beach house."

"Of course I'm sure. He has a gin palace moored behind it."

"Have you been here before then?"

"Sandbanks yes, but not to his house."

"How do you know it's his?"

"I'm a detective. I've seen pictures. I know about his properties. Just like I know that his brother has an even bigger place on Star Island."

"Star Island? Where's that?"

"Miami."

They walked down the lane. The white stucco mansion had an ornate green-tiled roof and Georgian windows. Surrounded by manicured Italian gardens with clusters of cypress and palm trees, the house could have been plucked straight off the cliff top at Cap Ferrat. All that was missing was a cascade of terraces leading to the azure sparkle of the Mediterranean Sea.

They stopped at the perimeter wall and looked around, checking that no one else was about.

"Follow me down here to the water."

They took a narrow, unlit path between two six-foot-high brick walls. Trees from properties on either side covered them from view. The moon was casting more light since the clouds had changed from black to grey. Its reflection on the water was visible at the end of the descending path.

Forsyth waded up to her knees to get around a galvanised metal security fence jutting out into the water. He followed her as she climbed onto a long pontoon that rose and fell with the tide. At the end was a ramp which moved with the pontoon up to a wooden jetty.

The fixed jetty led to the back of the property alongside two boat bays. They slowly climbed the steep wooden steps, timing the creaking of the timber with the clanking and groaning of the pontoon until they could see inside the grounds.

Archer noticed the nearest boat bay was empty, but the second boasted a sixty-foot luxury yacht with only the top deck visible. They climbed down into the empty bay and walked along another pontoon until they reached metal stairs at the end nearest the house.

He led the way up the stairs until he could see what was happening. Two men were talking against a whirring mechanical sound. They stood with their backs to him only twenty feet away beside a large swimming pool. The mechanical pool cover was being retracted to reveal a well-lit pool, with clouds of water vapour rising off it. Beyond the pool a man with white hair sat on the terrace smoking a cigar beside two large patio heaters.

Archer recognised him instantly. Peter Sinclair was as relaxed as a lord comfortably admiring his estate. One of the men at the pool moved away. Sinclair rose and walked towards the second man. He turned briefly to the side to watch the pool cover finish retracting. Archer recognised the man's profile from the penthouse. It was Clarke.

"The grounds are clear, sir. Haywood just checked them thoroughly."

"Keep the front gate manned. I need to have absolute privacy for an hour or two. Then we have a long night ahead of us. I'll buzz you when I'm ready."

"We'll be ready whenever you are, sir."

Clarke walked towards the side of the house, through a white painted gate, disappearing from view. Sinclair puffed his cigar several times before he walked back to the terrace. He left the cigar smouldering in an ashtray on the terrace table, opened the French doors and entered the house.

Archer looked for cameras and security lights then gave a thumbs-up sign to Forsyth as soon as he spotted a secure way to get to the house. They left the yacht bay and took a long perimeter route amongst the trees and bushes until they reached the far side of the terrace, thirty feet from the French doors. Looking through the windows along the terrace they quietly manoeuvred towards the door. Sinclair had absent-mindedly left it ajar a few inches.

The topiary screens next to the glass doors provided cover, the patio heaters an unexpected but welcome heat. Inside the house Sinclair was talking to someone. A female voice replied – it was Becky.

CHAPTER SIXTY-FIVE

The large entertainment area was opulent with colourful Picasso- and Hockney-style art hung on dark mahogany panelled walls above over-sized dark brown leather furniture. The circular log fire in the centre gave it a continental chalet feel, but the finishes seemed more in line with a luxury yacht than a house. It had a bar and home cinema, providing functional facilities for entertaining. An oversized fish tank lit with ultraviolet lights was the main showpiece between the bar and the seating area. The polished mahogany bar was high end with a samurai sword on display behind it. Sinclair placed an extra log on the fire while Becky sat on the huge sofa facing the fire and the bar.

Archer could see the side of her face. She was still wearing the orange tracksuit from the Boathouse, along with shiny cream stilettos.

"I couldn't care less about Louise. We're finished for good this time. She doesn't care about me, I don't care about her, so that's that. It's always got to be her way. She's just like you. That's why the two of you never got on," Becky was saying angrily.

"You rinse me for millions over the years, then you plan this revolting hoax and rob me blind with ransom threats. I was genuinely worried about you."

"You're such a liar. That's absolute bullshit and you know it. You were only worried in case it made you look stupid. You only care about yourself."

"Why did you do it to me?"

"Because I found out you were going to get rid of me."

"You found out I was going to divorce you?"

"Not divorce me. Have me killed."

"Bullshit."

"So you could marry a younger woman. I know all about it."

Sinclair looked down at the floor and thoughtfully stroked his neatly trimmed white beard and then his short white hair. He leaned into her personal space as if he was trying to intimidate her.

"Well it's true. I am going to divorce you. We've drifted apart over the last couple of years and I've met someone else." He stuck his chin out pompously.

"Louise found out from her Ukrainian friend. She told me everything."

"Oh right. I get it now. It was all her idea. I knew it. She's a real piece of work, that sister of yours. How much of my money have you given her over the years?"

"What's that got to do with anything?"

"She's a whore. She spends money like water. It's like pouring it down the drain with all her fucking parties and all her sycophantic cronies hoovering up mountains of Charlie in the toilets like there's no tomorrow."

"She tried rehab. You know she struggles with her addictions."

"She takes wads of money off you and spends it on any junk going. I suppose she's got you back into that old scene again? Or are you still just chilling out like a zombie on all your prescription drug cocktails?"

"You know exactly what the doctor prescribes for me. That half a Valium you gave me is wearing off. Where's my handbag? I need my handbag. I need my meds. I can't think straight without my meds." Becky's voice rose with panic.

"I'll get them as soon as we finish talking business. You agreed to tell me the exact location of my money. Now where is it?"

"I need to take the edge off first. I need a drink. Get me a drink."

"In a minute. What state is her business in?"

"Worse than ever. Her lifestyle is spiralling out of control. That's why she needs the money. She's run up huge debts. She's in over her head. You know Louise."

"I know she's a worthless flake. So what was the deal?"

"We agreed to split the money and go our separate ways."

Sinclair walked behind the bar, poured a shot of Jura single malt whisky and downed it in one. He turned around and looked at Becky. "Louise always was a selfish troublemaker. I honestly don't know why you bothered with her after all she's done to you."

"I did it for Amanda's sake. Imagine if Louise was your mother."

"But why take responsibility for her?"

"She's only a kid."

"But she's not your kid."

Becky held her head in her hands and screamed. "She is my kid."

"Bullshit. You're just being stupid now. You've never had a kid. The doctor told me." Sinclair laughed mockingly and poured himself another shot.

"You're such an arsehole. I had an abortion when I was sixteen. He didn't tell you that though, did he? He doesn't know everything and neither do you. She's the same age as the daughter I never had." Becky cried out loud and screamed, "I need my meds. NOW."

Sinclair took a deep breath. "All right, calm down. I'll get them. If you tell me who got you pregnant." He walked up to her and prodded her shoulder with his finger.

"What?"

"Who was it?" He leaned in closer. She moved back in disgust. He prodded her in the shoulder with his index finger to emphasise each word. "Who – Was – It?"

"My drama teacher, if you must know. I used to be in the drama club. We stayed late after school to rehearse for the school play. We were normally the last to leave the drama studio and then he would give me a lift home in his yellow MG."

"What happened to him?"

"He was afraid of all the scandal it would cause. The idiot killed himself when I told him I was pregnant. I said I'd tell his wife if he didn't leave her."

Sinclair returned to the bar and downed another shot.

"I want all my fucking money back. And the diamonds you stole from me. Then you'll leave the country. I'll give you ten million pounds and never want to hear from you again. If you agree to a quick divorce and go. You can use the company jet to travel anywhere, as long as it's far away from me."

"Where will I go?"

"Not Europe. Too close. Try Cape Town. Ten million will buy you a lavish lifestyle down there. It's a good climate and you can buy everything you'll ever need."

"Who is she, Peter?"

"No one you know."

"Who is she?"

He raised his eyebrows and nodded. A smile grew and he stood up straighter. He looked Becky directly in the eye. He smiled confidently.

"I met her in Paris this time last year. You didn't want to come. Remember?"

"How old is she?"

"Twenty-two. Austrian. Six foot tall. Blue-eyed blonde fashion model."

He stuck his chest out and his chin up in the air. His face beamed with pride.

"How do I know you'll let me live?"

"I gave you my word."

"That's not good enough."

"That's all there is."

He rummaged beneath the bar, picked up her red Hermès handbag and emptied it out over the bar. Ruffling through the contents he picked out four boxes of prescription drugs and waved them at her.

"Tell me now and you can have these back."

"I've taken a contract out on you as an insurance policy."

"On me? Don't be stupid. No one would be dumb enough to take it." Sinclair looked at her as if she was an idiot and laughed.

"The Ukrainians took it. And I paid them with your money." She laughed back at him, mocking his laugh before she flinched and looked at him apprehensively.

"Who would be that arrogant?" Sinclair scowled at her.

"Louise's friend."

"What's his name?"

"Uri Shevchenko."

"How much did he charge?" Sinclair stroked his beard pensively.

"Two hundred thousand pounds."

"Don't be stupid. That's way too much for a hit." Sinclair smiled again and wrote something down on a piece of paper.

"Louise owed them one point eight from business loans, so we gave him two million. If you let me go, I'll call the hit off."

"Tell me where the rest of my money is right now."

"I'll tell you where it is and I'll call off the Ukrainians if you let me go."

"Where's my money, you thieving cow? Tell me where it is before I lose my patience with you."

"And just for the record you were super shit in bed. So just remember that Miss Austria will be faking it. Now do something you're good at and fix me a Grey Goose."

CHAPTER SIXTY-SIX

Sinclair ignored her as he fed a shoal of small, red-bellied fish in the show tank with a single but larger crown-tailed fish from another tank. The shoal of fish went into a feeding frenzy. The ultraviolet-coloured water boiled as they fought over the fresh, colourful food. He watched the small fish attack it en masse until nothing was left. He turned to Becky and held his arms apart theatrically as if he were an impresario putting on a show. He bowed deeply towards her and then walked over to the log fire and grabbed the poker. He prodded the embers under the flaming logs and looked at her. His stare as cold as ice.

"You and those bloody fish," she sneered at him in disgust.

He left the poker in the fire, walked right up to her and slapped her hard on the cheek with the back of his right hand.

"Where's the money? Tell me where it is and you can have your fucking pills back."

"I need them now." She consoled her flushed cheek with her hand and stared back at him harshly but with a hint of doubt.

"Tell me where the money is. There's a divorce settlement drawn up and waiting for you to sign. Plus ten million pounds and a one-way ticket to anywhere far away."

"What's my alternative?"

"I think you know the answer to that."

Sinclair walked back to the fire and grabbed the hot poker. He pointed it at her and started to walk towards her, baring his teeth like a wild animal.

He began to shake with anger. "Do you want me to use the poker?"

Becky looked down at the floor as if caught in a trance.

"It's in a cottage in the Cotswolds."

"What's the address?"

"It's on a card in my handbag."

He left the poker next to the fire, returned to the bar and rummaged through the spilled contents of her handbag. He found the small card and read it out. She nodded and he made a short phone call, relaying the address. He then made her a Grey Goose vodka with orange over ice.

"Here you are. Your favourite drink."

"Where are my pills?"

"You'll have them back, with your settlement, if my men find the money."

She grabbed the drink off the bar and took it back to the sofa. She downed it in two.

Sinclair carefully picked up the sword from behind the bar. He slowly removed the blade from the wooden scabbard. It glistened under the spotlights.

"This is a very special sword. Look at it. A magnificent fifteenth-century Katana. Sharp as a razor. It's killed many men over the years. It once belonged to a famous Samurai and then to his son who was the most feared Ronin of all time. Now it's mine."

"Whatever."

Sinclair placed the gleaming sword delicately on the bar and picked up the phone again. He dialled a number and turned round, leaning against the bar with his back to her. Her eyes darted between him and the poker in the fire. She got up and walked quietly to the fire.

She picked up the poker and pointed it at the back of his head over ten feet away. She started to swing it back and forth as if she was hitting an imaginary object in mid-air. He was still talking on the phone with his back to her when she started to walk towards him, moving the poker down by the side of her leg. She stopped at the bar. She was within range.

Sinclair turned round and replaced the phone.

"Same again only lots more vodka," Becky said.

"I almost forgot how trashy you were. Very well, another one coming right up."

He fixed her another drink and took a single pill out of one of the boxes. Becky placed the poker against the bar and sat on a stool with her mouth open in anticipation.

"Just one until I get my money."

She took the pill and swallowed it without a drink. She grabbed the second drink, but stayed on the stool and drank it slowly through a bendy black straw. Sinclair poured another whisky and they drank in silence, staring at the cream phone on the bar.

It rang loudly, making Becky jump. Sinclair answered it and listened without speaking. He put the receiver back down and smiled at Becky.

"The address worked out."

"That was fast."

"I had men in the area."

"In the Cotswolds?"

"In the helicopter."

"Can I have another drink and my pills back now?"

"It seems like your young nephew was in the cottage having some fun. Some old whore his mother's age had him tied up in bed. Whips and handcuffs. He's a funny boy, that Christopher," Sinclair laughed out loud. "My men found everything except the two million you said you'd used. You're free to go. Do you want me to spare your sister?"

"You can do what you like with her. I never want to see her again."

Sinclair made another round of drinks at the bar. He then picked up a slim leather briefcase, placed it on top of the bar and snapped it open. He smiled to himself as he carefully extracted a thin document and turned it around to show Becky, pointing out parts of it on different pages.

"Here look," he pointed and then tapped the document. "The settlement figure is even spelled out. Ten Million Pounds."

"How will you pay me?"

"I'll have it transferred into your personal bank account tomorrow, less the two million you owe me, of course."

"Where do I sign?"

"You sign against the red sticker and I sign against the yellow sticker."

He presented the bare signature page to her. The red sticker was at the bottom pointing towards nothing but white paper. Above it a yellow sticker did exactly the same thing. Becky snatched the pen off the bar, scribbled her signature and printed her name and the date below it without reading the document.

Sinclair took the document and placed it back inside the briefcase.

"Put everything back in your handbag."

He handed her four boxes of pills and she grabbed them out of his hand. She took two more pills and put the contents back inside her handbag.

"Cheers." She raised her glass and drank the rest of her vodka.

"You can stay here tonight and take the Learjet tomorrow."

"I think one more drink should do it before I go to bed."

"Haven't you had enough?"

"One for the ditch. Neat."

"Very well."

Becky stood up. Her right heel keeled over, but she managed to grab the bar and save herself from falling over.

"I'll have it on the sofa by the fire and then go to bed."

"One neat vodka coming up. You better go and sit down."

Becky stumbled over to the sofa and fell into it. She rolled over and managed to sit up.

"What's taking you so l-o-n-g?" She started to slur.

Sinclair poured neat vodka in a fresh glass and took it over to her on the sofa, holding it by the base with a small black napkin.

"What about the o-r-r-a-a-n-n-g-e?"

Her eyes rolled around and her head wobbled as if she was catching it and then losing it again. Sinclair put the drink down carefully on the glass coffee table.

"What day is it, Becky?"

"S-a-t-u-r-d-a-y." Her head fell to the side and she slumped to the left, resting against a large cushion.

"Where are you?"

There was no answer. She was sprawled over the sofa on her back. Motionless.

Sinclair stared coldly. He looked sober and deadly serious.

He walked back to the bar and picked up the sword. Holding it gently, he stroked the polished blade and kissed it. "Business first."

He started humming as he took the divorce papers back out of the briefcase. Pulled the paperclip off and removed the last page. Grabbed Becky's pen out of her handbag and wrote something on the sheet above her signature. He placed the sheet of paper on the coffee table. Wiped the pen with his handkerchief and placed it in Becky's right hand for prints. He held it with the handkerchief and placed it on the coffee table next to the sheet. He did the same with the glass. He removed the pills from her handbag and scattered them across the table. He left them spread randomly over the table and placed the glass of vodka on top of the fake suicide note. Archer pushed the door open.

"What do you think you're playing at, Sinclair?"

CHAPTER SIXTY-SEVEN

Archer stood in the doorway and unholstered his gun. Sinclair jumped before turning around.

"Well, well. Look what the cat dragged in." His mocking tone and sarcastic grin showed no fear whatsoever. Archer pointed his Beretta at Sinclair's head. He knew Sinclair was unarmed.

"Trying to fake your wife's suicide? Leave her alone."

"Your too late, old boy. The spiked vodkas did the trick."

Archer looked at Becky's lifeless body slumped on the sofa.

"You think you can murder your way out of everything."

"Of course. Why not? I'm more powerful than you'll ever know."

"You're wrong. You're the weakest person that I've ever met."

A door crashed hard against the wall. Clarke burst through the doorway next to the bar and pointed his gun at Archer.

"Drop it, Archer. You're outnumbered."

"I've got a kill shot on your boss."

Haywood lunged through the same door and pointed his gun at Archer.

"See what I mean? You're outgunned."

Archer walked slowly towards Sinclair, moving away from the doorway. The two guns tracked his movement through an arc of over ninety degrees.

"Who's going to pay your wages if I kill your boss?"

"Drop it, Archer."

Forsyth entered through the French doors. Two bullets ripped into Haywood's chest. The gunshots surprised everyone except Archer, who shot Clarke in the chest and head before he could get a single shot out. The two bodies fell to the floor and slumped next to each other by the bar. Sinclair was stunned into statuesque silence as the two pools of blood on the marble floor merged into one.

Archer walked up to Sinclair and put the hot barrel of his Beretta against his temple, causing him to flinch and move his head backwards. Archer caught hold of him by the neck and held him at arm's length.

"One wrong answer and you get a bullet. Understood?"

"Yes."

"Do you own and operate a facility known as the Boathouse?"

"One of my companies does. Yes."

"Were you responsible for the death of my girlfriend, Alex?"

"Not personally. No. Contractors."

"Why?"

"She was poking her nose where she shouldn't have. Bloody journalists."

"You murdering bastard." Archer put his gun away. He grabbed Sinclair and wrapped his gloved hands around his neck. Sinclair's face went purple and his eyeballs bulged. Archer could feel his hands touching as they blocked Sinclair's air passage. Red veins stood out on the whites of Sinclair's eyes. They looked ready to burst.

A third armed guard entered through the main door near the sofa and raised his gun at Archer. Forsyth shot him in the head before he could pull the trigger. The gunshot jolted Archer from his stranglehold. He turned to see what had happened and released his hands from around Sinclair's neck. Sinclair fell and gasped for air loudly. He drew a long deep breath and then panted violently until his breathing slowed down. He was bent over, wheezing like a broken accordion.

Archer looked at him with contempt. "Tell me why you killed Alex." He could feel his anger welling up inside him. He was ready to erupt.

"We run the most secret facility in Europe. We'll kill anyone who gets close to it."

"Why haven't you killed me?"

"Davenport's protecting you."

"What?"

"Davenport masterminded it all. We give the British and American governments what they need to win wars and control foreign countries. Davenport conducts psychological experiments. I have all the power of private contractors at my fingertips."

"But Miles Davenport is not a killer."

"He's a monster. Your parents were going to expose him and so I had them killed. But don't bother looking for him. He fell out with some folks in Washington. He's gone into hiding. New face, the works."

It was all too much to take in and digest in one go.

"You killed my parents and Alex." Archer grabbed the back of Sinclair's silver hair.

"Stop him, woman," Sinclair said. "Show some compassion. I beg you."

"Hurry up, Archer," Forsyth said simply. "Finish off whatever you came here to do and let's get out of here."

"You're a moron, Archer. You'd better start running. You'll never get away with this."

Archer frogmarched him towards the fish tank. He pushed Sinclair's head under the water and held onto it firmly. He fought to keep it semi-submerged as large bubbles of air escaped from Sinclair's mouth. The piranha continuously tore into his flesh as a cloud of blood expanded inside the ultraviolet water.

Archer released the tight grip on his hair. Sinclair fell to the floor gasping for air. He rolled around coughing as he struggled to clear his windpipe and fill his lungs. There was no skin left on his face, just lumps of bleeding flesh hanging off it.

Forsyth sprayed the sofas and curtains with lighter fluid from a small yellow can and then made a continuous trail of fuel towards the fire. The fluid ignited with a loud whoosh and the flame followed the invisible trail back to the curtains, which instantly burst into flames.

Sinclair slowly pushed his body off the ground and crawled on all fours, regaining his breath before he stood up. He staggered towards Clarke's body, clearing his throat as the fire rapidly spread through the large room, engulfing it in flames that raged across soft furnishings, rugs and paintings. His hair and clothes were still drenched. His face was full of bleeding wounds.

He grabbed the gun from Clarke's hand, held it up and screamed like a psychopath in the middle of a prison riot.

"I killed your parents, you fucking moron," he yelled. "I shot the fuckers. Now it's your fucking turn. Where the fuck are you?"

He waved the gun around, unable to see clearly through the orange haze of bellowing fireballs. He held it at chest height and fired haphazardly around the room, smashing the fish tank and several bottles behind the bar until the clip ran out of bullets.

The water from the tank spilled towards the French doors. He threw the gun down and dodged the darting flames. Screaming incoherently as he crashed through the blazing doorway, onto the terrace, then stopped and froze before a fifteenth-century steel blade sliced right through his neck in one fatal blow.

CHAPTER SIXTY-EIGHT

I t was a week later. Archer walked along Walton Street from his house to his office on a cool Saturday evening. The clear sky was already starry and the air pleasantly fresh. He rarely used the office on weekends, but he had some time to kill before his six p.m. appointment.

His first-floor office was as deserted as expected. He swiped his card and entered the eight-digit security code. It was unusually dark and quiet without Zoe. No computer screens on. Not even the screensavers. He sat alone in the darkened office facing the window, his feet on a meeting table, and thought about Davenport, Sinclair and the Boathouse.

His eyes adjusted to the faint light from the street. It gently washed the room with shadows and outlines. He stared at Forsyth's generous gift. A two-foot-tall bronze sculpture of Lady Justice. The blindfolded moral force of the justice system. Balancing the scales of truth to measure both sides of the case. Holding a double-edged sword to symbolise the power of reason and justice. Like a judicial medieval knight.

He looked over at the gilt-framed canvas on the wall, darkened with horizontal shadows from the blinds. The two-hundred-year-old painting depicted a medieval knight riding on horseback across a stream, deep inside a forest. It was called Knight Errant. It had been a generous gift from one of his wealthier clients, for finding a stolen masterpiece.

He turned his head back towards the windowsill and focused on the highly polished fifteenth-century blade balancing on a small wooden stand.

He closed his eyes and took a long deep breath. His mind drifted off lazily. He thought about the good times with Alex and felt that he was finally ready to move on and live his life as best he could. He didn't feel good about what he'd done to Sinclair, but he didn't feel guilty about it either. Sinclair deserved it. He had no regrets, but the unpleasant act of revenge had only given him cold comfort. Miles Davenport had mysteriously disappeared without a trace, but he had no intention of looking for him. He had protected Sean from the murderers that ran the Boathouse, but he had also lied to him all his adult life – which meant that hypnosis would probably unlock his childhood memories. Did he really want to go through the inevitable pain those memories would bring? Probably not.

The computer drive he'd taken from Sinclair's briefcase was encrypted. Who knows what they might find if Zoe ever managed to crack the code.

Mobile phone GPS tracks and CCTV footage had proved that DS Lambert, the dirty cop, had killed Alex's friend Gillian King. With the comfort of not having the police or a car full of mercenaries chasing after him, he closed his eyes and sensed an unusual calmness emanating from the growing changes within. He felt released from the shackles of the past and in some strange way he felt renewed. The grief that he had carried around wherever he went was slowly lifting off his shoulders. The pain was still there, but it was bearable. Over the last week he had finally allowed himself to vent. He had stopped repressing his darkest feelings. Now he knew he could live with all that had happened. The future seemed less daunting. He had slept well all week and enjoyed running without feeling like he was constantly running away from something. He was comfortable with who he was. His life was not as he had planned or dreamed, but he knew he could make it work. He opened his eyes and felt surprisingly refreshed.

Forsyth texted him: *So far so good. Thanks for listening. SF xxx*

She had been a great partner and would become a close friend and possible business associate in the future. She had decided to move into her new flat and also to give her husband a second chance. They were going out for dinner tonight to see if it could work.

He kicked his feet off the desk, locked the office door quietly and headed downstairs to Morgan's Fine Art Gallery. There was a small champagne party to introduce three new artists to interested local collectors, and then it was off to Le Bistrot for a dinner date with Francesca Morgan.